BLACK MAJESTY

Book One — The Seeds of Rebellion

by

CHRISTOPHER NICOLE

BLACK MAJESTY

Book One — The Seeds of Rebellion

by

CHRISTOPHER NICOLE

Severn House Publishers

This first world edition published 1984 by
SEVERN HOUSE PUBLISHERS LTD of
4 Brook Street, London W1Y 1AA

Copyright © 1984 F. Beerman BV

British Library Cataloguing in Publication Data
Nicole, Christopher
The seeds of rebellion.—(Black majesty; bk. 1)
I. Title   II Series
823'.914(F)   PR9320.9.N5

ISBN 0 7278 1084 7

Printed and bound in Great Britain by
Anchor Brendon Ltd, Tiptree, Essex

This is a novel, but the events it relates are history. Henry Christopher, born 1767, died 1820, whose name became Henri Christophe, was a Negro slave who fought his way to power as the Emperor Henri I of Haiti. With his great compatriots, Pierre Toussaint l'Ouverture and Jean-Jacques Dessalines, he created a black nation capable of matching itself against the two foremost countries in Europe, England and France.

The quotations in this book are taken from *The West Indies: Their People and History* by Christopher Nicole.

Christophe was every white man's conception of the noble savage. Over six feet tall and built to match, he had the natural grace that both Toussaint and Dessalines lacked. He was as intelligent a man and as brilliant a soldier as the one, and as illiterate and lion-hearted as the other. He was born in one of the British islands – both Grenada and St Kitts have been awarded the honour – and although sold to a Frenchman at an early age, he preferred to retain the English spelling of his first name until his coronation. His personality attracted legend, and there are many conflicting stories of his youth.

Contents

Prologue

The rumble grew out of the still evening air, cascaded across the lush green of the sugar plantation, reached the heavy cedars of the forest beyond, echoed upwards into the foothills of the mountains which made a backbone to the island of Hispaniola and bounced back again across the quiet ocean. The sound might have been caused by a battle or by the first threatening groan of a coming earthquake; it might have been a volcano stretching or, more prosaically, the approach of a thunderstorm. But it was no more than the procession of three dozen barouches, gigs, phaetons, bounding behind their splendid horses, on the road to Plantation Vergée d'Or. It was 23rd March, 1765, and the Sieur de Mortmain was entertaining.

The Great House itself might have been on fire, so numerous and so brilliant were the candles and tapers, rushes and lanterns, which seemed to fill every window and flickered and swayed on every verandah. The polished floor in the great ballroom had been scattered with powder, the huge mahogany table in the enormous dining room sagged beneath the weight of countless dishes of food, West Indian – chicken and pork, smothered with peppers and cassereep, tuna fish and mackerel, caught off the coast of the plantation itself, avocado pear and eddo, sweet potato and roasted plantain – and European – sweetmeats and cheeses, best claret and finest brandies. The long row of portraits of previous Mortmains almost seemed to smack their lips as their severe gazes surveyed the scene beneath them.

Upstairs the bedchambers, each large enough to contain an average cottage, had been swept and polished, the beds overlaid with their pale covers decorated with the golden thread of the Mortmain emblem, the mailed fist, the snow-white mosquito nets withdrawn and secured to the high tents, ready to be released to protect those who would sleep from the countless insects which made up the Caribbean night, but for the moment not permitted to obscure for an instant the perfection they guarded.

And everywhere, in bedchamber and on gallery, on the main staircase and in the cavern-like entry hall, in the ballroom and in the dining room, in the study and on the verandahs, haunting the marble statues on the drive and the iron gates beyond, were the Mortmain servants. Every tall Negro – for Jacques de Mortmain recruited his domestic slaves rather as his idol, Frederick the Second of Prussia, recruited his guardsmen – was clad in a pale blue tailcoat, with gold thread at collar and cuff, white vest and breeches and stockings, and gilt-buckled black shoes, just as their female counterparts, hardly smaller, wore pale blue gowns with the Mortmain design, in golden thread, on their bodices, and white caps.

On the front verandah, waiting to greet the first carriage, were the three people who lived in this palace, and who owned everything, living or lifeless, on Vergée d'Or. Jacques de Mortmain, in a pale blue silk tailcoat with gold embroidery and buttons, a flowered silk waistcoat, with dark blue breeches, white stockings, and black shoes, the whole topped by a powdered and pommaded wig, suggested a gigantic bird of prey. He was above average height, but his sixty years made him stoop slightly, while his face was thin, dominated by the beak of a nose. His wife, some twenty years younger, revealed in her bloodless features the ravages of a lifetime in the tropics, the remnants of the bout of yellow fever which had once nearly killed her, and the continual malarial attacks which often sent her to bed with an ague. She wore a pink satin gown, carried away from her hips by enormous panniers embroidered in green and red silk; her wig, towering towards the ceiling, made her seem as tall as her husband, and winked with the sapphires which were her favourite stones, her malacca cane, which supported another enormous sapphire in its silver handle, reached her shoulder, and her fan was painted in the Mortmain colours of pale blue and gold.

Philippe, her only surviving son, stood behind his parents. He was twenty-two, and had but recently returned from Paris; the guests who were at this moment descending from their carriages would only remember him as a small boy, and he would remember them as very much his elders, or as grubby playmates. Now no one could doubt that he was a man, and more, that with his father clearly growing older and weaker every day he would soon be Seigneur of Vergée d'Or, owner of the greatest plantation in all St Domingue, grandest of *grand blancs*; not a man arriving tonight but would see in him a rival, not a woman but would see him either as a possible lover, if she was already married, or a possible husband, were she single. It was a thought at once exhilarating, and a little daunting to Philippe.

But he reminded himself that he would be a prize, even without his wealth. As tall as his father, and as slender, on his face the Mortmain nose fitted well between the high forehead and the wide mouth and big chin. He had refused to wear a wig, because it was absurd in the West Indian heat, certainly, but also because it would have concealed his own hair, which the Pompadour, on the one occasion he had met her, had remarked was the most beautiful she had ever seen, black and soft as night, a perfect match for his eyes. And for this of all occasions he preferred to dress quietly, a dark green coat over a gold-coloured waistcoat, and white breeches and stockings. If the ball was in celebration of the elevation of the eleven-year-old Prince Louis, grandson of King Louis XV, as Dauphin, there could be no doubt that Philippe was the true guest of honour.

The carriages were rolling to a halt before the marble staircase, and the first of the bejewelled and befanned ladies was being assisted down by white-gloved Negro footmen. Jacques de Mortmain's major domo snapped his fingers, and the orchestra struck up, while the maidservants hurried forward with goblets of iced sangaree.

Jacques de Mortmain kissed the hand extended towards him. 'Thérèse, how splendid to see you. You'll drink the health of His Highness?'

Thérèse de Milot raised her glass. 'And damnation to the English!'

Now the greetings, and the toasts, became general, and

the staircase became a long, glittering flow of people and comment, seeming the more brilliant because of the darkness which surrounded it.

Of varying shades. The overseers and their wives and children, whether *petit blancs* or mulattos, might be envious of their betters, but still were unable to resist the temptation to gather beyond the white palings of the gardens and watch the wealth from which they were forever excluded. Yet even they unthinkingly gathered into two groups. The meanest of the *petit blancs* would not allow himself to be a social acquaintance of the best mulatto, even if, under French law, any *café-au-lait* was born free. And the mulattos, of course, made sure they were nowhere near the *noirs*, who formed an even greater, and darker, concourse at the very end of the drive, from where they too, granted a holiday on this greatest of days, could stare and wonder, at beings as far above themselves, and as unaware of their existence as individuals, as was the very moon which was beginning to fill the sky and send a swathe of white light across the sea and the canefields and the forest.

And their numbers grew, constantly, as the maids and the coachmen of the guests, having discharged their immediate functions, left their carriages and joined the Vergée d'Or slaves. Opportunities for meeting those from other plantations, from the towns and the great houses of Cap François, were rare. Here was a chance to exchange gossip, to learn what was truly happening about them, in the world, no less than in St Domingue itself, to reunite with someone who had shared the horrors of the Middle Passage, or who had once been a slave on one's own plantation, perhaps to meet again a brother or a son, or even a husband, torn away for sale by the whim of his master.

And here too was an opportunity for plotting, for those who had at once the courage and the intelligence to suppose that the fact of their slavery was not an unalterable law of nature.

Into the crowd sidled one of the first of the coachmen to arrive, a little man, in his mid-thirties, who walked with a

12

limp, but who was greeted with some affection by everyone he passed. His black eyes searched the black faces in front of him until they found the one he sought, a powerfully built Negro whose heavy shoulders made him seem about to overbalance, and whose face was angry, as if there were a fire burning inside his brain.

'Jean François,' remarked the coachman, and walked on.

The big Negro hesitated but a moment, glancing to and fro, and then followed. The coachman was already beyond the crowd of slaves, taking the road towards the Negro village. His visits to Vergée d'Or were not to be wasted. But Jean François sweated. He was a recent arrival in Hispaniola, was not sure whom he could trust, and who would betray him to the whip, or worse, the wheel. Yet he was already a man of power amongst his people, by the very force of his character, the dominant anger of his personality. And he had been told that only the young coachman would be his equal.

Toussaint walked down the lane between the Negro huts, found the one he sought. Now the noise and the laughter and the glittering lights were far behind him, almost lost in the whisper of the trees and the soughing of the gentle wind. A dog barked in the village and then another, but both fell silent again as the two black men ignored them.

'You know she will be there?' asked Jean François.

'She will be there,' Toussaint promised, and turned aside, to pause before the cane mat which made a doorway to one of the smallest of the huts, at the same time motioning his companion to be silent.

They waited for some minutes, and then a whisper seemed to come from the mat itself. 'Who waits to see Céleste?'

'Pierre Toussaint,' said the coachman.

'Jean François,' said the big man.

'You are expected,' said the whisper.

Toussaint nodded, and held the mat aside, then followed Jean François inside. The hut was dark, save for a single guttering candle set in the earthen floor, sending shadows racing into the corners. It was noisome, and at first sight it

13

seemed unfurnished. The two men knelt, hands on knees, facing the flame and the woman beyond.

If she was, indeed, a woman. She appeared as no more than a wisp of scarlet cloth, for this evening she had put on her red turban; her face, so lined and gnarled it was impossible to gauge her age, seemed but a cage for her eyes. And like her visitors, she knelt, her fists clenched in front of her.

'What do two such men seek of a poor *mamaloi*?' she whispered.

'We seek knowledge, Mama Céleste,' Toussaint said. 'We seek a sign.'

'The war is over,' Jean François said. 'Our masters have been defeated, it is said. But they are still our masters.'

'We wish to know when it will be time,' Toussaint said.

'Time,' Mama Céleste whispered, and peered into the flame.

'Time,' Jean François said, his great fingers opening and shutting.

'Not yet,' Mama Céleste said. 'Not yet, O mighty warrior. Aye, mighty you are, of limb and mind, but not yet mighty enough. You will do nothing without the aid of Damballah Oueddo, without the presence of Ogone Badagris. Without them, without those they will send, who will be mightier warriors even than you, you will perish, and all who support you.'

'Then where are they?' Jean François' voice grew louder, and Toussaint shook his head, warningly.

'Who knows?' Mama Céleste said. 'They are everywhere, at all times. But only they know when they will choose to reveal themselves. And then they will come, as warriors even mightier than yourselves, men even bigger, and stronger, and more terrible in battle. Such men are only now about to be born, yet will they live, and prosper, in your cause. I can but tell you to prepare and be patient. When the time comes, you will know it. The white people will talk amongst themselves, and argue, and quarrel, and then they will set to killing one another, and the mulattos as well. Then, and only then, will Damballah Oueddo make himself

14

known to you.'

'And we will know him, when we see him?' Toussaint asked.

'There are many of our people, bigger than I,' Jean François said. And smiled, sceptically. 'Perhaps even mightier warriors, than I.'

'Black he will be,' Céleste said. 'Black as the night from whence he comes, and into which he will sweep the whites. And big he will be, a man of greatness apparent to all. Yet will his might be surrounded by beauty, and his blackness surrounded by light. By this beauty, by this light, shall you know him.'

PART ONE

The Slave

The West Indian planters and their families saw themselves as a race apart, creatures of unusual courage and ability, capable of creating vast fortunes under the most dangerous circumstances. They strode their verandahs like lion tamers, facing a horde of wild beasts kept in subjection only by terror. They placed their faith in the creation of an aura of personal ascendancy, of terrible omnipotence which permitted no opposition to, or even hesitation in, the carrying out of their slightest wish.

The symbol of this white supremacy was the whip.

Chapter I

THE CHILDREN

The Stamp Act, which aroused such a violent reaction in the North American colonies, evoked a similar response amongst the inhabitants of St Kitts, who not only destroyed all the stamped paper on their island, some two-thousand pounds worth, but sailed across to Nevis and repeated the deed there.

'Now then,' John Hamilton shouted. 'All together lads. All together. Charge.'

The men gave a whoop, and launched themselves against the iron-bound door, the log of wood they were using as a battering ram tucked under a dozen brawny arms. The wood crashed against the door, and the whole structure creaked.

'You'll cease this madness, Hamilton,' came the shout from within. 'I've muskets here. I'll blast you.'

'And hang for it,' Richard Hamilton shouted. 'Open up, Harley.'

'I'll see you damned first,' Harley shouted.

The men had paused, listening to the conversation, removing their tricorne hats to fan themselves and wipe their brows free of sweat as they awaited a signal from their leaders. The Hamiltons were cousins, their relationship immediately evident in the big, friendly features they each possessed, the wide mouth, too used to smiling for work of this nature, the thatch of curly brown hair, the lanky frame. It was in support of John Hamilton that Richard had brought his twenty men across the narrows from St Kitts to the much smaller island of Nevis. Here they had almost doubled the crowd; Nevis was one of the tiniest of the West Indian islands, hardly more than a huge mountain rising steeply from the sea to a height of more than three thousand feet. The village of Charlestown huddled at the foot of this immense extinct volcano, in the shelter of the only bay the island boasted, a collection of decrepit wooden shacks, of peeling paint and crumbling shingles, simmering in the afternoon heat. It contained hardly more than a few hundred people, and if most of them might have been expected to agree with their neighbours that the exactions of King George's government were rapidly becoming unbearable, they preferred to remain indoors, behind shuttered windows, and let others do their protesting for them.

'Break it down, Father. Break it down.' Little Alexander Hamilton, John's son, jumped up and down. The Customs House was one of the most solidly built structures in the town, yielding only to the church and the prison in the strength of its timber walls – but Richard Hamilton did not suppose it was going to withstand the efforts of a score of determined men.

'Again,' he shouted. 'Again.'

The men gave another roar, and ran forward. Once more the tree trunk struck the exact centre of the door and this time cracks appeared.

'Once more,' Richard shouted.

'There'll be a man-of-war here tomorrow,' Harley called. 'They'll have a yard-arm for you, Dick Hamilton. Oh, aye. And your people.'

Crash went the tree trunk and the door fell in. The men gave a whoop and swarmed over the shattered timbers, pausing only a moment at the sight of the Customs Agent, presenting a musket to them, then wisely throwing it to the floor in disgust.

'Just the paper, lads,' John Hamilton said. 'Just the paper. Don't touch a thing more. You'll send the account for this door to me, Ned.'

'Bah,' Harley said, sitting down at his desk and folding his arms. 'You'll not buy your way out of this.'

19

The men were carting great bales of stamped paper outside into the street, and now that the threat of bloodshed was averted, doors opened and people swelled the throng, chattering and sweating, sending nostril-tingling dust swirling upwards. It was a white crowd, although the people were as decrepit as their dwellings; their Negro slaves wisely looked on from a surreptitious distance.

'That is government property,' Harley said, coming to the broken door. 'And is worth two thousand pounds. I'll send you the bill for *that*, John Hamilton. And if it's not paid, you'll spend the rest of your life in a debtors' cell.'

'Twist his nose for him, Pa,' Alexander shouted. 'Twist his nose.'

'And your brood will starve,' Harley said, with some satisfaction.

'I'd not come outside if I were you, Ned Harley,' John Hamilton said. 'They might take to burning you along with the paper.'

The bonfire had already been lit in the very centre of the street, and the stamped paper was being hurled into the flames. Smoke drifted upwards into the still air; it would be seen by the watchers on St Kitts, who would know that the expedition had triumphed.

If that was the right word. 'What have we accomplished here, Dick?' John Hamilton asked his cousin, his exhilaration fading as the deed was done.

'An act of protest.'

'Will they not send more stamped paper? This time accompanied by soldiers?'

'I doubt the last. As for the stamped paper, why, we'll burn that, too.'

'We seek to defy the most powerful government in the world,' John Hamilton said. 'And that apart, have we not committed treason?'

Richard Hamilton watched the leaping flames, the cheering people. The entire white population seemed to have assembled now, and all were equally gleeful. He suspected that there was rum in the jugs being passed from

20

hand to hand.

'Not of the hanging variety,' he said. 'Not even King George would consider hanging an entire colony.'

'But he will wish to make an example of the ringleaders,' John said. 'Harley will not forget. That is a certainty. And if there *is* a frigate due . . . here in Nevis, I suspect we lack your stomach.'

Richard Hamilton frowned. 'Well, then, abandon this desert island and come to St Kitts.'

John pulled his nose. 'I am considering that very point. But there is naught for me in St Kitts. I doubt there is much for you, Dick. I'm for Virginia. If you can arrange me a passage.'

'Do you not suppose King George's warrants are served in Virginia as well?'

'Maybe they are. But it is a big country. There is room for a man to flap his wings. And they share our point of view, from what I've heard.' He rubbed Alexander's head. 'There will be more opportunities there for Alex than clerking in his father's store. You'll accompany me, Dick?'

'Not I,' Richard Hamilton said. 'I like to see the sea, when I awake, and before I retire. Besides, Jeanne is about to deliver.'

'Then you should be there, rather than here.'

'Politics first, personal matters after,' Richard Hamilton said. 'Besides, Marguerite is with her.' He watched the fire begin to die, the ashes drifting with the wind. 'But now it is done, I'll send the boat back for your things, John. And arrange passage to the mainland. We'll have you out of here before Harley's frigate can drop anchor.' He grinned. 'Our slave woman is about to give birth as well. We're doubling our establishment!'

From the deck of the sloop St Kitts loomed to the north. A considerably larger island than Nevis, it too was dominated by a single peak, the massive bastion of Mount Misery, which rose out of the centre of the island like a huge finger pointing at the sky. Well below it, and only six hundred feet above the harbour, the equally massive natural strength of Brimstone Hill, jutting away from the rest of the mountain, with the setting sun gleaming from the brass cannon guarding the embrasures cut into the living rock, reminded the watchers that this island had had to fight for its existence, more than once.

St Kitts was the oldest of the British West Indian colonies. Here Thomas Warner had led his tiny band of adventurers ashore a hundred and fifty years earlier, and from here, after settling with the Carib Indians, the Warners and their descendants had spread over the entire Leewards. Not without competition from the French, who until the Treaty of Utrecht only fifty years before, had shared the island, as the name of the main town, Basseterre, indicated. And even now a considerable number of French planters and merchants remained, despite the inconvenience inflicted upon them by the recently ended Seven Years War. For which, Richard Hamilton thought with some pleasure, he should be sufficiently grateful.

For as the sloop dropped her sails and came into the little wooden dock there was his brother-in-law, Maurice de Mortmain, standing in the crowd to greet him.

'Is it done, then?' Mortmain called, reaching for his hand.

'Aye.' Richard looked back over his shoulder; Nevis was only two miles away, and the smoke could still be seen drifting on the afternoon breeze.

'And no violence?'

Richard grinned. 'It was necessary to break down Ned Harley's door.'

The crowd cheered, and fell to shaking hands and slapping backs. Here at least there were no doubts as to whether or not destruction of the stamped paper had been their right as free-born Englishmen. Only Mortmain failed to share the prevailing jollity. He was in any event a serious man, rendered more so by the beak of a nose and the thrusting chin which was his family's hallmark, and also, Richard sometimes thought, by the whim of fate which had left him merely a poor relation of his famous and wealthy cousin in St

Domingue.

Now he said, 'You English. Were this still a French colony, messieurs, I do assure you this would be a hanging matter.'

'But it ain't a French colony, now is it, monsieur?' somebody said. 'We've a habit of seeing to our own affairs, here.'

Mortmain sighed. 'Until the frigate comes. Ah, well, we'd best make haste, Richard.'

The two men hurried up the street towards the shipping agent's office, above which Richard Hamilton lived. 'Is all well?'

'She was just beginning labour when I left,' Mortmain said.

'My God!' Hamilton began to run.

Now at last Mortmain smiled. 'But she is in good hands, Richard. Marguerite is experienced in these matters.'

He had seven children, where the Hamiltons possessed but one, at this moment, and he was on the porch to greet his returning father. 'Papa,' Christopher Hamilton shouted. 'Mama is crying.'

He was three, and had been promised a little brother. Hamilton took the steps three at a time, threw open the door at the top, ran across the tiny living room, burst into the bedroom, checked, gazed at this smiling wife. 'Jeanne . . .'

'Here she is, Uncle Richard.' Madeleine de Mortmain, at eleven the eldest of the five Mortmain girls, was holding the babe in her arms.

'She?'

'A girl, Richard,' Marguerite de Mortmain said. The sisters were remarkably alike, with yellow hair and soft, liquid features, which in Marguerite were almost doelike. If Richard Hamilton could be said to have married above himself in securing one of the Desmoins girls, Marguerite could have no doubt that she had aspired to the stars. Her father had been a bankrupt planter, no matter how superior even that might have been to a shipping agent. Maurice de Mortmain might be only his cousin's attorney for the

23

Mortmain St Kitts plantation, but the wealth was *there*. Yet she had, Richard Hamilton thought, contributed more to the marriage than her husband; with her as a mother Madeleine, in her mass of pale yellow hair, her nose delicate rather than beaked, her chin pointed, already promised beauty, hard to find in a Mortmain, and undoubtedly her younger sisters would also in time catch the eye.

'I am sorry, Richard,' Jeanne said.

'Sorry?' he shouted. 'To have you safe . . . to have you both safe . . .' He held out his arms, and the babe was placed in them, somewhat reluctantly, by his niece.

'What will you call her?'

Jeanne Hamilton sighed. 'She was to be a boy, and called Richard.'

'There is an equivalent,' Marguerite said. 'Richilde.'

'Richilde Hamilton,' Richard said. 'I like that name.'

'Then Richilde it shall be,' his wife agreed.

'With Jeanne as a second name.'

'Richilde Jeanne. Yes, indeed.' He turned his head as a fresh wailing came from behind him. 'What the devil . . .'

'Is me own, Mr Richard,' Henrietta said. Not for her a bedchamber filled with anxious relatives. She had given birth alone, had severed her own umbilical cord, and was already on her feet. She knew she was fortunate, in being the slave of a shipping agent rather than a planter, even if, as the only slave the Hamiltons could afford, she had more than enough to do. But both the Hamiltons were indulgent owners, who treated the big black woman as a friend rather than a servant.

'Bring him over here,' Jeanne commanded. 'It is a he?'

'Oh, yes'm, Mrs Hamilton,' Henrietta said, and placed the boy in her mistress's arms. 'He is a big boy.'

'Big,' Jeanne said in wonderment. 'My God! He must weigh all of ten pounds. Did he not harm you?'

'Well, I did be bleeding just now,' Henrietta said. She raised her skirt to peep between her legs. 'But I thinking it is stop.'

'What shall we call him?' Jeanne looked at her husband.

'Well, Henry for a start,' Hamilton said. 'As he is Henrietta's child. As for a second name . . .'

'Who was the father?' Mortmain asked, with obvious amusement.

'Well, Mr Mortmain, sir. . .' Henrietta looked embarrassed. She was not only a large woman, and able to make her feelings felt, she was also extremely handsome.

'He'll be a playmate for Christopher,' Jeanne said. 'We'll call him Henry Christopher. How's that, Henrietta?'

'Why, mistress, that is very nice.' She gazed at Richard Hamilton. 'You ain't going sell he, Mr Hamilton? You ain't going sell he?'

'Not while I can afford to keep him, and you,' Hamilton agreed. 'As the mistress says, he'll be a playmate for Kit. Besides . . .' he placed Richilde in her mother's other arm. 'He's Richilde's twin. Well, almost.'

He stood back to look at them, the one so white, the other so black; the pair, so beautiful.

Richard Hamilton raised his eyes from the paper he had been studying, gazed across the desk at the man standing on the other side. 'This is madness, Troughton. You must know that.'

The Customs Agent sighed. 'No doubt what you did was madness, to others. Governments must govern.'

'At a distance of four thousand miles? Let them allow us a government of our own. Or at least representation in theirs.'

Troughton sighed again. 'I am not here to discuss politics, with you, Richard. I am here to present a simple fact.'

'Of my arrest? You'll have a riot on your hands.'

'Aye. What I am showing you there is merely the warrant. I am in possession of letters as well, instructing me not to force the matter until the frigate arrives.'

'The frigate,' Hamilton remarked contemptuously. 'Always the frigate.'

'She is really on her way this time, Richard. From Kingston, with a company of soldiers as well as her normal complement. She is, I quote, to restore the islands to their duty.'

'Their duty.' Hamilton got up, stared out of the window at the ships lying in the bay, loading sugar from lighters. He pointed. 'There is our duty, Troughton. To grow sugar, and to ship it, so that Farmer George can grow even richer. You will have a riot.'

'I am aware of it. But the frigate *is* coming. You will have some deaths on your conscience.'

Hamilton chewed his lip.

'Which is why,' Troughton went on, seeking to take advantage of his friend's doubt, 'I have come here at all. To give you time to consider.'

'What do you recommend?'

'Your cousin John seems content enough, in Jamestown.'

'You'd have me run? Anyway, Johnnie is a factor. He needs but a roof over his head and some goods to sell. I am a shipping agent.'

'Do they not have ships out of Virginia? Johnnie will provide you with introductions.'

'And the planters here?'

'Will find somebody else to organise their cargoes for them. They will have to. Believe me, Richard, it is the best way. It is the only way. You cannot defy King and Government, and Navy as well.'

'Ned Harley,' Hamilton growled. 'I should sail across to Nevis and wring his neck.'

'Then would you be wanted for murder as well. And he was only doing his duty when he lodged charges against you.'

'As you are only doing yours in arresting me.'

'I hope I am doing my duty as a friend, first, by giving you time to remove yourself.'

Richard Hamilton looked down into the yard, where the cradle waited in the coolness of the shade. It had been Jeanne's decision that the two babies should share it. In many ways she was treating the slave boy as if he were the son she felt she should have had. But Henry was such a smiling, happy child it was difficult to resent it, no matter

26

what problems Hamilton might see looming in the future.

'I have a family,' he said. 'My daughter is still at the breast.'

'I know that,' Troughton said. 'Perhaps you should have considered them sooner.'

'You'd have me expose them to a sea voyage, and then a search for employment, and indeed, sustenance?'

'You'd have them starve, while you kick your heels in prison? Or even worse? It could come to that: you have defied His Majesty. You have a brother-in-law, Richard. Surely he could care for your wife and children until you have found your feet.'

Richard Hamilton sat behind his desk again. This was his home. It had been hard in the beginning, but he had done well, and been happy. And become a leader in the community, at least that of the Basseterre merchants. Nor had any of the planters, his social betters, either refused his company or attempted to dissuade him from leading their protest. But he knew them well enough, even Maurice de Mortmain – or especially Maurice de Mortmain, who lived in continual fear of his famous cousin's disapproval, which might leave *him* destitute – to be sure not one of them would raise a finger in his defence. And if the townspeople would be more faithful, as Troughton had pointed out, a few staves and pistols would hardly accomplish much against the cannon of a frigate, the muskets of a company of foot.

Did he regret what he had done, that sunlit day nearly a year ago? Only the consequences, not the deed. But how many men, he thought with wry humour, must have had an indentical reflection at some time in their lives? And did his ever restless spirit not thrill to the idea of once again adventuring, even without Jeanne? Or was the thought of being entirely his own man again the most exciting of all?

He raised his head. 'How long have I got?'

'A year,' Richard Hamilton said. 'Hardly more than that. You've my word.'

Jeanne Hamilton smiled through her tears. 'And I'll count

27

on that. I cannot help but feel once you set foot on that ship I will never see you again.'

'I'm not that easy to lose.' He kissed her again, then lifted his son from the floor. 'You're going to look after your mother for a season, Kit.'

'I want to come with you, Father,' Kit shouted. 'I want to fight the Indians.'

Richard Hamilton held him close. 'I'm not going to fight any Indians, Kit. I'm going to work. And you'll be coming soon enough.' He set the boy down again. 'Then you'll have to work, too. But meanwhile, you'll look after your mother, and you'll care for you sister, and you'll see to Henrietta and little Henry, and you'll help Uncle Maurice in everything he decides. You understand me?'

Kit was biting his lip, determined not to cry in front of his French cousins. But without success. Great tears rolled down his cheeks. Richard was glad to turn away. 'Marguerite.' A hug and a kiss.

'We'll look after them for you, Richard,' she said. 'It was a proud thing you did. It'll come right in the end. It must.'

'In the end.' He reached past her to shake Maurice's hand. ''Tis a heavy responsibility I load on to your shoulders, old friend.'

'A welcome one,' Mortmain promised him. 'They will prosper, as I prosper, until you are ready for them.' But his forced smile was sad, his thoughts easy to understand. Richard Hamilton was fleeing, to be a wanted felon. So John Hamilton, by report, had prospered. He was older, as his family had been older. He had always been more serious-minded than Richard.

But then, Richard thought, Maurice had always been a pessimistic man, so it was natural for him to view the future with concern. He squeezed the fingers a last time, looked over the seven children, who ranged from Etienne, at fourteen already almost a man, serious of face like his father, constantly putting on his brand new tricorne hat and then taking it off again to finger the braid at the brim, to little Annette, only two, waiting in the arms of her nurse. They

28

were all blonde, all slender, all serious. He could never tell them apart.

He gave them a collective embarrassed smile, turned to Henrietta, who carried a babe in each arm.

'I too sad to see you going, Mr Richard,' Henrietta said. Her gaze drifted to Maurice de Mortmain, and then away again.

'Mr Mortmain is a good man,' Richard said. 'He will be a good master. You have naught to fear.'

'He ain't going sell we, Mr Richard? He ain't going sell my Henry?'

'No,' Richard said. 'He has promised me that. He won't sell you.' He smiled at her. 'You will be better off on the plantation than you are here.'

'But he going put Henry in the field,' Henrietta said dolefully.

'Now, that I cannot say,' Richard said. 'Henry will have to work. You do understand that, Henrietta?'

'Yes, sir, Mr Richard. I understanding that. But if he get put in the field he going get the lash. I knowing that.'

'He need never be whipped, if he works well. It is up to you to make sure he learns that.'

'Field slave must get the lash,' Henrietta said. 'I knowing that.'

'Not if you train him well,' Richard repeated. He chucked his daughter under the chin. 'He'll have Miss Richilde to care for.'

'Oh, he going do that,' Henrietta promised. 'I going train him to do *that*.'

'Well, then ...' Richard Hamilton looked back at the people in the room, picked up the small carryall in which were his clothes. 'One year,' he said, and went outside.

There he paused to set his tricorne on his head and faced the people who waited to say goodbye.

'You don't have to go Richard,' said one of the men who had accompanied him to Nevis. 'Say the word and we'll fight that frigate. We've those guns up on Brimstone.'

'And become relvolutionaries?' Richard clapped him on

29

the shoulder. 'I'd not wish that on any man.' He went down the stairs, exchanging farewells as he did so.

'Only a year,' Marguerite de Mortmain said, and put her arm around her sister's shoulder. 'It will seem no time at all.'

'I shall never see him again,' Jeanne Hamilton said, her voice flat.

'Oh, come now,' Maurice de Mortmain said, glancing anxiously at his wife.

'I shall never see him again,' Jeanne repeated. 'I know it.' She touched her breast. 'Here. I shall never see him again.'

The children hurried through the long grass, panting, stumbling, sweating, effort oozing from every pore, trying to keep up with the General. Who now came to a halt, holding up his hand, so suddenly that Richilde Hamilton cannoned into Lucy de Mortmain, and Henry Christopher, bringing up the rear as usual, cannoned into Richilde.

'Here,' Kit Hamilton said; he spoke French, as the children were encouraged to do about the plantation. 'This is a good defensive position.'

The grass dissipated itself in a patch of bog, some twenty yards across, beyond which there was a stand of trees.

'I don't think it's good at all,' Lucy said, sitting down to peer at a scratch on her leg; a thorn had torn the stocking to get at the white flesh beneath. She was thirteen years old, actually a year older than the General, and was inclined to argue.

'They'll attempt to dislodge us with missiles,' Kit explained, his big, friendly Hamilton features expressing good-humoured patience. 'But we can sit here all day.'

'I don't see why we should sit here at all,' Lucy said, taking off her hat to fan herself, sending pale blonde hair tumbling. 'I want to go home.'

Kit sighed. 'We have to defend the stable,' he said. 'That is the whole object of the game.'

'I think it is a silly game,' Lucy declared. 'I don't see why we have to play soldiers all the time. I think we should play kings and queens. I think we should have a ball. I think you

30

should ask us to dance.'

Kit glanced at her in exasperation, and then looked at his sister and the black boy. Who stood together, as they always did. They were the youngest of the children, just eight, and always did exactly what Kit told them to. In many ways he was a father to them. They didn't have any other. Well, Richilde thought, Henry didn't, certainly. And if he did, it wouldn't matter. Henry was a slave, and belonged to Mama. She supposed *she* had a father. No one seemed to know for sure. Mama would never talk of him.

'We are playing soldiers,' Kit said. 'Because that is what Louis and I like to play. And you agreed to it, too, Lucy.'

'That was before it got so hot,' Lucy said, disagreeably. 'I want a glass of coconut water. If we go back to the house Henrietta will give us a glass of coconut water.'

'Ssssh,' Kit said. 'And lie down. They're here.'

Richilde immediately threw herself full length in the grass, regardless of the damage to her white dress. Henry lay beside her, panting. Lucy sighed, and also lay down, beside Kit. They peered through the grass, watched the other children coming out of the trees beyond the bog. Louis de Mortmain was first. He was fifteen, and dominated Kit, in their choice of games, much as Kit dominated the younger ones. With him were his other two young sisters, Annette, who was nine, and Françoise, who was eleven. With perfect symmetry, the Mortmains had had their children one every other year for seven births. Richilde thought it would be wonderful to have a lot of sisters, even if she was perfectly satisfied with a single brother; besides, Henry really acted as another brother. But sisters! Often Annette and Françoise and Lucy went into a huddle together, from which she was excluded, because she was too young, they would say, but she knew it was because she was only their cousin. And then there was Catherine, so dignified and aloof, at seventeen, and even more Madeleine, already married at nineteen, to whom they could turn for advice, or sympathy. Madeleine and Catherine were both perfectly willing to give Richilde advice or comfort as well, but it wasn't the same.

31

Besides, they all had a father, too. A real father.

'We'll let them know we're here,' Kit whispered, and stood up to wave his arms. Louis started forward immediately, but checked as his shoes slipped in the mud.

'You come back here,' Françoise shouted. 'You'll get all dirty.'

'Now then,' Kit said, crouching beside them again. 'While they're thinking about how to get across, we'll start a flanking movement. You and me, Lucy.'

'I thought we just had to stay here, and stop them from getting to the stable,' Lucy objected.

'If we don't outflank them, they'll outflank us, soon enough,' Kit pointed out. 'That is elementary military strategy. Besides, it's what Frederick would do. It's what he did at the Battle of Leuthen. He made a demonstration in front of the Austrians, and then marched more than half his army round their flank while they weren't looking, and beat them all up.'

'Frederick,' Lucy grumbled. 'Always Frederick. He's a *Prussian*. Why can't we fight like a French general?'

'Because the French generals always lose,' Kit said brutally. 'Now you two, listen. Show yourselves every so often, just to remind the enemy that we are still here. And when you hear me shout, launch a frontal attack. We'll catch them in the rear.'

'Across that bog?' Richilde squeaked.

'It's not as deep as it looks. You can take off your shoes and stockings. Now remember, wait for my shout. Come on, Lucy.' He crawled away to the left, and Lucy, after a moment's hesitation, followed him.

'If I get my legs all muddy,' Richilde said sadly, 'Mama will be so angry.' But she took off her shoes, pulled her skirt up to roll down her stockings. It did not really occur to her to disobey Kit.

Henry watched her with interest; as he wore only a pair of white cotton drawers he had nothing to take off. Nor did his presence embarrass her. He was her twin, Mama always said, which suggestion would send Henrietta into peals of laughter.

Besides, he was interested in other things. 'This Frederick,' he remarked. 'He is a real man?' He also spoke fluent French, overlaid with the soft West Indian brogue.

'Of course,' she said. 'He is the King of Prussia.'

'Kings ain't good,' Henry said. 'That is what I hear your mummy say.'

'You are talking about King George,' she said. 'He is King of England. He is a bad man, Mama says. But most kings are quite good. This new king of France, Louis the Sixteenth, he is a good king, Uncle Maurice says. And Frederick is a great king. He wins all his battles. And he builds lovely palaces. Miss Fitzgerald teaches us about him in the schoolroom.' She paused, her mouth a huge O, distorting her features which, like her Mortmain cousins, contained enough of her mother's looks to dilute the Hamilton strength – 'She'll never be beautiful,' Jeanne Hamilton would say. 'But she won't be ugly, either.'

The schoolroom was the one place Henry was not allowed to enter, their lessons the one amusement he never shared; it was against the law to teach a slave to read or write. And she wouldn't hurt Henry's feelings for all the world. 'Uncle Maurice has a book about him too,' she said. 'With pictures.'

Henry laughed, and leaned forward to ruffle her mane of curling light brown hair, making her flush. She adored his sudden, intimate gestures, so disconcerting when coming from a black boy. If the truth were told, Richilde was afraid of black people, the field hands, great big men and women who carried fearsome long knives called machetes, and stared at her with huge dark eyes. Louis had told them all horrible stories of a slave revolt only twelve years ago in a place called Berbice, a Dutch colony situated on the mainland of South America, when all the white people had been chopped up by the machetes, and, apparently worst of all, a Dutch girl named Miss George had been kept a prisoner by the blacks for several weeks before she had managed to escape. Richilde was not at all sure how being kept a prisoner could actually be worse than being chopped by a machete, but Louis assured her that it was, and Françoise had supported him, rolling her eyes and saying, 'It's horrible, you'll know when you grow up.' So presumably it was horrible.

But of course black people were not really the same as Henry, who with his friendly features and his wide grin *could* have been her brother, except for his colour. And who was her friend.

Now he said, 'You going show me those pictures, some time?'

'Some time,' she agreed, and turned away from him to peer through the grass. 'Are they still there, do you think?'

'I think they gone home,' he said. 'To drink coconut water.'

'Oh, they can't have,' she protested, and stood up, to kneel again as a clod of earth flew through the air towards her, followed by several others. 'They're still there.'

'Why they like to be soldiers, all the time?' Henry asked, lying beside her. 'Kit and Louis.'

'All boys like to be soldiers, all the time,' Richilde said, wisely. 'Don't you wish to be a soldier, all the time?'

'How can a slave be a soldier?' he asked.

She frowned at him, disconcerted by his sudden gravity. And by the realisation that he *was* a slave, which he had never actually put to her before. In any of its aspects.

Her thoughts were interrupted by a creaking of wheels, the stamp of hooves. She rolled over, on to her back, looked up at the pony and trap, at Etienne de Mortmain, coatless, sleeves rolled up his muscular arms and head shaded by an enormous straw hat, strong fingers tight on the reins. Beside him sat his sister Catherine, also sheltering beneath a straw hat, but looking much more elegant in a pale green gown, with a matching chiffon scarf round her neck and drifting behind her in the breeze set up by their progress.

Etienne brought the trap to a halt as the two children started out of the grass. 'Richilde?' he shouted. 'Whatever are you doing?'

'Just playing, 'Tienne,' she said.

34

His gaze shifted from her to Henry. 'You'd best get up,' he said. 'We'll drive you to the house.'

'Oh, but . . .' she looked across the bog at the trees.

'Do as 'Tienne says, dear,' Catherine said.

Richilde hesitated, then ran to the trap. Henry followed more slowly.

'You'll not ride, Henri,' Etienne said. 'I'll attend to you later.'

'I'm Henry,' Henry protested. 'Not Henri.'

'God damn you for being a mutinous black dog,' Etienne shouted, his hand flicking the whip to send the thong curling towards the little boy. 'You are anything I care to call you, boy. Now get yourself back to the house.' He jerked the reins, and the trap started to move. Richilde, just climbing into the back, nearly fell over, and had to hold on to both sides. Kneeling, she looked back at Henry. In avoiding the whip he had fallen over, and was only now getting up again, to gaze after the vehicle with smouldering black eyes.

The Mortmain plantation of Marigot was situated on the north eastern side of the island. Here was Windward, where the trade winds never ceased, and the great Atlantic rollers, hardly broken by the presence of the neighbouring island of Antigua, hull down upon the eastern horizon, constantly pounded the beach. It was a cool place, as compared to the more gentle living on the protected, Leeward, side. But Richilde loved the sea, the smell of it, the feel of it, the sound of it. She adored it when Miss Fitzgerald would allow them to walk on the sand, without their shoes and stockings, skirts held to their knees as they paddled on the edge of the waves. She dreamed of one day actually entering the tumbling waters, of feeling them pick her up and roll her over, of fighting with them. But that of course had to remain a dream. Miss Fitzgerland would never hear of it. If the slaves occasionally bathed in the sea, it was not something that a white person, and more especially a white lady, would ever consider doing.

The road from the orchard and the stream, where the

children played most of their games, skirted the top of the beach before turning inland towards the plantation house. Marigot was a large estate, by the standards of St Kitts; it covered some hundred and fifty acres and required over a thousand field slaves. The canefields stretched away to the north and west, under the very shadow of old Mount Misery, which seemed to hang directly above the trap as it entered the drive. Here on Windward the plantation house was the first building encountered, to make sure it remained upwind of all the smells and sounds from the slave village, as well as the plantation farm, and the factory, its red brick chimney a lone sentinel against the green of the fields and the trees carpeting the lower slopes of the mountain.

The factory was silent now, the plantation itself quiescent. It was the quietest part of the year, with the young cane, the ratoons – shoots taken from previously cut stalks and transplanted – all growing well, and with the grinding season still several months away. Richilde thought grinding almost as exciting as the sea. Then the plantation seemed to shake itself, and awake from a long sleep. The huge iron rollers would turn, crushing the canestalks, and screaming against each other almost as if the cane itself was crying out for mercy, the chimney would start belching black smoke, and a steady mound of glorious sweet brown sugar would accumulate in the storerooms, into which the children were often allowed to drive their fingers to consume whole handfuls of the delicious granules. While the scent of fermenting molasses would pervade the whole plantation, for the sugar which could not be properly crystallised, because of impurities, was not wasted, but converted into the plantation's other main product, rum. Sometimes, when Uncle Maurice was in a good mood, the children would be allowed mugs of the incredibly heady white liquid, which would send them into giggles and then a deep and dreamless sleep. Once the rum had been purified, and coloured, it was regarded as too strong for them.

Of course grinding had a dark side, too. Uncle Maurice was really quite an indulgent master. Today, for example, as she could see beyond the house, there were only four men occupying the stocks. This was sufficiently unpleasant, she supposed, as they were naked, and only given water once a day, and for the rest had to sit out in the sun, without even a hat, and unable to swat or scratch the insects which clustered on their skins, while the other slaves were encouraged to throw rotten fruit at them, which not only left an unpleasant smell but attracted even more insects. However, white people in Basseterre who had committed a breach of the peace were similarly incarcerated, save that they were allowed to retain their clothes for the sake of decency – which did not seem to matter in the punishment of the blacks – and unless one of the slaves had been especially wicked, such as insubordinate to an overseer, they would not actually be flogged. Uncle Maurice did not flog his slaves himself; like most planters he employed a professional, called a jumper, a man who went from plantation to plantation, offering his services. This was because the whip used to discipline the slaves was not an ordinary cat-o-nine-tails, but a cartwhip, a single long thong of leather, with a piece of steel embedded in its tip. Thus where the cat soon became matted with blood and flesh and dwindled into a single broad paddle – which no longer hurt, according to Etienne – the cartwhip went on cutting and hurting with every blow. Carelessly used, it could kill, very rapidly, and there was no planter who wished to destroy property he had paid good money for – none that Richilde had heard of, anyway.

But during grinding the overseers used their whips freely, and the slightest slackening of effort was rewarded with a flogging. Much as she loved the taste and smell of the sugar, the hustle and the bustle, she dreaded hearing the piteous screams of the wretches, men and women, strung up on the triangles to suffer; she would run to the bedroom she shared with Annette and Lucy and pull her pillows over her ears.

A sudden terrifying thought crossed her mind that Henry had been guilty of insubordination to Etienne. But Henry could not be flogged. He was her friend. Her twin. And he was only eight years old. And most important of all, he was a house, not a field slave. House slaves were only flogged if they actually attacked a master or mistress.

Yet he would certainly he punished.

'We were only playing soldiers,' she ventured.

'Alone, in the grass?' Catherine turned her head to look at her, not very severely, Richilde was happy to note, but frowning as she inspected her more closely. 'Where are your stockings and shoes?'

'I took them off.'

'You are getting too old to romp with slave boys,' Catherine said. 'And he is getting too old to be allowed to play games with you. He should be put out to work.'

'He is going to be put out to work, Etienne said, not turning his head, as he was concentrating on avoiding the ruts and pot holes in the drive. 'I intend to see to that.'

'Oh, but . . .' Richilde bit her lip. It really wasn't much good arguing with 'Tienne, who saw himself as very much the young master. Uncle Maurice would see her point of view. And certainly Aunt Marguerite. She wasn't at all sure about Mama any more. She was very moody; sometimes she would be quite kind and understanding and then at other times she would look at Richilde as if she really didn't know who she was.

The plantation house was the biggest building Richilde had ever been inside; it would have made two of even Government House in Basseterre. It gave the impression of being only a single storey with an attic, because the downstairs was a mass of large galleries, protected by a deep sloping roof, out of the centre of which the upstairs rose like an afterthought; but the upstairs, small in comparison with the rest of the building, contained six bedrooms. It was a happy place, where the sea breeze constantly soughed and the servants smiled, and of course, with so many children about the place there was always laughter or shouting or screaming or banging going on somewhere in the background. Richilde could not imagine living anywhere else. According to Kit, she *had* lived somewhere else once. She had been born in the little room above the Shipping

Agent's Office on the waterfront in Basseterre, because that was where Father and Mama had lived. She had seen the place, on one of their rare visits to town, and she found the thought quite incredible. Certainly she could remember nothing of it. Marigot was her home.

The trap pulled to a halt in front of the wide front stairs, and Richilde jumped down. She wanted to be first into the house, first to see Uncle Maurice, first to explain the situation. She ran up the steps, skirts clutched in front of her, only then realised that she had left her hat and shoes and stockings in the long grass. Mama would be furious. Uncle Maurice was very generous, but Mama could never forget that she and her children were nothing more than poor relations.

But surely they would still be there tomorrow.

'Uncle Maurice.' She burst into the office. Uncle Maurice only went aback – into the fields – once a day now that he was getting old, and spent the rest of his time working on the account books. Now he looked up with an expression that was at once tired and pleased; Richilde knew that he was very fond of her, where perhaps he found his own daughters rather tiresome – she never asked for anything.

Except today. 'Uncle Maurice,' she said. 'We were playing a game . . .'

'She was rolling about in the grass by the orchard, with that black boy,' Etienne interrupted, coming into the room and throwing the satchel he had been carrying into a chair. 'Half naked. It was quite disgusting.'

Maurice de Mortmain frowned at his niece. 'Were you doing that, Richilde?'

'It was a game.'

'Catherine saw it,' Etienne said.

Mortmain looked at his daughter, who waited in the doorway.

'Yes, papa,' she said. 'It really was quite disgusting.'

'It was a game,' Richilde shouted. 'All the others were there. They were hiding in the trees. We were playing soldiers.'

'That boy must be punished,' Etienne said. 'It is quite insufferable, allowing him to play with the children. And he was rude to me, answered me back. He should be whipped, and then put in the field.'

'You can't, Uncle Maurice,' Richilde begged.

Maurice de Mortmain looked at the tears gathering in her eyes, then at his son. 'Are there letters?' he asked, buying time.

'Several.' Etienne opened the satchel, placed the mail on the desk. 'About Henri Christophe . . .'

'His name is Henry,' Richilde said. 'He was christened Henry. He wants to be called Henry.'

'He wants?' Etienne sneered. 'A slave boy?'

'My God,' Maurice de Mortmain said, and held up the black-edged envelope. 'From St Domingue.'

Etienne frowned. 'Uncle Jacques?'

Mortmain slit the paper, took out the sheet inside, scanned it. 'Uncle Jacques is dead,' he said. 'Philippe says he never truly got over Tante Marie's death. We must . . .' he frowned as he continued to read. 'My God,' he said again.

'Papa?' Catherine came into the room.

Maurice de Mortmain stood up. 'Go and fetch your mother. And Aunt Jeanne. And find all the children. I wish to see them here. Immediately.'

'But what's happened, Papa?'

Maurice de Mortmain looked as if he had seen a ghost. 'Philippe wishes me, us, to go to St Domingue,' he said. 'To live at Vergée d'Or. Fetch your mother.'

'It seems that Philippe has decided to reorganise the estates,' Maurice de Mortmain said, surveying the family gathered in front of him. 'He has been studying our returns, and he is of the opinion that Marigot is no longer an economical proposition. Besides, he apparently does not like owning property on an English island. So I am to place the plantation on the market.'

They stared at him, unable to comprehend.

'Sell Marigot?' Marguerite de Mortmain asked at last.

'But . . . this is our home.'

'We are to make a new home, in St Domingue,' Mortmain
explained. 'Philippe is very generous in what he says. He
says he feels sure that I, with my great experience of
planting, will be of tremendous assistance to him on Vergée
d'Or. He also says that he looks forward to providing a home
for all of you.'

'St Domingue,' Etienne said. 'The greatest colony in the
entire West Indies. Oh, it will be marvellous.' He squeezed
Catherine against him. 'You'll find a rich husband, in St
Domingue.'

'Leave Marigot?' Marguerite de Mortmain said, half to
herself. 'That is quite impossible. You must write Philippe,
Maurice, and tell him that it is quite impossible.'

'My dear,' Maurice de Mortmain said, 'Philippe is now the
head of the family. He *owns* Marigot, just as he now owns
Vergée d'Or. If he has decided to sell, there is nothing I can
do about it. Besides, there is sound economic sense in what
he is saying. Only the big plantations are making the same
profits they used to. Marigot is really too small.' He
attempted a smile. 'And as Etienne says, in Cap François
Catherine will be able to find a rich husband. Why, all the
girls will be able to find rich husbands.'

'And Madeleine?' Marguerite demanded. Madeleine de
Mortmain had done the best she could, in St Kitts, and
married an English planter.

'Well . . . she will be able to come and visit us, from time
to time.'

'Time to time?' Marguerite shouted. 'She will be hundreds
of miles away. Hundreds.'

'I am sorry, Marguerite,' Maurice de Mortmain said. 'But
we do not have any choice in the matter. If Philippe has made
up his mind. . .'

'Philippe,' his wife sneered. 'Always Philippe. You would
take orders from a man half your age?'

'Philippe is not half my age,' Maurice said, mildly. 'He is
thirty-one. That is not half my age.'

'You are fifty-two. Are you going to take orders from a

41

man twenty years younger than yourself?'

'I am in no position to do otherwise, my love. Would you have us starve? All of us?'

Marguerite de Mortmain bit her lip, and flushed.

'I cannot go to St Domingue,' Jeanne Hamilton muttered.

'Why not?'

'Richard will not know where to find me.'

Maurice exchanged glances with his wife, who put her arm round her sister's shoulder.

'Richard will find you, my dear,' she said. 'If he ever comes to look. But you know that not even that nice boy Alexander has heard from him in five years. He went off into the West to seek his fortune, and has just disappeared. You must accept the fact that he is dead.' She raised her head, to look at Kit, almost defiantly, Richilde thought. But she was saying that Father was really dead. Richilde wanted to burst into tears, even though she had never seen the man. And yet she didn't, because of the excitement which bubbled through her. Of course they had to go to St Domingue, with Louis and Annette and Françoise and Lucy. Even with Etienne and Catherine. St Domingue was the greatest of all the West Indian colonies, whether English or French. Everyone said so.

'I think you children should run off and play,' Maurice de Mortmain said. 'Aunt Jeanne and Mama and I have things to discuss.'

Richilde raced through the drawing room and out to the back verandah. Henry Christopher sat here, fanning himself, with her hat. He had brought her shoes and stockings as well.

'Oh, you darling,' she cried. 'Thank you ever so much.' She sat beside him, kissed him on the cheek, held his hand. 'Henry, you'll never believe what has happened.'

'Your daddy has come home?' he asked, hopefully; his mother had brought him up to believe that he was still Richard Hamilton's slave, rather than a Mortmain.

'No.' Richilde's smile died. 'Aunt Marguerite says he is dead.'

'He ain't dead,' Henry declared. 'He can't be dead. Not Mr Hamilton.'

'I don't know. Oh, I wish I knew. But Henry, we are to go to St Domingue. All of us. We are leaving Marigot, to go and live with cousin Philippe at a place called Vergée d'Or. It is a most splendid place, Tante Marguerite says.'

'St Domingue?' He frowned at her. 'But that is French.'

'Well, I am half French.'

'I am English,' Henry said.

'Well, you will learn to be French,' she said. 'You will love it there, Henry. St Domingue is the place to be. It is the most wonderful place on earth. Everyone says so.'

Chapter 2

ST DOMINGUE

Only in the still young colony of St Domingue, with all the hinterland of Hispaniola available for expansion, were Frenchmen to be found who wished to become West Indians.

'Cap François,' Louis de Mortmain told the children, 'is the Paris of the Western Hemisphere.'

And even Richilde, prepared to be sceptical, was forced to accept the suggestion that here was a city transported from the very heart of European civilisation to grace the magnificently lush green of the mountains and the forest which had dominated the skyline for the past three days as the sloop had skirted the coast. She had, of course, seen pictures of European cities, without ever relating them to reality; Basseterre had always seemed the ultimate in civilised living for her. But, as they disembarked from the boat on to the greenheart dock, it occurred to her for the first time that Basseterre was in reality nothing better than a fishing village.

The other children were no less impressed, and she could tell that even Mama and Aunt Marguerite, and Miss Fitzgerald, for all their pretence at sophistication, had had their breaths taken away by the splendour about them. By the buildings: every one seeming to be new and most splendidly appointed; by the architecture, which cascaded from turrets and high balconies to verandahs and patios, to massed beds of multi-coloured flowers, to ornate and voluptuous, and quite indecent – to Richilde's eyes – statues, carved from the purest marble, to the tall trees leaning across the wide boulevards, their branches a glitter of crimson flowers. And then by the kaleidoscope of humanity which bustled everywhere, *grand blancs* displaying the latest in silk satin, ostrich feathers drooping and décolletages plunging; *café-au-laits* gossiping on street corners, brown faces animated, gowns like multicoloured firework explosions, heads bound up in no less brilliant bandannas; or *noirs* gleaming with sweat and endeavour working on the docks. And then by the variety of scents and aromas, almost every one pleasant, which arose from the perfumed gardens and the no less perfumed bodies of the population; by the accumulation of vast ships anchored in the harbour, and most of all by the deference paid to them as soon as it was learned that they were Mortmains, and bound for Vergée d'Or. Because waiting for them on the dock was an army of carriages and equipages, and several white men, supported by a regiment of slaves . . . but no Seigneur de Mortmain for whom they had been waiting in a state of some apprehension.

'I am Fedon,' the first white man said. He looked every bit as well dressed as Uncle Maurice, who was wearing his best coat and a new pair of white stockings, and far more confident. 'I am the Sieur de Mortmain's attorney. Welcome to St Domingue. Ladies.' He kissed Aunt Marguerite's hand and then Mama's.

'My cousin is not in town?' Uncle Maurice asked.

'Ah, no. The Sieur de Mortmain seldom visits Cap François. And these are the children? How nice.' His eyebrows arched as he obviously counted, and arrived at eight. 'How nice,' he said again, and looked at the Negroes. 'There was no necessity to bring any blacks.'

'These are personal servants,' Aunt Marguerite explained.

'Ah,' he said again. 'Allow me to introduce these gentlemen.'

There were six more white men, all apparently overseers on the plantation, who were assigned one to each carriage. Richilde found herself in the last, with Annette and Kit and

Lucy, and a man named Morin. She wished to ask how the slaves, or at least Henry, would get out to the plantation, but she didn't dare. Instead she gazed out of the window as the carriage rolled through the streets, at the people who hastily moved out of the way the moment they saw the Mortmain crest, and saluted.

'Cousin Philippe must be very popular,' Lucy observed.

'Popular?' Monsieur Morin considered. 'He is very powerful. He is the richest man in St Domingue, and St Domingue is full of very rich men.'

'Are you very rich?' Kit asked, with that terrible directness of his which Richilde often found embarrassing.

Monsieur Morin merely looked at him. 'I work for the Sieur de Mortmain,' he said.

Now they had passed the last of the houses and were riding along a beaten earth road next to the beach, with the great rollers thundering on their left, and the huge mountains rising away to their right; in between there were cultivated fields, and in the distance dark forest.

'You will like it here,' Monsieur Morin said. 'It is the best place on earth.'

'Is the plantation far?' Lucy asked.

Monsieur Morin allowed himself a smile. 'You have been on the plantation for ten minutes.'

'Have we?' Richilde cried, speaking for the first time, and craning her neck to look out of the window. 'But there is no cane.'

'We grow other things on Vergée d'Or besides cane, mademoiselle,' Morin said. 'But you will see cane soon enough. Vergée d'Or is a large place. Look there.'

Canefields! Which stretched for as far as the eye could see. Just as the road stretched for as far as they could see, too; she realised that they had been travelling long enough to have ridden from Marigot into Basseterre, and they had been on the plantation all the time.

But then she saw what appeared to be a large town, although the houses were all low and small, and there were no church steeples.

'The Negro village,' Morin said.

'How many slaves do you have?' Kit asked.

'It is difficult to be precise,' Morin said. 'About seven thousand.'

'Seven *thousand*?'

'We have eight hundred white people too,' Morin said. 'Well, whites and mulattos. They live over there.'

Beyond the slave village there was a town of elegant houses and grassy lawns. Richilde found that she had taken off her hat and was scratching her head. She suddenly felt like a midget. Even the trees which lined the road seemed to be larger than any she had seen before, while the factory, which now came into view as the road at last turned away from the sea coast, made Marigot's seem no larger than a workshop.

Morin was smiling at their amazement. But now, like a good magician, he produced his *pièce de résistance*. 'If you look up there,' he said. 'You'll see the chateau.'

To begin with Richilde could only make out a stand of enormous trees, beneath which the carriage was now making its way. Then it stopped, and a blue-coated Negro footman was opening the door and another was waiting to help her down. Their wigs were powdered, their feet encased in brilliantly polished black leather shoes. Behind them was a regiment of blue and white clad Negresses, bowing and clapping their hands to welcome the guests, who gathered in a nervous huddle on the patio, all, even Uncle Maurice, looking up in amazement at the turrets which overhung them, at the balconies and the wings, at the brick patios which surrounded the lower floor and could only be insulted by being called verandahs, at the raised rose gardens which fringed the grand staircase, at the horde of servants which lined the walkway, at the mass of white people who waited beyond, and then at the man who was at this moment descending the staircase like a king.

Because he is a king, Richilde thought. Philippe de Mortmain has to be a king, to live like this.

Philippe de Mortmain looked surprisingly young. Richilde

47

remembered that he *was* much younger than either Uncle Maurice or Aunt Marguerite or even Mama, but still he was over twenty, which necessarily made him old, like Etienne or Madeleine. Yet the fact was that he did not look a great deal older than Etienne.

He possessed, of course, the Mortmain features, prominent and sharp, and the Mortmain height, with a breadth of shoulder which made him seem larger than he actually was. And surprisingly, amongst all the brilliantly dressed overseers and servants, he alone wore nothing but a shirt and breeches, tucked into black riding boots. But she observed, as he approached them, that the shirt was best cambric, and even that would have been unnecessary to delineate him as the master of Vergée d'Or. He moved with an unconscious arrogance, an utter certainty of his wealth and power, and of the lack of it in all those beneath him. Including his own relatives.

'Maurice,' he said, kissing Uncle Maurice on both cheeks. 'How splendid to see you. Marguerite.' He kissed Mama's hand. 'Jeanne? Yes, indeed. And these are the children?' He shook hands with Etienne and Louis, standing beside each other, paused in front of Catherine. 'But you are a beauty, dear cousin,' he said softly, and brought a rush of colour to her cheeks. 'You are all beauties,' he said, kissing Françoise and Lucy and Annette in turn, and arriving at Kit. 'And you?'

'Christopher Hamilton, monsieur,' Kit said.

'Ah. The English children. Then you will be Richilde.'

Her knees felt weak, and knocked together. She couldn't speak.

He smiled at her. 'Another beauty on its way,' he said. 'Vergée d'Or will glow. It has not glowed for too long. Now I know you will all wish to see your grandparents. Maurice, we'll talk when I return.'

He gave them a collective smile, went down the marble steps to where a horse was being held for him by a Negro groom, and where half a dozen other white horsemen, also dressed for the fields, were gathered, like military staff surrounding a general. Philippe de Mortmain raised his riding crop, and the little cavalcade moved off.

Marguerite de Mortmain said something in an undertone to her husband, who hastily frowned and shook his head. Clearly their cousin was not to be criticised, no matter how obviously he might treat them like his other myriad possessions.

'You going come with me, mademoiselle,' a voice said, and she discovered one of the Negresses at her elbow. She looked left and right, realised that each of them was being taken in hand, almost literally, by an attendant. And the others were already walking away, so that she was being left behind; even Kit was walking beside a Negress. She wanted to run, but the woman at her side was maintaining a most stately tread, and she made herself keep pace.

They climbed the stairs, past the white women and children, who smiled and bowed and greeted them; Richilde realised that they had to be the families of the overseers, who now started to drift away as the new arrivals reached the upper porch and were escorted through enormous double doors held wide by attentive black footmen in blue and gold liveries. Here was a gallery, big enough, she supposed, to contain the entire Marigot Plantation House, stretching almost out of sight in the distance, filled with a cool breeze coming in from windows at the far end, and circulated by fans which turned softly, suspended from the ceiling and worked by young black boys, all wearing the Mortmain livery. The walls of the gallery were hung with portraits of severe looking men with the pronounced Mortmain features, punctuated with women of varying attractiveness, but every one with an arrogant tilt to her head, a sneer of utter contempt on her lips as she looked down on the people below.

'We going this way,' the Negress said, and led Richilde through one of the many doors opening off the gallery. Once again she looked anxiously after her cousins, and more especially Kit, but he was being led through another of the doors. Now she found herself in a carpeted hallway; at the end of which was a staircase, leading down again, and then another hallway, this one with windows opening on to an interior garden, a place of lawns and flower beds, with a fountain in the centre, and entirely surrounded by the rest of the house, which she realised was built in the form of a gigantic hollow square.

Now they were ascending another staircase. She realised that she was quite lost, doubted that she could ever find her way back to the main part of the house. Except that she could always ask, because every doorway was guarded by a blue and gold liveried footman who bowed to her.

'This your bedroom,' the Negress said.

Double doors were being opened, and Richilde entered a cavern of a chamber, filled with exquisitely carved furniture, and containing a tester bed in the very centre of the floor; the drapes, needless to say, were pale blue and gold.

'But . . . where are Lucy and Annette?' she asked. On Marigot they had shared a room, and indeed a bed.

'They got room,' the Negress said. 'Not far from here. I will show you. When you done bathe.'

'Bathe?' But she was very hot and sticky. And the woman was already giving instructions to half a dozen maid servants who were bringing ewers of water, some hot and steaming, and others obviously cool, while two footmen were placing an ornately moulded tin tub in the centre of the floor. Others now bustled in with her box, containing her clothes and her dolls; it looked pitiable in the midst of so much elegance. As would her clothes, she realised; she had worn her best gown to land, on Mama's instructions, and it did not match the dress worn by the Negress. But then, she thought, even Mama would look like a poor relation in these surroundings. Because she *was* a poor relation.

The Negress smiled at her. 'You are sad,' she observed. 'There is nothing to be sad about. Vergée d'Or does be a happy place, for you. I am Amelia. I going look after you. You all get out,' she said to the maids and footmen, her tone suddenly brisk. 'The Mademoiselle going bathe.'

The bustled from the room, and Richilde allowed herself to be undressed and seated in the tub, to have Amelia scoop

50

water over her shoulders before applying a deliciously scented soap to her flesh.

'This is your home, now,' Amelia said. 'You going live here, and you going marry here, and you going die here. And you going be happy here. The master does like everybody to be happy. He does get very angry if somebody ain't happy. And you don't *ever* want to make the master angry. No, ma'am.' She straightened, stood almost to attention. 'Now Madame Jacqueline come.'

Richilde hastily wrapped herself in her towel, turned to face the woman who had just opened the door, and found herself staring in surprise. Madame Jacqueline clearly had Negro blood; Richilde could estimate at a glance that she was probably a quadroon, that is, one of her grandparents had been a Negro. Like so many women of her racial characteristics she was remarkably handsome, tall and strongly built, with almost perfect features, and glorious straight black hair, which clung, strand to strand, almost as if it were stuck together with glue. But the surprising thing about her was her gown, which was of dark green damask, the rings on her fingers, emeralds which winked at Richilde with incalculable value, her décolletage, and the utterly regal fashion in which she moved and carried herself. And spoke.

'You will be the English girl,' she said.

And the most surprising thing of all was that she was hardly older than Catherine, Richilde decided. She had to remind herself that whereas in the English colonies, people of colour, in whatever degree, were born slaves and remained slaves, unless manumitted by their masters, in the French colonies it was the reverse, and a single drop of white blood, sufficient to classify one as a *café-au-lait*, guaranteed freedom for oneself and one's dependents. Even more, in the French colonies mulattos could own property and accumulate wealth. As this girl had obviously done. Or someone had done for her.

'Yes, mademoiselle,' she said. ı am Richilde.'

Jacqueline smiled. When she smiled she was quite beautiful. 'We shall be friends, you and I,' she said. 'Now get dressed. Haste, Amelia.'

Amelia hurried, and Richilde found herself hurrying too, although, however wealthy she might be, this Jacqueline had to be her social inferior. But she was utterly ashamed of her gown; her best one was lying soiled on the floor, and this one had a darn where she had snagged it on a branch.

Jacqueline continued to smile, 'Dressmakers will be here first thing tomorrow morning,' she said. 'We must have you looking your best.' She took Richilde's hand. 'I will see to it personally.'

They walked through the galleries, passed the bowing footmen. 'Do you live here?' Richilde asked.

'But of course.'

'Oh,' Richilde said. Because she couldn't, however hard she tried, figure out what her new friend might do here. On the other hand, she was most certainly her friend; they had now regained the main gallery, and Jacqueline was introducing the people in the pictures. 'Pierre de Mortmain was the founder of the family fortune,' she said. 'He was a *boucanier*. A *matelot*. Do you know what that means?'

'I don't think so,' Richilde confessed.

'He and a boon companion, a *matelot*, lived right here in St Domingue when the whole island was owned by the Spaniards. They killed the wild cattle which used to roam these plains, and still do, in the interior. They smoked the meat, turned it into *boucan*, hence their name. And they fought against the Spaniards. Until eventually they found some small boats, with which they started attacking Spanish coasting vessels. They formed themselves into a sort of navy, the Brethren of the Coast. Pierre de Mortmain was one of the most successful. He eventually became a pirate, and was very famous. But he never forgot St Domingue, and his son created his plantation. There is no greater plantation in the entire Antilles, than Vergée d'Or.'

'Why is it called Vergée d'Or?' Richilde asked.

'A vergée is a measurement of land. Did you not know that?'

'I think so,' Richilde said, doubtfully.

'You are English,' Jacqueline said, with the faintest suggestion of contempt. 'You think in terms of acres. A vergée is about a third of an acre.'

'Oh, but . . .' they had reached a window, and Richilde looked out at the sweep of canefields in the distance.

Jacqueline laughed. 'Of course. There are thousands of vergées composing Vergée d'Or. But that is what Ranulf de Mortmain, old Pierre's son, called it. Because he began with just one vergée, but he called it the golden one, because he knew it would grow. He knew the wealth of this soil. And do you know that was only one hundred years ago? Ranulf de Mortmain was Philippe's great grandfather. No more.'

It was the first time that Richilde had heard anyone refer to the Seigneur by his Christian name, except for Uncle Maurice, and Uncle Maurice always used it with a great deal more respect than Jacqueline had just done.

'But what relation are you to the Seigneur?' she asked. Because white men did have mulatto relations, even in St Kitts, although they were not as a rule allowed around the house.

Jacqueline smiled. 'I am not a Mortmain. My name is Chavannes. I am merely Philippe's housekeeper.'

'Oh,' Richilde said, not understanding at all, either how someone so very young could possible be a housekeeper, or how a housekeeper could possibly refer to her employer in so familiar a fashion.

But if she was in a position both of knowledge and authority, and as she was being so very friendly . . .

'May I ask you a question?'

'Of course,' Jacqueline said.

'We brought some domestic slaves with us from St Kitts. Do you know if they have come out to the plantation?'

'I should think so,' Jacqueline said. 'It really wasn't necessary, you know. Indeed, I think Philippe may be rather displeased when he discovers that. He gave orders that Marigot was to be sold, together with its slaves.'

'Oh, but these are people we've always had. Especially Henry Christopher. Why . . .'

'Henry Christopher?'

'My twin,' Richilde said.

'Your what?'

'It's what Mama always says. It's a family joke, really. We were born on the same day. He's been my playmate ever since. Do you think we could go and find him? I really would like to know that he has settled in all right, and is being looked after.'

Jacqueline Chavannes had stopped walking, and was gazing at her in total amazement. Then she suddenly gave a peal of laughter. 'Why, yes,' she said. 'I think we *should* go and find this twin of yours.'

Jacqueline hurried Richilde along the gallery and on to the porch at the head of the great staircase. Here were Françoise and Lucy, standing together to admire the gardens and the trees.

'Oh, there you are, Richilde,' Lucy cried. 'Are you coming to explore?'

She glanced at Jacqueline.

'Mademoiselle Richilde is coming with me,' Jacqueline said. 'Come along, mademoiselle.'

Richilde gave her cousins an apologetic smile, hurried down the stairs behind her friend. 'Couldn't they come too?' she asked as they reached the bottom.

'Only if you wish them to,' Jacqueline said.

'Oh, but . . . well, they are the Mortmains, you know. I'm only a poor relation.'

Jacqueline gave another of her peals of splendid laughter. 'But that is why I like you, my dear girl. Because you are not a Mortmain. I am not a Mortmain either. That is why we are going to be friends, you and I.'

Richilde didn't understand her at all, but now she was again lost in wonderment as they entered the ground floor of the chateau, through an entry hall every bit as wide and as high as the great gallery, but this one hung with swords and muskets and pistols, and instead of windows or corridors leading off, here were great arches, those on the right giving into a magnificent withdrawing room, an expanse hardly less

54

than a vergée itself of polished parquet flooring, littered with incidental tables made from carved wood and with equally splendidly moulded brass trays resting on top, containing a variety of ornaments, and comfortable chairs, arranged in groups, a spinet and, at the far end, a billiards table, while the whole was cooled by great glass doors which opened on to another patio behind which was yet another rose garden surrounded by a lawn as smooth as baize.

The arches on the left gave access to a dining room hardly smaller than the withdrawing room, where there was an enormous mahogany table, around which were some forty-eight chairs; the walls were lined with polished mahogany sideboards, laden with silver cutlery, with decanters of wine and brandy, while above them hung pictures of horses' heads.

'Philippe maintains a stud,' Jacqueline said, carelessly.

They had now walked the length of the hall, to where a red velvet curtain hung from the high ceiling. Jacqueline parted this curtain, to reveal that the corridor continued, with doors leading to pantries, where slaves were industriously cleaning silver, doors leading to storerooms, where other slaves were loading bottles or boxes, a door leading to a cool room, where the walls were lined with zinc and the floor was covered in sawdust, to keep the great blocks of ice from melting too quickly, and where whole carcasses of cows and pigs hung from the ceiling.

'Where does the ice come from?' Richilde asked in a whisper, fanning herself against the heat in the corridor.

'It is brought down from Newfoundland,' Jacqueline explained. 'Philippe maintains special ships for the purpose.'

They passed other doors leading to what were obviously cellars, and then at the end there was another curtain, and they entered an enormous kitchen, filled with wood burning ranges, with low tables at which slaves were cutting up pieces of pork for the evening meal, supervised by a large black man.

'This is Lucien,' Jacqueline explained. 'Lucien is the head cook. Mademoiselle Richilde is English, Lucien.'

Lucien kissed her hand, to her surprise. 'You going eat well here, mademoiselle,' he said. 'Everyone does eat well on Vergée d'Or.'

'We are seeking the black people from St Kitts,' Jacqueline said.

'Oh, yes, Madame Jacqueline,' Lucien said. 'They done been take to their place.'

'Then we shall find them. Come along, Richilde.' Once again she took Richilde's hand, and this time led her through the back door and on to another patio, fringed with fruit trees rather than flowers. While Richilde puzzled over another mystery; why her new friend was called madame, when she was clearly a mademoiselle, both by virtue of her age and because she wore no ring.

'The domestic slaves,' Jacqueline explained, 'do not live in the slave village. They have their own houses out the back, here. These houses are much nicer than slave barracoons. It is a great privilege to be a domestic. You must hope that your people will be able to retain their positions.'

'Oh, but they must,' Richilde cried. 'Henrietta and Henry Christopher must, anyway. Uncle Maurice promised.'

Jacqueline squeezed her hand. 'It is always a mistake to become too fond of servants,' she said. 'Just as it is a mistake to become too fond of animals. Pets. They always die, or get sick, or have to be put down. It is far better to remember, always, that they are just sent to please us.'

Richilde bit her lip. Even her cousins did not understand that Henry could be a friend, and not a servant. She could hardly expect this girl to understand. Except that this girl's grandfather, or more likely, her grandmother, must have bridged the gap between the races. She wondered if she dared ask her about that.

They walked down a smoothed earth avenue between coconut palms, with a stream bubbling on their left, and Richilde realised with a leap of her heart that they were only a few hundred yards from the sea. And once again an Atlantic facing beach, with rollers tumbling over the reef to come surging in as surf on to the sand itself. She wondered if it would be possible to swim here. Of course Miss Fitzgerald would forbid it here as much as in St Kitts, but this girl might allow it.

There were so many things she wanted to ask Jacqueline. So many things she felt she *could* ask her, where she had never felt that about a single human being before.

'Here we are,' Jacqueline said, as the avenue made a slight dogleg to the right, and they came upon another small village, a place of some elegance, where the cottages were separated by masses of pink-flowered oleanders, and the scent of jasmine was heavy in the air, while each cottage, Richilde observed, possessed a sizeable vegetable garden at the back. The place seemed deserted, as of course nearly all the domestics were up at the house, but there were one or two women with babies at their breasts, and several small children.

'We seek Henrietta, from St Kitts,' Jacqueline said.

The woman she addressed curtseyed. 'She does be just down the road, Madame Jacqueline.'

'Thank you,' Jacqueline said, courteously. 'Would that be your friend, Richilde?'

'Henry,' Richilde shouted, running forward. 'Henry!'

Henry Christopher's somewhat solemn face lit up, and he in turn left the little house and ran on to the street. 'Richilde,' he shouted. 'But I did wonder where you was. You are up at the Great House?'

'Oh, yes, Henry,' she said, like him speaking English without thinking. 'Henry, you must see it. It is like nothing you can ever have imagined.'

'Like something King Frederick must have built,' he said, grinning.

She squeezed his hands. 'Just like something he would have built. I can't wait to show it to you. I'll show it to you tomorrow morning.'

Henry's smile had faded. 'I don't know what I going be doing tomorrow, Richilde,' he said. 'These people say I got to go in the field.'

'Never,' she said. 'I'll speak to the Seigneur. We'll both

speak to the Seigneur, won't we, Jacqueline?'

'I think,' Jacqueline said, 'that to begin with you should make a habit of speaking French. The Seigneur does not like English, or anything about the English. And secondly, you, boy, Henri Christophe . . .'

'My name is Henry Christopher,' Henry said.

'Yes, boy. But it is Henri Christophe in French. Do you not speak French?'

'He speaks French,' Richilde explained. 'But he likes his name to be spoken in English.'

'He likes?' Jacqueline raised her eyebrows. 'Well,' she said, 'I think, if you mean to talk to the Sieur about your friend, Richilde, you should do so now.' She pointed, beyond the village, to a track which led back into the canefields, and up which the Sieur de Mortmain was at this moment riding, followed by his six overseers.

Philippe de Mortmain drew rein beside them. He did not frown, as he did not smile. His expression never altered at all. At yet Richilde suddenly felt as if someone had emptied a bucket of ice cold water over her.

'You, boy,' Philippe said to Henry, who was staring at him. 'You are from St Kitts?'

'Yes, sir,' Henry said, in French.

'Then you have much to learn. And the first thing you have to learn is that you do not look at me. Not ever. Do you understand me? When I am near, you stand with bowed head.' Philippe de Mortmain pointed with his riding crop at the women and children. 'Like those people are doing. Do not let me see your head raised in my presence again, or I shall be angry with you. Do you understand me, boy?' he asked, as Henry continued to stare.

'Yes, master,' Henry said, and hastily lowered his eyes to gaze at the dust. But Richilde could tell that he was angry, or afraid; his legs were trembling.

'Then you will do well here,' Philippe de Mortmain said. He turned to Jacqueline. 'And you, madame? What devilry are you up to now?'

Jacqueline did not appear to take offence. 'Mademoiselle

58

Richilde wished to discover if her slave had safely arrived, monsieur,' she said.

Richilde glanced at her in surprise; the quadroon had used the Seigneur's Christian name so freely up to this moment.

'And so I brought her down here to see,' Jacqueline said.

'This boy is your slave? Philippe de Mortmain enquired.

'He belongs to Mama, monsieur,' Richilde explained, 'But he is my friend.'

'Indeed?'

'Her twin,' Jacqueline observed with a smile.

'Explain.'

'We were born on the same day,' Richilde said. 'Almost the same minute, Mama says. So we are friends.' She was encouraged to be bold. 'You won't put him in the fields, monsieur? Say you won't. He is very good about the house.'

'Is he now? And what are you called, boy?'

'I am Henry Christopher,' Henry said.

'Henri Christophe. It has a certain ring to it.'

'Henry Christopher,' Richilde said. 'It is an English name.'

Philippe de Mortmain gazed at her for some seconds, then the grim face broke into a smile. 'Then Henry he shall be,' he agreed. 'How old would he be, if I may be so ungallant as to enquire a lady's age?'

'I am nine years old, monsieur,' Richilde said.

'The devil you are. He also looks older. He shall be my postilion. Will that please you?'

'I do not know what that is,' Richilde said.

'My groom,' Philippe de Mortmain said. 'He will stand on the step behind my carriage, and hold the door for me when I wish to get down. And for you, Mademoiselle Richilde, whenever you drive with me. Would you like to drive with me?'

'Oh, monsieur, could I?'

'You shall,' Philippe de Mortmain said. 'Beginning now. Now you shall ride with me.' He stooped from the saddle. 'Give me your arm.' She held up her right arm, had it seized in a powerful grip, and a moment later was seated behind him. 'Hold me round the waist,' he commanded. 'And you, boy, report to Jean François at the stables, and he will show you to your duties. Gentlemen.'

Once again, to Richilde's total surprise, he neither addressed nor looked at Jacqueline Chavannes, as the little cavalcade moved off towards the house. Richilde looked back at the girl, watched her trudging up the road behind them, with the dust from their hooves settling on her hair and her beautiful clothes and jewellery. And on her face, which was twisted in a mixture of anger and contempt.

The mystery deepened when Jacqueline was not present at supper. Indeed, Richilde did not see her again after she returned to the house, because it was time to join the rest of the children and exchange information and wonder at what they had discovered during their explorations, before they were called in to take their places at table. Philippe de Mortmain had arranged it so that they all sat at one end; he really was a much more friendly person than he appeared, even if he largely ignored them, preferring to talk with Uncle Maurice and Father Thomas, his chaplain, about all the unrest in the mainland British colonies.

'Madness,' Uncle Maurice asserted. 'I felt the same thing when poor Richard and his cousin stirred up all that trouble in the Leewards. And where has it got them?' He looked sympathetically at Jeanne. 'Now there is going to be a lot of trouble for the Americans.'

'I wonder,' Philippe said.

'Well, if the British have sent over an entire army . . .'

'Armies are all very well,' Philippe said. 'When there are other armies to oppose them, when there are garrison towns to be captured, with their stores of food and munitions. I have often thought, for example, that we here in St Domingue could declare our independence, and secure it, even against a French army.'

'But, my God,' Uncle Maurice said. 'That . . .'

Philippe smiled. 'Is treason? I do assure you, my dear Maurice, no one is going to arrest the Sieur de Mortmain for treason, nor anyone who is under his protection.' His gaze swept the table. 'But it is a point worth considering. Paris is often every bit as absurd as London. It will certainly be interesting to see how the Americans manage with their revolt. But that is sufficient politics for one night. Marguerite! Jeanne! Are you satisfied with your apartments?'

'They are magnificent,' Aunt Marguerite said. 'Quite beyond my expectations. I do not know how to thank you.'

'Then I suggest you do not try. I am but filling the house, with the right people. It is a crime for a house like this to be occupied only by a lonely bachelor.'

'None the less,' Marguerite insisted. 'Jeanne and I cannot just accept your hospitality. We must play our parts, as Maurice will play his. As you *are* a bachelor, Philippe, perhaps you will let us manage your household for you?'

'But monsieur already has a housekeeper,' Richilde said, without thinking, and blushed scarlet as every head turned to look at her.

'Go to your room, miss,' Mama said. 'How many times have I told you never to speak at table unless addressed?'

'Oh, but . . .' Richilde stood up, biting her lip to keep back the tears.

Philippe de Mortmain smiled at her. 'May I beg an amnesty, as this is her first night here, Jeanne? Sit down, child. She is right, you know. I do have a housekeeper, with whom Richilde has already become friends.'

'Oh,' Marguerite said. 'A . . .' she glanced at her husband. The word, and its various connotations, was not unknown in the English islands.

'I have, in fact, several housekeepers,' Philippe said, smiling at his cousins. 'Each of whom has certain duties to perform. I do assure you that there is no need to concern yourselves with any domestic matters. Rather would I have you rest and enjoy yourselves, and perhaps play the hostesses when we decide to entertain. There has been a sore lack, for both Papa and myself, since Mama's death.'

'I wonder you have not married,' Jeanne Hamilton ventured.

Philippe's gaze swept the table. 'I have never yet found

61

the woman with whom I would choose to spend the rest of my life,' he said. 'But now . . . who knows. I suspect my quest may be coming to an end.'

Richilde discovered that he was looking at her.

'He's going to marry Catherine,' Louis de Mortmain said. 'No doubt about that.'

The meal was over, and the grown-ups, along with Etienne and Catherine, were seated on the outside patio while the younger children had been dismissed to the far end.

'Oh, that will be exciting,' Lucy said. 'We'll all be bridesmaids. Won't we all be bridesmaids, Françoise?'

'He can't marry Catherine,' Françoise declared.

'Why not?' Louis demanded.

'Because we're all cousins,' Françoise explained, triumphantly. 'You can't marry your own cousin.'

'But we're only second cousins,' Kit said. 'At least. Come to think of it, I don't suppose Richilde and I are related to him at all. But certainly he can marry Catherine, if he wants to.'

Why do they all think he wants to marry Catherine? Richilde wondered, her heart pounding. He was looking at me. And he likes me. That was obvious. And as Kit had just pointed out, they were not even related, except by marriage. Of course he was old enough to be her father, but many girls married men old enough to be their fathers. And marriage, to Philippe de Mortmain . . . Why, it would mean that she would be mistress of all this. Françoise and Lucy and Annette, and even Catherine . . . and even Etienne, the wretch, would have to call her madame, and be polite to her, and do what she said . . . and then Jacqueline could be her housekeeper as well as Philippe's, and go on being her friend, as well. She felt so excited she thought she would burst.

But she hated it when the others kept talking about Catherine. The trouble was, Catherine was old enough to be married now, while she wouldn't be old enough for ages.

62

And perhaps Philippe did not want to wait very much longer; he was certainly very old. Her excitement was replaced by utter misery.

She was distracted by the arrival of several white men, with their wives, coming out of the candle-lit gloom of the patio.

"You'll have met Fedon, my attorney,' Phillipe de Mortmain said. 'His wife, Antoinette. And . . .' the names drifted into the darkness. Richilde was not really interested in them. She found herself wondering what Henry Christopher was doing, down in the domestics' village, whether he was thinking of her, and how he would take to his new duties, as a postilion. It sounded fearfully grand, and it suddenly occurred to her that when next she saw him he would be dressed in the Mortmain colours; undoubtedly the uniform would suit his already tall and muscular frame.

The evening filled with a vicious snarling, and she instinctively moved closer to Kit as she watched half a dozen large dogs being brought out of a gateway leading to the rear of the garden.

'They are only puppies, really,' Philippe explained. 'When papa died, I had his dogs put down. They were his. A dog can only have one master. So then I had to start from scratch with these pups. They are barely a year old. But they are good dogs, eh, Robert?'

The big Negro holding the leashes grinned at the white people. 'Oh, yes, sir, master, they are good dogs. They good and fierce. Nothing but red meat for them.'

Richilde watched the dogs' teeth as their lips drew back, and she clutched Kit's hand.

'Well, then,' Philippe de Mortmain said. 'I trust you have arranged a demonstration?'

'Yes, sir, master,' Robert said. 'They waiting now.' He gave a whistle, and once again the gate swung in to allow five men to enter, four of them dragging a fifth, who writhed and fought as he was pulled to the centre of the lawn beneath the patio. Richilde stared at him in horror, realising that he was naked, and smeared in blood, although she could see no sign of any injury.

'Master,' the man shouted. 'I begging you, master. Hang me, master. Hang me.'

'I am giving you the chance of life,' Philippe said, getting out of his chair to stand at the top of the steps. He snapped his fingers and the four men released their victim, immediately moving in front of him so that he could not climb the steps. 'That way,' Philippe said, pointing into the darkness. 'And you had best make haste.'

Jeanne Hamilton gave a gasp, and Maurice de Mortmain also got up. 'Philippe,' he said. 'You cannot be serious.'

'The fellow is due to be hanged for stealing,' Philippe said. 'As he well knows. This way his death will serve a purpose. And who knows, he has a sporting chance. Long odds, perhaps, but still a chance.'

'But Philippe . . .' Maurice grasped his cousin's arm. Philippe looked down at the hand on his sleeve, and Maurice slowly released it. 'Not in front of the women and children. I beg of you.'

'It will not be in front of the women and children,' Philippe said.

'Father Thomas,' Maurice de Mortmain appealed.

'It is the Seigneur's will,' the priest said. 'And the man is, in any event, condemned.'

Philippe was pointing at the black man. 'I told you to make haste.'

The man stared at the white man who was condemning him, then at those who sat or stood around him. Tears were rolling down his face. But he understood that further pleading was pointless. His tongue came out and circled his lips, and Richilde tried to imagine what thoughts must be going through his mind, whether he was considering an attempt to get up the stairs to attack his executioner, and realising that he would not make it. She felt sick.

The man turned, gave a despairing wail, and ran into the darkness.

'Count to ten,' Philippe said.

Jeanne Hamilton leapt to her feet, hurried across the

patio, grasped Richilde's arm. 'Bedtime,' she gasped. 'Come on, hurry.'

But I want to stay, Richilde thought. I want to watch, or at least hear. I want to feel some of the hate which has suddenly filled the evening. The hate and the fear and the bloodlust, all mingled together.

Chapter 3

THE MARCH
TO YORKTOWN

The fleet commanded by de Grasse recruited free men, of whatever colour, in Martinique and Guadeloupe and St Domingue and, as many of these volunteers were slave owners, there were also black servants on board the ships which dropped their anchors in Chesapeake Bay. Legend has it that amongst those who witnessed the surrender of Lord Cornwallis were a mulatto freeman named Chavannes and a Negro slave named Henri Christophe.

'Good morning, madamoiselle,' Phillipe de Mortmain said, smiling at Richilde. Who hesitated, like a thief caught in the very act, exposed in the centre of the great gallery. Because she did not even wish to see him, much less speak with him. Her confused emotions of last night had settled into the certainty that he was a monster. Mama had called him that, and for once Richilde had agreed entirely with her mother.

'I am going into Cap François,' Philippe said, coming closer. 'And I would like you to come. I promised you a ride in my carriage, remember? You will be able to see your friend Henry at work.'

'Oh, but . . .' She bit her lip.

'Madame Jacqueline is coming too,' Philippe said.

She so wanted to ride in the carriage. She so wanted to see

Henry. As if she could ever look Henry in the face again. Henry, all of the slaves, would know what had happened. Would know that she had been seated on the patio beside this man when he had ordered the destruction of one of them, in the most terrible fashion.

She looked past him, saw Kit, just appearing from his bedchamber. Oh, darling Kit. 'Can Kit come too? My brother,' she explained, as Philippe looked vaguely puzzled.

'But of course. The more the merrier, eh?' He threw his arm round her shoulders as he walked her towards the porch. 'We are riding into town,' he told Kit. 'Your sister and I. And she wishes you to accompany us. She does not wish to ride with me alone. She thinks I am cruel.' He gave her a squeeze. 'Do you not, Richilde?'

'Oh, I . . .' She was having difficulty breathing.

'It was a cruel thing to do, sir,' Kit said. 'It will make your people hate you.'

This time Richilde lost her breath altogether. But Philippe de Mortmain did not appear to take offence. Indeed, he smiled.

'My people hate me anyway, Christopher,' he said. 'And they hate you as well. Not for being cruel. Merely for having the complexion you possess.' He escorted them on to the porch, from where they could look down the great staircase, at the outside patio where they had sat last night, with the lawn beyond. Richilde expected it to be splattered with blood, or at least trampled and muddy – but it was as smoothly perfect as it had ever been, its borders patrolled by a platoon of slaves who knelt or squatted, each armed with a machete, chipping away at the weeds. Beyond, in the distance, they could make out other slave gangs heading into the fields: groups of fifty and sixty men and women, each similarly armed, each led by a single white man on a mule.

'They hate us,' Philippe observed. 'For being here, while they are there. Do you know how many slaves I own, Kit?'

'Monsieur Morin said about seven thousand,' Kit said.

'Give or take a hundred, yes. And I have seven hundred white or mulatto residents on the plantation as well, but of those, two thirds are women and children. Now what do you suppose stops that weeding gang down there from running up these steps and cutting the three of us to pieces? I assure you that they all know what happened last night.'

Richilde found that she was holding his hand, and his fingers gave her a reassuring squeeze.

'It is simply fear,' he said. 'It is a nameless, unconscious fear. I am the master. I possess the power of life and death over them. Were I to give an order now, I could have them all hanging in fifteen minutes. What is more, I could order that gang to hang one of their own number, and I would be obeyed without question. Because of their fear. And I will tell you this, Christopher Hamilton. The very moment those slaves, or perhaps even one of them, ceases to know absolute terror whenever I approach, then are all of our lives in danger. Remember that. The responsibility will soon be yours, no less than mine.' He pointed. 'The carriage.'

'Henry,' Richilde shouted, and ran down the stairs, only remembering to pause, and look over her shoulder at Philippe, as she reached the bottom.

Philippe smiled. 'Does he not look splendid?'

Henry Christopher stood beside the carriage, holding the door for them He wore a pale blue tail coat decorated with gold braid, pale blue stockings, and black leather shoes with gilt buckles. Kit realised that he had never seen Henry with shoes on before. Today he also wore a white powdered wig. And he carefully studied the ground as his master approached.

'You look splendid, Henry,' Richilde said.

'I thank you, mademoiselle,' he said. Always before he had called her Richilde.

'I entirely agree with mademoiselle,' Philippe de Mortmain said, giving Richilde a hand up into the carriage, where Jacqueline Chavannes was already seated, dressed as usual as if she was going to a ball. Kit sat beside her, and Henry closed the door on them. Then the driver, a very large black man named Jean François, flicked his whip and the carriage rolled down the drive. Kit looked out of the window to see

Louis standing on the porch, gazing after them, a puzzled expression on his face.

He glanced at Jacqueline. He and Louis had sat up talking for a long time last night; Louis had indeed advanced a similar reasoning to that of Philippe de Mortmain in explaining why his cousin had acted as he did. Kit had not agreed with him, as he did not agree with him now; Uncle Maurice, for instance, had maintained discipline on Marigot, where the proportions of white to black had been even more dangerously low, without ever descending to downright cruelty. But he and Louis had soon carried their discussion to more interesting topics. Louis had asserted that Madame Chavannes had to be Philippe's mistress. Both boys were just becoming old enough to understand the differences between the sexes, the delights which undoubtedly lay in front of them. Which, they both felt, were perhaps already available, when they looked around themselves at the scantily clad Negresses, many of them hardly older than themselves, and decidedly attractive in their slender, hard muscled and yet well breasted, bodies. Supposing their respective mothers would not be furious at the very idea. But none of the black girls in any way compared with this elegant and utterly composed creature, who now conversed with Philippe de Mortmain, calling him monsieur, but smiling and apparently content with her situation. To possess such a woman . . . Kit flushed as she suddenly turned her head and found him looking at her.

They were amongst houses, and people. The carriage pulled off the main thoroughfare into a side street, and came to a halt. Henry Christopher immediately opened the door, and Philippe de Mortmain got down. 'I shall not be long,' he said. 'You may visit your family, Jacqueline.'

'Thank you, monsieur.' She allowed Henry to take her hand, descended herself. 'Would you like to come for a walk, children?' she asked.

Did she really think he was a child, Kit thought angrily? But he climbed down and, with Richilde, followed her across the street and round the corner, into a small haberdashery, where the people serving behind the counter were clearly Jacqueline's relatives.

'This is my father's shop,' she explained. 'Papa, I would have you meet Monsieur Christopher Hamilton, and Mademoiselle Richilde.'

They shook hands with the old gentleman, whose features possessed many more Negro characteristics than those of his daughter.

'They are now living at Vergée d'Or Great House,' Jacqueline said. 'We are friends.'

'It is nice out there,' Monsieur Chavannes agreed. 'The Seigneur de Mortmain is a very kind man. He is very generous.'

Richilde looked at Kit, who raised his eyebrows. He wondered if this man knew the position his daughter occupied? Of course he would know. And was happy that it should be so, because to him Philippe de Mortmain was a kind and generous man. As no doubt he also knew of the inhumanity of which Philippe was capable, but which in no way affected him, or Jacqueline. Kit felt quite sick at the thought of ever possessing such power over other human beings. Not that he ever would, of course, as he was a Hamilton and not a Mortmain. And yet, in his remark this morning, Philippe had almost suggested . . .

'And this is my brother, Jacques,' Jacqueline was saying, introducing a young man who had just come from the back of the store. He was younger than his sister, certainly, not a great deal older than himself, Kit estimated, but lacked her open expression, and indeed, scowled at the visitors.

As Jacqueline observed. 'We must be getting back to the carriage,' she said, taking Richilde's hand. 'The Sieur de Mortmain was merely visiting his bankers. He will be ready for us soon.'

They emerged into the glare of the street, for the sun was by now high in the sky.

'Why doesn't he like us?' Richilde asked. 'Your brother?'

Jacqueline smiled, but it was one of her bitter smiles, this time. 'He envies you your white blood,' she said. 'He would

70

be as you.'

'Don't you want to be like us?'

She shrugged. 'I'm happy.'

'Mulattos are much better off in the French colonies than in the British,' Kit observed. And then glanced at her to see if he had offended her.

'That is quite true,' she said seriously. 'But it is also the cause of my brother's anger. Ten years ago, a mulatto had exactly equal rights with a white man, here in St Domingue. But my people became too wealthy, and too arrogant. And the whites grew to hate us. So they had laws passed against us, and now, why, we cannot wear clothes or jewellery of more than a certain value, and our menfolk cannot bear arms. We must know our proper place.' Her lips twisted.

'But you dress like any white woman,' Richilde said.

'Ah,' Jacqueline said. 'That is because I am under the protection of the Sieur de Mortmain.'

And despite what you say, Kit thought with a sudden flash of insight, you hate us just as much as your brother does.

'Why did the Sieur de Mortmain take us into town, instead of the Mortmains?' Richilde asked.

'Like I told you.' Jacqueline said. 'Because you aren't Mortmains. The Seigneur thinks very deeply. He plans all the time. You are, like me, nothing without him. This pleases him. And that is why we should be friends. Us three.'

Kit hadn't actually thought of it in that blunt fashion. But he supposed she had to be right. They of all people couldn't afford ever to quarrel with Philippe de Mortmain. Or even not to take his side.

Jacqueline paused on the street corner, gazed at the carriage. 'Like them,' she said, half to herself.

The children peered past her shoulder. Jean François had descended from his perch and was deep in conversation with another black man, obviously also a coachman, because he wore livery and a wig, although he was nothing like Jean François in appearance, but was small and narrow shouldered, and stood awkwardly, as if one leg was shorter than the other.

'Is he a Vergée d'Or slave?' Kit asked.

Jacqueline shook her head. 'But Toussaint and Jean François always seem to have much to discuss. If they are not careful they will both wind up on the wheel.' She jerked her head to where Henry Christopher waited, by the door, but obviously listening to what the two men were saying. 'Your friend too, Richilde. I should warn him against bad company, if I were you.'

Vast clouds of smoke rolled above Vergée d'Or, seeming to reach upwards into the heavens to mingle with the rain clouds which every noon gathered above the mountains. The plantation was grinding.

Grinding on Marigot had been a hectic affair, Kit Hamilton remembered. But it was nothing compared with here, where the concentrated efforts of nearly eight thousand people were dedicated to producing a new record crop. He had now experienced three of these annual cataclysms, and each one had left him more amazed, and emotionally drained, than the one before.

The smoke, rising in the air in a column for three hundred feet before spreading to obliterate the morning sky like some portent of inescapable doom. But rather was it a portent of inescapable wealth. It was a sweet-smelling smoke, which titillated the nostrils even as it filled the lungs. And beneath it, the furnace that was Vergée d'Or, the smell of the boiling sugar cane, and then the boiling sugar, and then the boiling molasses, filled the air, the mind, the body, even the soul. During the grinding season, a normal diet was impossible; everything tasted sweet. But then, during the grinding season, nothing was normal.

Gone were the lazy mornings spent riding the paths between the canefields, the huge lunches, the jolly evenings sitting on the patio drinking wine, the trips into Cap François, the fencing lessons and the shooting practice which Philippe de Mortmain regarded as an essential part of the daily routine of every white man on the estate. Gone even was the siesta considered so important to Europeans; even at two in the afternoon, when the sun ruled the heavens, the work went on. Although not even the sun, a Caribbean sun, huge and round and fiery and imperious, could penetrate the smoke blanket which covered the plantation. The sun could do no more than add its heat to the inferno below. Yet it was scarcely noticed.

The plantation made Kit think of the tales he had heard of the great slave revolt in Berbice, on the mainland of South America, sixteen years before, when the rampaging blacks had destroyed everything in their paths. For before grinding the canefields must be burned, to remove the possibility of snakes or poisonous insects attacking the cutters. Thus over a month earlier had the great smoke clouds first rolled across the landscape, and the brilliant white sheets in the Great House become dotted with black wisps of ash, which dissolved into filthy smudges whenever touched. The house servants had been the first to find their work doubled, as they washed and scrubbed and cleaned.

The fires smouldering, the fields had been assaulted with knife and machete. Philippe de Mortmain had himself led the van of the charge, supported by his overseers, by his cousins Etienne and Louis, and even, this year, by Kit himself, at last considered old enough, at thirteen, to control a work gang. Behind them the slaves had marched like an army advancing in extended order, shouting and cheering, driven always by the ear-splitting crack of the whip, and followed by the squealing axles of the carts on to which the cut stalks had been thrown.

Once this work had been properly commenced, Philippe left it in the care of Fedon, and attended to the factory. For the previous six weeks this had been made ready, with grease and polish, to take away the rust and the faults which would have accumulated during the growing season. Now it had been put to work. The selected slaves, great strong young fellows, had mounted the treadmill, the signal had been given, the whips had seared their backs, and the huge wheel had started its ponderous action.

Then it had been time to light the boiling fires. Special fuel had been stored for this purpose over the previous weeks, dried wood and straw. By now the first cartloads were bouncing down the tracks from the canefields, heaped with cut stalks, already turning from green to yellow, still showing the scorch marks from the flames; the casualties, Kit thought fancifully, despatched from the battlefield, where the dreadful work of execution went on and on.

The carts were drawn by mules bred specially for this purpose, up to the raised man-made mound behind the factory, where the giant chutes awaited. Here there also waited another regiment of slaves, controlled and marshalled by Maurice de Mortmain, and armed with spades and pitchforks. These dug into the canestalks and tumbled them down the chute, and thence into the first of the rollers, this one a system of interlocking iron teeth, which seized the cane and crushed it into splinters. The dreadful sound rose even above the whine of the treadmill and the gears, while every so often a stalk escaped, to fall over the side and arrest the process with an almost human scream of tortured metal. To discourage this were some forty picked hands, for time was not to be lost repairing machinery. Here was a dangerous job, and Kit could still remember, at last year's grinding, the truly inhuman scream which had followed the disappearance of a black man's hand and forearm, his fingers caught by the ceaselessly rolling drums.

That poor fellow had died from loss of blood and shock. But no one had had the time even to notice his passing. And he had soon been forgotten, as the mangled cane was thrown out the far side, on to another chute, before being forced through another set of rollers, these no more than barrels, touching each other as they rotated, which seized the shattered stalks and compressed them, causing the first drops of the precious liquid that would eventually be sugar to drip into the gutters beneath.

But still the cane's ordeal was unfinished, for there was yet another chute, and yet a third set of rollers to be negotiated, these so close and fine that their squealing creak against

74

each other dominated all other sounds inside the factory. Here the last of the juice was squeezed free, and the stalks were left no more than wisps of useless wood.

Yet not so useless that they could not still be consumed. A sugar factory produced its own fuel, its own energy, whenever possible. Beneath the last of the rollers was an immense pit into which the stalks fell. But here again was a platoon of slaves with pitchforks and spades, for off the side of the pit there led a channel to the fires, and in this gully there were more carts and sweating labourers. The stalks were loaded on to the carts, and carried to the great furnaces.

This truly was the end of their journey, until they were belched forth to darken the sky as black smoke. But the juice had only just begun its travels. The gutters from beneath the rollers and the crushers ran down to the vats, huge iron tubs set exactly over the never cooling furnaces. Here the liquid bubbled and leapt, a witch's brew, constantly being combed through with nets at the end of long sticks held by the factory hands. Beyond were more gutters, more cauldrons, more furnaces, and not until Maurice de Mortmain was satisfied with the quality was the cane juice allowed to flow off into the cooling vats. These were also set over a pit, and had perforated bottoms. For as the liquid cooled, while the precious crystals would cling to the sides of the vats, the still molten molasses would slip through the sieves and into the fresh vats waiting beneath.

The manufacture, storage, and bunging of the hogsheads was a separate industry in itself, employing another horde of slaves under the supervision of Monsieur Huges, the head carpenter. And always there were the book-keepers, commanded by Monsieur Ferry, a dapper little fellow who wore spectacles, and was never to be discovered without a notepad in one hand and a pencil in the other, listing, evaluating, checking.

Nor was even the complete hogshead the end of the process, for the molasses in turn were drawn down yet another gutter, to yet more vats, and these were kept simmering, while the additives were carefully measured, for Vergée d'Or, like every other sugar plantation, manufactured its own rum. Here waited the head chemist, Monsieur d'Albret, a happy fellow who had to spend most of his day tasting the slowly fermenting liquid; there was more red in his nose then ever came from the sun.

But perhaps d'Albret was symptomatic of the whole, because, remarkably, Kit thought, grinding was a happy time, or at least a distracted time. There was not an able-bodied person on the plantation, from Philippe de Mortmain himself down to the smallest Negro boy or girl who did not work harder this month than throughout the rest of the year taken together. Only the white women and their children were exempt from labour. And yet, the change from the unending field work, the making and mending of roads, the back-breaking weeding, the repairs to houses, was itself pleasant, and during the grinding season there was no daily punishment parade. The whips cracked ceaselessly, and the men and women worked until they dropped, for the ships were coming, and would be in Cap François on the appointed days to load, and the life of a slave, valuable enough as part of the estate's assets, became trivial if set against any damage to the crop caused by a delay in shipment. Thus they remained too busy to be miserable.

Except perhaps those with too much intelligence for their own good. For as Kit walked his mule down the road from the factory, his spell of duty over for the day, towards the relative peace and sanity, and more important, the hot bath and the change of clothing, of the Great House, he encountered Henry Christopher.

Even the coachmen were required during grinding, to drive the largest of the carts. Henry, for all that he was only twelve years old, expertly controlled the two mules who drew his enormous load, a pile of canestalks which reached several feet above his head. No doubt he too was pleased to be doing something more than riding beside Jean François but he did not look happy. The laughing boy who had played with them on St Kitts might never have been. Henry already had the physique of a young man, taller than Kit himself, and quite as broad, and his face had assumed the grimly gaunt characteristics of so many slaves. Now he merely touched his forehead in respect as his old friend rode by. They were friends no longer. On Vergée d'Or there were masters, and there were slaves, and fate had decided that Kit should go one way and Henry the other. Which was a pity, Kit thought; he still liked the boy, still felt that they had the capacity for friendship. And Henry surely knew that it was due equally to Richilde and himself that he had been spared the torments of the field, the indignities of the slave compound.

But he seemed aware only that they had made their choice. And resented it. Kit somehow felt responsible for the black boy's future, because he was their slave. He certainly did not want Henry to be unhappy. That way led to irrational acts the consequences of which not even himself or Richilde would be able to save him.

And it wasn't as if there had ever been a choice. Philippe de Mortmain, for whatever reasons of his own, had given the Hamilton children the chance to escape their predestined role of permanent poor relations. The Mortmains had not liked the way in which their great cousin, over the past three years, had paid more attention to Richilde's progress on the spinet or with the needle, than any of Françoise or Lucy or Annette's efforts, had encouraged the marriage of Catherine to François the son of a neighbouring planter, Thomas de Milot, when she would obviously have made so perfect a wife for himself . . . But there was nothing they could do about it, either. What Philippe de Mortmain decreed, so it was.

Richilde had accepted this more easily than himself. But then, she came into less contact with the actual working of the plantation. For such was the fear that the very presence of Philippe de Mortmain inspired that there had never again been any necessity for him to reveal that mailed fist which was his treasured family emblem, at least before the ladies. Kit often wondered, indeed, if that first night, so shocking in its suddeness, had not been as carefully calculated as everything else the Seigneur did. In which case he was indeed a monster. A monster who intended to marry his sister.

But a monster who was also probably the wealthiest man in the West Indies, which in 1779 probably meant the world, and a monster who had never been anything less than unfailingly kind and generous to them both, and to Mama, for all that she daily seemed to fade as she dreamed more and more of her long lost husband who was only a distant memory to Kit.

So where did that leave him? A lifetime of security, as brother-in-law to the Sieur de Mortmain, provided that he stayed at the monster's shoulder, which would necessarily require him to become a monster himself? He really could see little alternative, however much he wanted one.

He approached the plantation from the western side, walking his horse beside the beach as he neared the domestics' village, drawing rein with a frown as he watched the woman walking on the sand, loose gown flowing in the constant sea breeze, hair drifting. She, like him, was still out of sight of the village, and she was utterly unaware of his presence, half hidden as he was by the trees. He watched in consternation as she stopped walking, lifted the gown over her head and threw it on the sand, revealing that it was her only garment, and then slowly walked down the beach towards the water. Because Jacqueline Chavannes was also spared the travails of grinding. Her labour was only to be performed in bed, beneath her master.

He became aware of a fresh rash of sweat, and of a sudden pounding of his heart, as he gazed at that body, so strangely light brown, so gleaming in the afternoon sunlight, so perfectly shaped, from high, pointed breast through softly curving buttock to gently muscled calf. And covered in such firm velvet flesh, to suggest that within was a volcano of passion, waiting to be released.

But it was the Sieur de Mortmain's passion. Jacqueline had, in fact, kept herself aloof from Kit over the past couple of years, where he had hoped their friendship would grow.

78

She and Richilde were still as thick as thieves. They sewed together and they walked together, and undoubtedly they talked together. About what he did not know and could not discover, for Richilde, as she entered puberty, was also less of an eager playmate than before, kept to herself, adopted a serious demeanour, except when in the company of her mulatto friend. Who was, he supposed, in many ways replacing the elder sister she had always wanted and never had. Which was just as well, because relations between her and the three younger Mortmain girls daily became more distant. They openly disdained Richilde's preference for a coloured girl, as they disparagingly put it. But there was nothing they could do about that either, save privately sneer over the peculiar etiquette that forbade the quadroon ever being allowed to join them for meals or entertaining, or in church. Richilde was the Seigneur's favourite cousin, and Jacqueline Chavannes was his favourite housekeeper. There was not anything even Uncle Maurice and Aunt Marguerite could do about that last, however much they obviously disapproved.

But the growing rift between the families was being extended to himself as well, and he had no older playmate. Save for Louis. Louis alone, with his relaxed approach to life, did not seem to find it uncongenial for the Hamiltons to have so advanced themselves. 'I tell you honestly, Kit,' he would say. 'I doubt I shall ever make a planter. I have not the stomach for it. You are welcome to my share.' Louis was a good fellow, but a frightful bore. It occurred to Kit for the first time in his life that he was lonely. And that his loneliness might be heading him into forbidden paths. For he had released the rein, and the mule was making its way forward, guided by his knees, on to the sand. And now the woman heard him, and turned sinking as she did so until only her head was exposed, frowning, and then smiling, as she recognised him.

'Why, Kit,' she said. 'Why do you not come in? The water is deliciously cool.'

He dismounted, wondering if he dared, wondering if it

might be possible, in the cool intimacy of the sea, just to brush against her velvet skin, to discover if she was indeed as delightful to touch as she was to observe.

But would she not be angry if he undressed before her? Even supposing he could bring himself to?

Yet she had invited him. And she had not been angry at his staring at her. Now she gave a low laugh and stood up. He supposed he would never forget that picture, of water dripping from hair and from chin, from nipple and from slowly uncovering pubic hair, as she waded towards him. 'Are you afraid of me?' she asked. 'I think you are.'

'I . . .' He licked his lips.

'I have seen you watching me,' she said. 'Just as I have watched you grow. I have known that one day you would seek me out.'

'I . . .' His tongue seemed stuck to his head.

She had come right up to him. Now she put her hands on his shoulders, drew him forward, kissed him gently on the lips. He could not stop himself. His hands closed on her ribs, and then slid down over her rounded hips. Her flesh was indeed like velvet, and seemed to glow beneath his touch. And her fingers were releasing the buttons on his shirt.

Her mouth turned up to his, and a moment later they were kneeling, and then lying, on the sand. He attempted to protest, to remind her that he had spent the day in the factory, that he was covered in grease as well as sweat, and smelled of smoke, but it really did not seem relevant. Here was the culmination of every vague stirring within him for the last three years, since he had first set eyes on her, and since he had first become aware of his own manhood. And in her arms all consideration of the past, the future, even the present, seemed irrelevant – until he had climaxed and rolled away from her, to lie on his back and gasp for breath, and become very aware indeed of who and what he was, and even more, what she was.

She knelt beside him and smiled at him. 'Fifteen years old,' she said. 'They are the best.'

He raised himself on his elbow. 'You . . . my cousin . . .'

80

'Oh, I shall not tell him. Unless I have to.'

'Eh?'

Again that liquid smile. 'You belong to me, now. You must never forget that. To me.' She shook her heavy wet hair in his face, scattered sand. 'And only me.'

He frowned at her. 'I don't understand.'

She sat on her heels. 'It is very simple. I do not find your cousin a very exciting man. Yet must I lie with him. He bought me as if I were a slave. He settled all my father's debts for him, if Papa would allow me to come out here. I was but sixteen. And should I leave, why, he would bankrupt Papa. But I do not want to leave. Why should I be poor? And yet, I may be forced to leave, when your sister grows up. Because she is what Philippe really wants. A wife whom he has trained from a very early age, to like the things he likes, to think as he does, to live as he wishes. Besides, she is what Mama Céleste promised him.'

Kit frowned at her. 'Mama Céleste? Promised?'

Jacqueline kissed him on the nose. 'You are too young to know of that. Yet Philippe will marry Richilde. And when that time comes, I may need someone to turn to.' She sighed. 'It will not be very long, now.'

'Me?' He sat up in alarm. 'You must be mad.'

'You,' she said. 'And you will not refuse me. The Seigneur will be amused to learn about us. Then. He would not be amused now. Were I to tell him what happened here this afternoon, he would beat me. But he would also send you from the plantation. He might even change his mind about Richilde. And he will certainly send your arrogant little black friend into the fields. And there would be the end of all your hopes and ambitions. So we will not tell him, and we will be friends, and we will be allies. And we will both be happy. I will make you very happy, Kit Hamilton.' Gently she pushed him back to the sand again. 'Oh, very happy.'

As if he could ever be happy again. That evening, and every evening for the rest of grinding, he seated himself as far as possible from Philippe de Mortmain, convinced that he would betray himself, his guilt, his surging desire. To which was now added the misery of jealousy. Because Jacqueline would be waiting, alone upstairs in the huge suite she shared with her master, to make him every bit as happy.

'Poor Kit is overtired,' Aunt Marguerite said, ruffling his hair. 'It is hard work.'

'But good work,' Maurice de Mortmain said. 'We have topped the record.'

'As we have done every year for the past three,' Philippe said. 'Since your arrival, indeed. I never doubted that with you here, Maurice, the plantation would go from strength to strength. But now it is all but done. You will be able to laze again, Kit.'

Kit joined in the laughter. Suddenly he was a conspirator. It was not something he had ever intended. He wondered if Henry was similarly unhappy because he too was a conspirator, remembered that day, so long ago now, that Jacqueline had pointed to the little lame coachman, Toussaint, whispering to Jean François. He had encountered Toussaint often since, when going into Cap François, had invariably been greeted with the utmost courtesy. Toussaint was, indeed, a most courteous and popular man, apparently amongst white people as much as black. Even Philippe de Mortmain always gave him a greeting. 'The most intelligent Negro I ever met,' he would say, and utter one of his short laughs. 'The only intelligent Negro I ever met.'

'I wonder you do not buy him for yourself,' Richilde had once remarked.

'I would,' Philippe had replied. 'But the scoundrel Milot will not sell. At least, dear Thérèse will not sell. She regards Toussaint as her prize possession. Mind you, I'm not sure it wouldn't be a mistake. One does not really want an intelligent Negro around the place, especially as coachman, where he can meet others. Look at Jean François, now. He is ideal. He has not a brain in his head. And the same goes for your young Henry. You can see that at a glance.'

Which was absolute nonsense, Kit reckoned. Henry had brains all right. It occurred to him that Henry was quite

82

capable of conspiring. But conspiring to do what? Except perhaps run away, either to perish in the jungle, or be recaptured and flogged to death. Kit doubted even Richilde would be able to save him if he attempted anything as foolish as that. Supposing Richilde still wanted to look after him at all.

But it was his duty to look after both of them and, as Richilde clearly no longer needed his care, that left only Henry. He could not doubt that Jacqueline was probably right, and Henry would share in his disgrace, when it inevitably came.

'Now I have great news for you,' Philippe said, actually leaving his chair to stand before them. 'It arrived three days ago, but I have kept it to myself until today, until grinding had been completed. Because it will affect us all.'

'News?' Maurice de Mortmain frowned. 'From France?'

'Indeed, from France. You will hardly disagree, dear cousin, that the failure of Burgoyne's expedition against the Colonies from Canada, indeed, his surrender, has put an end to British hopes of reconquering America?'

'Well,' Maurice said. 'I wouldn't go so far as to say that. The British . . .'

'Bah,' Philippe said. 'The British. Always the British. This time they are going to receive a beating, I can promise you that.' He looked around him with a triumphant air. 'Because His Majesty had decided to throw the weight of France into the struggle.'

'What did you say?' Maurice shouted.

'I mean that, very shortly, France will be declaring war upon Great Britain,' Philippe said.

'War?' Aunt Marguerite cried. 'Oh, my God! Not again. The last time . . .'

'They had the better of things,' Philippe agreed. 'This time things will be entirely different.'

'War,' Jeanne Hamilton moaned. 'War.'

'War,' Etienne de Mortmain shouted. 'We shall lick them this time. I know it.'

'We all know it,' Philippe declared.

'But . . .' Maurice de Mortmain was obviously confused. 'You said, very shortly. Then how do you know of it?'

'We have been advised by fast sloop. A great fleet, commanded by the Admiral de Grasse himself, is on its way to Cap François. It is intended for America, to land an army to support the colonists. It is necessary for the fleet to be actually there when war is declared, or at least very close, or the Royal Navy may well intercept it. But the Governor-General was informed in advance, because it is de Grasse's hope to recruit here, and in the other French colonies.' He looked at the three young men.

'It seems madness,' Maurice de Mortmain said. 'For a monarchy to fight another monarchy in support of rebels. Suppose we here in St Domingue were to copy the Americans?'

'Well, now,' Philippe said. 'There would be quite a situation. But first we will fight for these other colonists. And make friends with them, eh, as we all share the same hemisphere. I have no doubt at all that several of them will volunteer for the colours. But I thought that one of you might like to lead the way. Etienne?'

'Eh?' Etienne twisted in his seat. 'Well . . .'

'Not 'Tienne,' Aunt Marguerite declared. 'It can never be 'Tienne. Why, Philippe, he is your heir.'

'Yes,' Philippe said, somewhat drily. 'As you say, not Etienne.'

'I will volunteer, monsieur,' Louis said, getting up.

'You, boy?'

'I am seventeen, monsieur. Quite capable of bearing a musket.'

'It will hardly come to that,' Philippe promised. 'I will get you a commission, I promise you. But I am proud of you, boy. Proud of you.'

War, Kit thought. Against the British. But he was British himself. No, he wasn't; he had been born in St Kitts and was French by adoption. The British had driven his father into exile and probably death. His every instinct cried out to him to support the Americans.

Just as his every instinct cried out to him to escape Vergée d'Or, at least for a while, to think, and to avoid the baleful influence of Jacqueline Chavannes.

'I would like to volunteer also, monsieur,' he said.

'You?' Philippe looked amazed.

'You?' Jeanne Hamilton shouted. 'My God, not you.'

'You, Kit?' Richilde asked. 'Why you?'

'Because . . . because Father is in America, somewhere,' Kit said. 'I know it. And cousin Alex is certainly there. My family, all fighting against the British. I should be there too.'

'Spoken like a man,' Philippe said. 'But do you not suppose that you are rather young?'

'I am fifteen,' Kit insisted. 'And I am as tall as Louis. I am a man.' If you only knew how much of a man, dear Philippe, he thought. He looked from left to right, defiantly. 'It is more my fight than any of yours.' He smiled at his mother. 'Who knows, I might find Papa for you.'

'But who'll look after you?' Jeanne wailed. 'Out there, all on your own?'

'That is an important point,' Philippe agreed. 'You will both need servants.'

'Why . . .' Kit grinned at them, all of his problems suddenly falling into place. 'We'll take Henry Christopher. Who could ask for a better servant than that?'

'The column will advance.' The colonel spoke quietly, hardly seeming to be addressing more than his immediate subordinates, his voice certainly not carrying to the mass of white clad infantry standing rigidly to attention behind him. But now those subordinate officers drew their swords and pointed them at the distant earthworks which guarded the town of Savannah, the drums began to roll, and the soldiers marched forward.

Kit's stomach rolled with the drums, and his mouth was dry. It was only just past dawn, and he had been unable to digest any breakfast. He glanced quickly to the left, saw Louis also advancing, fifteen yards away, sword pointed at the British position, face grim with determination. Then he

85

looked forward again. It had been impressed upon the volunteer officers that they must always look to the front.

Yet he was continuously aware of Jacques Chavannes' eyes, fixed on his back. He did not suppose it was at all coincidental, really, that the mulatto should have volunteered for the American expedition; half the mulattos in Cap François had taken the opportunity to fight alongside the whites. Nor could he suppose it strange that the young man should be in his regiment, his company; there were only two regiments of volunteers from St Domingue, one from Cap François in the north, and one from Port-au-Prince in the south, and they both came from Cap François. And presumably he was not even the only officer in this army who had made a mistress of the sister of one of the enlisted men. But he was certainly the one with the guiltiest conscience.

Made a mistress of Jacqueline Chavannes. There was humour. She had taken him, because she had felt like it, because she was bored with Philippe, and because she had surmised that he might one day be useful to her. He was the one to be pitied, not her.

What thoughts to be taking into battle. Because now the active army was advancing, towards the little balls of white smoke which broke into spreading cloud above the British lines. Undoubtedly, early as it was, the defenders were fully aware of the French and American plans, no doubt because the fleet had wasted hours yesterday, and a great deal of powder and shot, in a futile bombardment of the defences.

A cannonball bounced over the ground towards him. He had the greatest urge to jump to one side, but dared not. Instead he watched it pass him, and listened to screams from behind. But he dared not turn, not even to see if Jacques Chavannes had been hit. He must always look towards the enemy.

The pace was quickening, and remarkably he had not been wounded. Now he could see soldiers manning the redoubts, mustachioed fellows in very dark blue coats with bright yellow waistcoats, and huge, braided grenadier bonnets, obviously Hessians, the mercenary Germans hired by King George to fight his colonial war for him. They were preparing to fire a volley, as soon as the French and Americans came within range. Kit almost hesitated, then forced himself onwards, watched the ripple of smoke, felt the rush of hot air, and still remained standing. But standing, now; not advancing. From behind and to either side there came cries of dismay, and he realised that the other officers were retiring. He looked to his right, watched Louis run back towards the men he had been leading.

Kit turned right around, his whole being consumed with an angry frustration, an immense desire to rush forward all by himself, to conquer the hated Germans or die in the attempt. But his own column had also dissolved, and was retreating out of range, leaving several of their comrades tossed about the meadow like so many white sacks, bicorne hats rolled away, muskets and bayonets useless toys, blood already coagulating as the sun rose.

And now too he could smell the death, mingling with the powder which hung in the still air, mingling too with the sweat and the fear, as he found himself also running after the defeated Frenchmen. He wanted to catch them up, to belabour them with the flat of his untried sword, to drive them once again into the assault. But when he reached them he did nothing. He had run away as well, and besides, there was a senior officer, mounted, telling them to fall in and march back to their cantonments. There would be no more fighting today. Or ever, perhaps. Watching the conflict had been the Admiral, as well as the army commanders, and now the Admiral turned away in disgust; the dawn assault had been his idea, as had been the preliminary bombardment.

He found himself amidst the tents of the regimental camp, already being stowed. 'We are to leave,' Louis de Mortmain said. 'Savannah is too strongly defended.'

Kit stopped in front of Jacques Chavannes. 'Why did you not follow me?' he asked. 'We could have won, had you followed me.'

'I ran because the others ran, monsieur,' Chavannes said.

'I would have followed you, master,' Henry Christopher said. His face was as grimly stern as ever. 'Why do you not give me a musket?'

'Now you know that is nonsense, Henri,' Louis said. 'We cannot arm our slaves.'

Henri opened his mouth to protest against the misuse of his name, caught Kit's eye, and shrugged. 'Yet these Americans fight to avoid being slaves themselves,' he said.

'You talk too much, boy,'Louis snapped. 'And think too much. Watch yourself.' He stalked away.

'He is right, Henry,' Kit said. 'About talking. And even perhaps thinking. There is a time for everything.'

'And now is not the time for me,' Henry said thoughtfully. 'But I am thinking only on military matters, master. As you have taught me to do.'

'Military matters,' Kit said bitterly. 'The ease with which an army can be routed?'

'The ease with which an army can lose heart, certainly,' Henry agreed. 'But even more important, the strength of a defensive position, well held. Even Frederick the Great would have found Savannah difficult. That is something to remember, master.'

Even inside the tent ice formed beneath the ground sheets, crackled as they moved; outside the snow clouded down in a constant blizzard, driven by unceasing winds. This winter of 1780 was even worse than the last, and that had been bad enough. Kit huddled in his greatcoat and shivered, watched Louis de Mortmain attempting to light a pipe, listened to Henry's teeth chattering; the black boy felt the cold more than any of them.

On Vergée d'Or they would still be celebrating Christmas. Certainly they would drink a toast to absent friends, and Mama and Richilde would shed a tear for him, as no doubt Aunt Marguerite would shed a tear for Louis, and Henrietta for her Henry. But they could hardly drink a toast to the coming victory.

It had been the Admiral's decision to move the French

army north after the abortive onslaught on Savannah. It was still supposed by the Americans that the main British effort would eventually rise out of New York, where General Sir Henry Clinton was in overall command of the British forces in North America. Thus they had sat around their various encampments and occasionally engaged in a skirmish with the redcoats while the British had been allowed to overrun Virginia and Georgia and the entire southern half of the country. It had hardly seemed an adequate strategy to Kit, brought up on the aggressive notions of the great Frederick, but then there did not seem any coherent strategy evident in any of the Americans' plans; they did not even allow their commander in chief, a Virginia farmer named George Washington, a free hand in whatever he might attempt to do, but subjected him to long-distance control by a committee of civilians.

The French soldiers had at the least been cheered by the arrival of a general officer to command them, Jean Baptiste Donatien de Vimeur, Count de Rochambeau, a veteran of both the War of the Austrian Succession and that Seven Years' War in which Frederick of Prussia had earned his reputation as the greatest soldier of all time. Kit had felt rather ashamed as he remembered their childhood games when he had teased the Mortmains with the fact that the French generals had always lost their battles; Rochambeau had been one of those generals. But he was at least a professional. And yet his arrival had made very little difference either to their success or lack of it. They had merely spent more time during the summer drilling. And even that had been preferable to sitting around their tents in the deadening cold, waiting for something to relieve their boredom.

'I wonder you do not take a pipe,' Louis said, at last puffing happily. 'It is a great solace.'

'I suspect it would freeze to my lips,' Kit said.

'You are a sad fellow,' Louis commented. 'Well, I shall go for a walk. There are some women down by the canteen. I saw them there this morning.' He winked. 'A fellow must endeavour to keep from freezing.'

'Good luck,' Kit said, and pulled his greatcoat tighter yet.

Louis regarded him for some seconds. 'I think your master is sickening, Henri,' he said. 'You'd best see to him.' He lifted the tent flap and stepped into the snow.

'It is a fact,' Henry remarked. 'A woman would be good for you, Master Kit.'

'What do you know about women?' Kit sneered, instantly regretting his mood.

But Henry did not take offence. Henry never took offence, no matter how Louis might treat him. Although he could no doubt, even at thirteen years of age, take Louis in one hand and break his neck. Kit wondered if he realised that. If slaves ever dared have thoughts like that.

'I know nothing about women,' Henry said. 'Save that they are soft, and good for men.'

'Have you ever had one?' Kit asked, with genuine interest. Here was a possible way of getting inside that massive black head.

'How I am going to have a woman, Master Kit?' Henry asked.

'Oh, I had supposed, down in the slave village . . .'

'Nobody ain't having any young woman without the Seigneur saying so,' Henry pointed out. 'He does like to select. And the old ones, what they are going want with me?'

You might be suprised, Kit thought, but he did not say it. 'You will have a woman, soon enough,' he said.

'Oh, yes,' Henry agreed. 'I have been told this. By the time we return to St Domingue I shall be a man, and right for being a father.' He gave one of his very rare smiles. 'Unless I am a very old man by the time we return.'

'Yes,' Kit said, thoughtfully. 'Have you ever thought, Henry, of *not* returning to St Domingue?'

The black boy stared at him.

And Kit flushed; he had uttered an only half-formed thought. 'It is that . . . well, I doubt the Seigneur is doing me, or anyone, a favour by attempting to turn me into one of his family. I am not, and never shall be. And I doubt I really

90

wish to be a planter.'

'You have too kindly a nature, to be a planter,' Henry observed.

Kit's flush deepened. 'I . . .' he groped for words. 'I would like to see the world different, to be sure. Were it possible. But as it is not . . .'

'You going to stay here?' Henry was incredulous. 'Them British will hang you.'

'It's a big country,' Kit said. 'We could go west, into the wilderness.'

'We?'

'I should take you with me, of course,' Kit said. 'You are my slave. You are my responsibility.'

Henry looked at him for several seconds. Then he said, 'I am your mummy slave, Master Kit. Just like I am my mummy son. I must go home to St Domingue.'

'Oh, but . . .' Kit looked up as the tent flap was raised, and a man stepped inside. The visitor wore the blue coat and tan breeches of an American soldier, but also the red waistcoat of one of General Washington's guard, just as his sword and epaulettes denoted an officer. He was no one Kit had even seen before, although there was something familiar about his big, handsome, good-humoured face.

He looked at Henry first, frowned, and then at Kit, and smiled. 'I seek a certain Christopher Hamilton, serving with the Touraine infantry regiment.'

Kit scrambled to his feet, saluted. 'I have that honour, sir.'

'I knew it.' The officer held out his hand, then spoke in English. 'I have the honour to bear that name also, sir. Your cousin, Alexander Hamilton, at your service.'

'Alex?' Kit allowed himself to be embraced. He had heard so much about this man, from Mama, without ever having seen him before, to his memory. 'But . . . how did you know I was here?'

'I was speaking with the general,' Alexander Hamilton said. 'Your general, who told me there were several young men from St Domingue in his force, and I knew that was where you had gone, so I examined the lists. But it is good to

91

see you, I can tell you that. I remember you, you know, when you were just a child. And you had a sister, just born.'

'Richilde?' Kit said.

'That is right. The prettiest babe I ever saw. That was just before I left the island for Virginia. Why, she must be a big girl now.'

'Thirteen years old,' Kit said. 'This is Henry Christopher.'

Hamilton glanced at the Negro boy, without interest.

'He was born in St Kitts, also,' Kit explained. 'The same day as Richilde.'

'Indeed, I remember your father telling mine of the event,' Hamilton agreed.

'As no doubt you remember my father also,' Kit said.

'Why, yes, boy, so I do.' Hamilton's face became grave. 'As you do not. That is sad. He stayed with us, for a season, when he first came from St Kitts, and then he went west. There are great forests to the west, Kit. No man knows for sure how far they stretch. But that was twelve years ago. He would have returned by now, were he coming back.'

Kit nodded. 'It is something we have learned to face. But you . . . you have prospered?'

'I am a captain,' Hamilton said proudly. 'In the Continental Army. And more . . .'

'And an outlaw when this rebellion finally collapses,' Kit said.

Hamilton frowned. 'It is not a rebellion, Kit. It is a war. A war of independence. And it will not collapse We shall win it, if we have to fight for fifty years.'

'We shall not win it by sitting here freezing,' Kit said.

'This is hardly the season for campaigning,' Hamilton pointed out. 'Although General Washington has campaigned in the winter, certainly. Four years ago he crossed the Delaware on the ice to defeat the Hessians at Trenton. But now he thinks of larger victories. Come. I would have you meet him.'

'Meet General Washington?'

'Of course. That is what I have been trying to tell you. I am his military secretary. Come along.'

92

'But ... my God,' Kit hastily straightened his tunic, attempted to smooth his breeches. Henry held a mirror for him.

'The general has spent five winters at this war, Kit,' Hamilton said. 'He will be glad to see you clothed and shod, no more. But wear your sword. You are a soldier.'

'Of course.' Kit buckled on his belt, placed his tricorne on his head. 'Henry ...'

'I will have supper ready for your return, master,' Henry said, bowing.

'He will make a good worker,' Hamilton said, as they hurried through the snow. 'If he is but thirteen, he will be a big fellow. But you are a shade too friendly with him, Kit. Believe me, black bucks understand only the lash, the discipline of fear.'

Kit opened his mouth to argue, then thought better of it. It was difficult to explain to anyone the exact relationship he had with Henry. It was not something he was sure he could explain to himself. And he certainly did not wish to quarrel with this long lost cousin, so strangely and happily reappeared.

Now they were being challenged and then saluted by sentries, and in place of tents there were huts of logs, with proper roofs, and welcoming wisps of smoke rising into the still air. And finally, a doorway, guarded by a private soldier dressed much as Hamilton, who in turn presented arms. Hamilton opened the door and ushered Kit inside, into a delightful warmth and a surprising amount of light. To the left was a small table on which were the remains of a sparse supper; to the right was a much larger table covered in maps; both supported several candles. At the rear of the one room hut there were two cot beds, separated by a grate in which there was a roaring fire, and on one of these there sat a man, coatless, gazing at the roof with both hands apparently attempting to fit inside his opened mouth.

Kit paused in surprise, uncertain whether or not to salute, then took his cue from Hamilton, who merely came to attention.

'My cousin, sir,' he said. 'Lieutenant Christopher Hamilton, of the Touraine regiment.'

George Washington slowly straightened, dried his hand on a towel. 'Have you sound teeth, lad?' he asked.

'Sir?'

'Because if you have, you are a lucky fellow. Preserve them, Christopher Hamilton. Perserve them as if they were gold.' He gave a brief smile. 'Or they soon will be, and will hurt the more for that!' He stood up, well built without being tall, face dominated by a massive jaw and a pronounced nose, and by the clearest eyes Kit could remember. 'Welcome.' He held out his hand, and after a glance at Hamilton, Kit took the proffered fingers. 'Sit down, Lieutenant,' Washington said. 'Alex, pour us a glass of wine. It is a chilly night. Your name is not French, sir.'

'Indeed not, sir. I was born on the island of St Kitts. My father was a cousin of Captain Hamilton's.'

'But you were recruited in Cap François.' Washington's gaze played up and down him, taking him in.

'I live with another cousin, sir. A French planter, in St Domingue.'

'And volunteered,' Washington said, raising his glass. 'I drink your health. And now you wonder what you have done, to be sitting here in the cold and the damp, fearing a British onslaught.'

'Well, sir . . .' Kit flushed with embarrassment.

'Believe me, Mr Hamilton, so do I, from time to time,' the general said. 'War is often a frustrating business. Have you studied it?'

'Indeed, sir, I have spent much time on the campaigns of Frederick the Great.'

'And you fight for the French?' Washington raised his eyebrows. 'But you could hardly have found a better teacher. Tell me what you consider the secret of his success.'

'Concentration, sir,' Kit said, his eyes sparkling as they always did when he thought of Frederick. 'Concentration, on the battlefield, against a portion of the enemy, by skilful use of the ground to disguise his movements.'

94

'Admirably put. And that, Mr Hamilton, is the most difficult of all the martial arts. Concentration on the battlefield. Yet the concentration of forces against an enemy weak point is the whole secret of victory.' He finished his drink, stood up. 'We shall have to find somewhere for us to concentrate, Mr Hamilton, your French and my Continentals. Then we also might gain a victory. It has been a pleasure, lad.' Once again he held out his hand.

The armies marched south. Long forgotten now where the freezing winds of the winter. Now it was high summer, and they knew only the heat and the dust. When they halted for the nights, Kit thought he would have given a great deal for a blast of cold air. But always there was Henry, waiting with a cooling drink, preparing their bivouac – they no longer possessed a tent. Henry was happiest in the heat. Besides, he, in common with everyone else, was happy to be on the move, with a purpose. Supposing they knew what it was.

There were a great number of soldiers; this was by some way the largest army Kit had ever seen, perhaps ten thousand Continentals and some seven thousand French. Their uniforms were new, their muskets were clean, they had ample supplies of powder and shot. They were accompanied by a train of the new Gribeauval artillery, reputed the finest in the world. He supposed they must be one of the best equipped armies ever in existence, a far cry from the tales Alex had told him of the early days of the war, when the men had barely had sufficient powder to fire a volley, or shoes to cover their feet, of that winter in Valley Forge when the army had all but distintegrated, had only been kept in being by the indomitable spirit of its commander.

But more important, now, they were all professionals. The Americans by five years of warfare, the French either because they had always been regulars, or because, like Louis and himself, and Jacques Chavannes and all the other colonial volunteers, they had been trained to perfection over the past year.

Only their destination remained a mystery, locked in the minds and hearts of Washington and Rochambeau. And their immediate aides. Alex undoubtedly knew of it, in his demeanour, his cheerful confidence, but he knew how to keep his general's secrets. In the beginning it had been supposed, with much grumbling, that they were again retreating. This was because in the early summer the allied armies had taken up a position before New York, where the main British armament, and Sir Henry Clinton, lay. The expectations of a battle, perhaps the battle which would decide the war, had been high. For the first time the Continentals, with French support, were preparing to take on the British veterans in an open field, with some prospect of victory.

But once again nothing had happened. The armies had faced each other, and drilled, and skirmished, and exchanged cannon fire, as each long, lazy day had succeeded the other. Kit's sword had still never been contaminated by blood. If this was warfare, he had supposed, then it was a remarkably wasteful way of spending one's life. Louis had enjoyed it. Louis just enjoyed being in uniform, and he did very well with the women who always hung around the encampment. But women were not for Kit Hamilton; he had no intention of catching his feet in another snare such as Jacqueline Chavannes, however often he wanted, and envied, his cousin's easy facility.

Henry had fretted too. He considered himself a part of this army, even if he possessed no uniform, carried no weapon. Their success was his cause for joy, their failure cast him down as much as any white man. In this attitude he was unique. The other black servants – and there was a considerable number, including quite a few from St Domingue and even one or two others from Vergée d'Or, accompanying those overseers who had also volunteered – were content to enjoy life. However much leather they had to polish, however often they had to erect and then dismantle tents, however long they marched behind their masters, inhaling dust, this life had to be better than that on a plantation. They would be happy if the war should never end. Henry seldom mingled with them, spent his leisure moments in solitary contemplation, staring at the drilling soldiers, gazing at the brilliant uniforms with obvious envy, polished Kit's sword with loving care. This was an experience he would remember all of his life, Kit knew. It would, no doubt, be the great experience of his life, the only experience of his life worth remembering. Certainly if he intended to go back to St Domingue.

But that must wait on the end of the war. Which did not seem any closer. Except for the excitement in the air. It had begun the night, only a week ago, when their colonel had come round, very quietly, and told them to prepare to move out before dawn, speaking with each officer in turn, and reminding them that they must leave their tents standing, their camp fires burning. Certainly it had seemed that they were running away, from an as yet untried enemy – save that some two thousand men under Colonel Heath had remained behind, to keep those camp fires burning, to convince General Clinton, and his seventeen thousand men, that the entire allied army was still waiting for him to come out.

It had seemed an elementary manoeuvre, but it was none the less apparently successful for that. They did not know if the British had as yet discovered their departure, but in any event the enemy had to be several days behind in the race to wherever they were going.

'Except,' Henry said, 'that the British have the Navy. They can move by sea.' Because they marched close by the coast, and every so often saw the rippling waters.

'God damn you for a pessimistic black boy,' Louis grumbled. But the fact was undeniable, and a couple of days later they saw the fleet, a huge array of yellow-varnished three deckers, moving slowly south with all their canvas spread before the light northerly breeze. Kit thought it the most beautiful sight he had ever seen, even as he hated them.

'They *are* beautiful, lad,' said Colonel Dufour, sitting astride his horse to watch them.

'And they carry the end of all our hopes, sir,' Kit said.

Dufour laughed. 'You mistake the situation, boy. Those ships fly the fleur de lys. That is Admiral de Grasse's fleet. We have caught Admiral Graves napping.'

A fleet, and an army, moving together. Concentrating. This then was the campaign on which General Washington had been brooding, last December. The next day they arrived at the promontory called Head of Elk, gazed at the huge, slow-moving Chesapeake Bay, at the forests and streams which surrounded it, the occasional hamlets which dotted the shore – and the French fleet, waiting at anchor, to transport them further south.

'There is a town at the bottom of this bay,' Alex said. 'Called Yorktown. It is garrisoned by the British Army of Virginia. That is our destination.'

The guns roared, continuously, and from their positions the soldiers could watch the bursting plumes of smoke and masonry, no doubt mingling with arms and legs, flying into the air as each shot struck home. It was horrifying, and yet it was magnificent.

The British were entirely surrounded, by the French and Americans on two sides, by the James river on the other two sides. yet the river would have been sufficient to make Yorktown impregnable, with the support of the Royal Navy. This was the fear of both Washington and Rochambeau. They knew that Admirals Hood and Graves were hurrying to the rescue of their beleaguered countrymen, and they knew too that while the Compte de Grasse still patrolled Chesapeake Bay, where the River James debouched into the sea, the British had won too many naval victories over the French to say what would happen when the two fleets met.

Thus the reason for haste. There were eight thousand redcoats inside the town, commanded by Lord Cornwallis. Could they be forced to surrender, coming after Burgoyne's disaster at Saratoga four years ago, and with Clinton unable to make any headway in the north, then no one could doubt that the British position would be incalculably weakened.

'The regiment will advance,' Colonel Dufour said, and Kit drew his sword. Once again he was aware of the stomach-churning excitement of going into battle. But this time there were no doubts, and he did not suppose there were any doubts behind him, either. He was a professional, as were his men. They knew what they were about. The assault would be costly, but if they could dislodge the British, drive them back into the town proper, enable the great guns to be advanced to a position from whence they could fire into the houses themselves, then Cornwallis's position would become untenable. Normally such a manoeuvre would be accomplished by means of parallel trenches, which would slowly approach the enemy while enabling the besiegers to remain under cover. This was the art of siegecraft. But there was no time for siegecraft, with the Royal Navy at sea.

The drums began, the boys marching immediately behind the officers, their sticks thumping the *ra-ta-tat* which enabled the men to keep step. And now the guns from the redoubts were firing back, those that remained; most had been overturned by the French fire. And yet there were sufficient. Once again a cannonball bounced across the uneven ground towards Kit, and once again he heard yells and moans from behind him. But his gaze was fixed on the parapet in front of him, and the men who waited there. Not Germans, now. These were truly men in red coats and white breeches, his own countrymen, and the Union Jack waved above their heads. No doubt there was even someone in that trench named Hamilton. But they were fighting for tyranny, and he was fighting for freedom.

He had the strangest thought: would Henry Christopher consider he was fighting for freedom?

A man stood on the parapet, his musket levelled. Kit could do nothing about him, save keep on walking. This was his duty, as an officer. He watched the musket move, watched the puff of smoke, and felt nothing. He had been told that he would feel nothing, when he was hit. At least for a while. And he was till walking forward, while the man had lowered his musket and was presenting it like a pike, with his sixteen inch bayonet thrusting from the muzzle. It came at Kit's chest, and he knocked it aside with his sword, prepared for a thrust, and watched the man fall backwards, arms and legs suddenly scattered. He glanced to his left, and Jacques Chavannes grinned at him; smoke still drifted from his gun muzzle.

'We fight together, monsieur,' the mulatto said.

'Together,' Kit agreed, and dashed forward again, realising that he had never actually looked into the Englishman's face. But the man before him now wore a moustache and a sneer and carried a sword. Their blades clashed and Kit whipped his to and fro, forgetting much of the fencing he had been taught at Vergée d'Or in his anxious haste to beat down his assailant. The Englishman slipped and fell, and Kit felt a crunching beneath his blade. He looked down in horror, at the blood spurting upwards, at the expression on the man's face, of surprise and dismay, as he died.

Slowly he withdrew the sword, stared at the dripping blood, so bright for the moment, only then recalled that he was in the middle of a battle, jerked his head so hard his bicorne fell off, gazed forward, and watched the redcoats hurrying back to the next line of defences, several hundred yards away. Some of the French sent bullets after them, most just stood and cheered, and the cheering spread right round the line of redoubts to signify that they had all been captured.

'You are hurt.' Henry handed him a water bottle, began feeling his arms and legs and chest; the white uniform was splattered with blood.

Kit drank deeply, gave the bottle to Louis, who was panting at his elbow. 'Not my blood,' he said. 'But Henry, you should not be here.'

'I followed the advance,' Henry said. 'I ain't never seen anything like that.' He took the sword from Kit's nerveless fingers, knelt to clean the blood away, using the dead arm of the English officer. 'Now you are a proper soldier, Master

100

Kit.' He raised his head, his expression filled with admiration, and envy. He would like to be able to kill, Kit thought. But who?

'A great day.' Alexander Hamilton pulled his horse to a halt, leapt from the saddle to shake Kit's hand. 'A brave assault. The general is delighted. Look there.'

He pointed to where the cannon were already being dragged forward, careless of dead and wounded they might crush in their gunners' haste to get them in position and resume the bombardment before the British could launch a counter attack.

'Then we have them,' Henry shouted, slapping his hands together in glee.

Hamilton gave him a curious glance, then turned back to Kit. 'All depends on the navy, now. Listen.' Even above the shouting of the excited French, the bugle calls and the rattle of hooves, they could hear the deeper booms of the heavy cannonades, thudding out of the bay. 'They have joined battle, Graves and de Grasse.'

The tune played by the band, appropriately enough, was called *The World Turned Upside Down*. But apart from the music, there was no movement amongst the watching men, and had the drums and bugles ceased, Kit supposed there would not have been a sound, either.

The French, no less than the Americans, were too conscious of the immensity of what had happened. They had not believed it, six weeks ago, when after an ineffectual cannonade, the British fleet had hauled away again and left de Grasse master of the Chesapeake. Such a thing had never happened before in all the annals of the interminable conflict between English and French. They had not believed it as their heavy cannon, moving ever closer, had pounded Yorktown, and all within it, to pieces. Here too was a unique mishap for the British military machine which less than twenty years before had rampaged the length and breadth of the world, never tasting defeat. And the culmination of their disbelief had come only two days ago, when a red-coated drummer had mounted the parapet outside battered Yorktown, and beaten a parley.

Now they were left with a feeling of utter exhaustion, as the redcoats marched out of the surrendered town, rank upon rank of them, and slowly piled their arms before Generals Washington and Rochambeau, Lafayette and Greene. There could not be a man present, Kit supposed, who did not know that he was stepping into history. Yorktown had to rank as the day the Thirteen Colonies secured that independence they had so rashly declared five years before, just as for the men whose ancestors had gained Agincourt, Crecy and Poitiers, it had to be the most disastrous defeat since they had fled from Hastings before the Norman invaders.

He glanced at Louis, to see what his feelings were. But Louis was merely looking hot and bothered at having to stand so long in the sun. His imagination could not soar above the commonplace, the obvious, that this campaign had at last been successful, that tonight there would be more wine than usual to drink, and that the women of Yorktown would undoubtedly be most accommodating to an officer in the conquering army, especially one with money in his pockets.

Henry knew what had been accomplished. His eyes shone as he gazed at the sight, and his hand and arm twitched as Kit returned to the encampment. Kit could tell what he was thinking, held out his own hand, had the fingers seized in that strong grip.

'I have seen history, Master Kit,' Henry said.

'My own thoughts,' Kit agreed. And smiled. 'So you see, Henry, that even strongly defended fortresses can be taken.'

Henry watched the British, now forming lines, an army without its weapons, awaiting the will of its conqueror. 'Them boys say eight thousand surrendered,' he observed.

'Something like that.'

'Then they should not have been taken,' he said. 'Not by seventeen thousand.'

Kit frowned at him. 'They were outnumbered by two to one.'

102

'Armies have fought before, at greater odds,' Henry said. 'Frederick has done so. You have told me that, Master Kit.'

'Well, yes,' Kit said. 'Perhaps the British were badly led. Perhaps their mistake was to allow themselves to be bottled up in the first place. But once they were there . . .'

'They let the guns get too close,' Henry said. 'Had they stopped the guns getting too close, even if they had had to die doing it, they would have held the town. Those men did not wish to die for their King. What is the point in going to war for a King, Master Kit, if you are not prepared to die for him?'

Kit scratched his head. 'You do think too much, Henry,' he said. 'I shall have to consider that one. Alex!'

Once again a handshake and an embrace. 'It is over, Kit. Thanks as much to your good fellows as to ours. Over. The General is sure of it. You will be going home.'

'Home,' Kit said, thoughtfully. Home to Vergée d'Or, to having to treat Henry like the dirt beneath his feet, to the futile amusements of the plantocracy, the unchanging rhythm of the planting seasons. Home to Jacqueline Chavannes, and Philippe. Home to conspiracy, to an awareness that he did not belong, and could never belong. The Hamiltons were not planters, and had never been planters.

'The thought does not seem to please you,' Alex said.

Kit flushed. 'Perhaps I have too much enjoyed being able to speak my own language, these last two years.'

Hamilton studied him for a few minutes. Then he said, 'Then why not continue to do so?'

Kit's heart leapt. 'Is it possible?'

'If you will swear allegiance to the Stars and Stripes. You have fought for it.'

'Willingly,' Kit cried. 'Oh, willingly. But . . . Mama? Richilde?'

'I will have you transferred to an American regiment,' Hamilton said. 'The general will attend to it himself. You are one of us, far more than a Frenchman. Then, when the war is over, we will set up in business, you and I, and then you may

103

send for your mother. And Richilde.'

'If she will come,' Kit said thoughtfully. 'She is by way of being betrothed.'

'At thirteen? She must be quite a lady. Well then, you have naught to worry about, there.' He clapped his cousin on the shoulder. 'You will visit her, I promise you. But you are right, this is the land of the future, the place to make your home and your fortune. I have never regretted a moment since I landed here. Will you give me your hand on it?'

'Willingly.' Kit held out his hand, and glanced at Henry. 'And Henry?'

'You may keep your slave, of course. He also will do well in America, if he will but work. And you have never criticised him for lack of that.'

'Well, Henry, how about that for a future?' Kit asked.

Henry's face was sad. 'I am your mummy slave, Master Kit,' he said. 'And St Domingue is my home, now. It is there I have to go. I will return with Master Louis.'

Kit opened his mouth, glanced at Alex, who was regarding the pair of them with a puzzled expression on his face.

'Besides,' Henry said. 'You will need someone to tell your mummy that you are well, and will be better. I will tell her that, Master Kit. And Miss Richilde.'

Chapter 4

THE COACHMAN

*In an age of exceptional military commanders, Toussaint
must rank as the most remarkable. Napoleon had at least
spent his youth at a military college; Toussaint had spent
his driving a coach. In everything he was self-taught, but
so successfully had he accomplished his own education
that long before the first disturbances he was highly
regarded by his owner and his fellow Negroes alike.*

'Wake up, sleepy head,' Jeanne Hamilton said. 'And
many happy returns.'

Richilde sat up, pulling straying hair from her eyes. The
room seemed crowded, with Mama, of course, and Aunt
Marguerite, with Françoise and Lucy and Annette, with
Miss Fitzgerald and Amelia.

'How does it feel to be fifteen?' Aunt Marguerite asked,
and kissed her on the forehead. Aunt Marguerite was being
very generous about the whole thing, although Jacqueline
was positive that she must have prayed for Richilde's death
a hundred times. Richilde had not believed that for a
moment, but at the same time she knew that Aunt
Marguerite had to be thinking that were she *not* here, then
one of her own daughters might be in this happy position –
as both Lucy and Françoise were past sixteen – might
already be the mistress of Vergée d'Or.

She was so excited she wanted to burst, as she accepted
their presents, hugged and kissed them one after the other.
Miss Ftizgerald was last. Today even her habitually stern
face was relaxed; indeed, she appeared on the verge of tears.

'I will bid you goodbye now,' she said. 'I would not spoil your betrothal.'

'But . . . you're not leaving today?' Richilde cried.

'I am leaving Vergée d'Or today,' Miss Fitzgerald said. 'I will remain in Cap François until my ship is ready to sail. That will be next week.'

'But . . . why are you leaving at all?'

Miss Fitzgerald smiled through her sadness. 'Because my task is finished here, Richilde. You are the last of the children. And today you are no longer a child.'

'But . . . the wedding . . .'

'Will not take place for another year, my dear girl. I have things to do with my own life.'

She was lying, Richilde knew instinctively. She had indeed developed the art of knowing most things instinctively, because she was never told anything, never actually instructed in what was about to happen, or what was not about to happen. The plantation, no doubt from years of often frightful experience, responded instinctively to the Seigneur's wishes, and over the past six years of her stay here Richilde had become an extension of those wishes.

She did not know why, or how. Her life seemed to have been taken over from the day she had set foot in St Domingue. Sometimes she felt vaguely resentful about that. But only sometimes.

She leaned back in her bath to allow Amelia to soap her, feeling vaguely surprised that Jacqueline had not yet come in to congratulate her. But Jacqueline was a law unto herself. She would be along.

She had come here, *expecting* her life to be taken over. There it was. They all had, summoned by the great man to do his bidding, and that first day she had been overwhelmed by the splendour with which they had suddenly been surrounded, by the personality of Philippe himself, and by the shocking evidence of his cruelty that first evening. Richilde thought that only Kit had ever been able to stand back and look at the plantation, and their new life, with any detachment. Which probably accounted for the haste with which he had wanted to get away from it, at the first opportunity. Dear Kit. They had received only a handful of letters, but even Mama was reassured; the French army did not appear to be doing sufficient fighting for his life to be in any danger. According to Kit, both Henry and himself, and even Louis, were having the times of their lives. Dear Henry. It was impossible to confess that she missed him even more than she missed her brother. But she did. And yet at the same time was happy that he wasn't here, exposed to the risks of being a plantation slave, the whims of her future husband.

Because she knew now that not even she would be able to protect him should he fall foul of the Seigneur. Philippe de Mortmain could be, as she had observed that first night, a monster. She saw little of his ice cold rages. Vergée d'Or was so enormous that everything to do with the field slaves was more than a mile away from the chateau, and the young ladies were not encouraged to visit the factory or the barracoons. She had not seen a slave flogged since coming here, much less heard one wailing his misery. Yet these things did happen and, according to Jacqueline, they happened much more regularly than ever on Marigot. Philippe de Mortmain did not employ a jumper; he required his own overseers to be experts in handling the cartwhip, by constant practice, just as he himself was an expert, by constant practice. According to Jacqueline, he ruled his plantation like the most omnipotent of Asian despots, and even to look him in the eye was, for a black person, an immediate reason for punishment, as she remembered his threat to Henry, again on that unforgettable first day. Nor could she doubt that Jacqueline, for all her tendency to exaggerate, was telling the truth. She had observed a fraction of his true demeanour on that day, and she often enough saw Uncle Maurice come in from the factory, trembling and sweating, reaching for the wine bottle in an attempt to blot out the dreadful scene he had just witnessed.

And this was the man she was going to marry. The man to whom, today, she was about to be formally betrothed. This too had been decided that first night. She had known it then,

107

without understanding it, any more than she truly understood it now. Once again Jacqueline had an answer. 'He has chosen you because from the start he could see that you would be more beautiful and have more character than any of your cousins, and because, more important, the others are *his* cousins, too. His father married a cousin, and out of nine children, only Philippe survived. He fears for the future, and with more reason than most,' she would say, enigmatically. 'He wants a wife who will be everything to him.'

As Richilde had been groomed to be. She played the spinet, because he enjoyed hearing the music. She had not been taught embroidery since the age of thirteen, because Philippe did not consider it a necessary accomplishment for a lady, surrounded as she was by servants. He wished her to be able to converse like a man and so, where her cousins had been provided with needles, she had been provided with books. Mama had been scandalised. But undoubtedly books were far more interesting than tapestry.

But was she not scandalised by the whole thing? Without knowing what to do about it, or even if she wanted to do anything about it. She had not been less overwhelmed, from her first moment on the plantation, than any of the others. And she had been more overwhelmed by his kindess to her. She had known him as a monster, that first night – but as a handsome, gay, enormously wealthy and powerful monster, who was offering to share all of that power, all of that wealth, with her. Well, she did not suppose he actually intended to share it. But providing she did as he required, was all that he required, she would have the use of it.

She chewed her lips and Amelia, now patting her dry, clucked her tongue disapprovingly. Amelia, terrified that the slightest blemish would form on her skin, trailed behind her with a parasol whenever she would go walking abroad. She had never dared broach the subject of a swim in the sea to her maid. She was more afraid of Amelia's disapproval than of Miss Fitzgerald's. Besides, it would be different when she was married.

To a monster. To the most exciting man in the world. Besides, he had explained and she could understand the reasoning behind his deliberate harshness. He was protecting her as much as himself, as much as his plantation. And he was acting no differently from any other planter. If she doubted, if she feared, if she hated what he had to do, it was surely because she did not come from planting stock. She would have to learn. She *was* learning. Philippe de Mortmain was her gateway to the stars. She would not find another.

The Seigneur stopped speaking, the crowd of whites and mulattos politely applauded. Do they envy me, Richilde wondered? She stood beside her future husband on the upstairs porch, looking down the sweep of the great staircase at the people gathered below. Or did they not envy her as she had never envied, for example, the Queen of England, because hers was a rank and a position beyond envy? But what of those gathered behind her? Even Etienne was forced to stand there today, his Milot bride at his side. Claudette de Mortmain was a lovely and charming girl; Etienne had done well for himself, even if his marrying the sister of Catherine's husband was but another example of the inbreeding which was apparently practised by all the *grand blancs*. But even the wife of the heir must necessarily stand behind the future mistress of Vergée d'Or; because, Richilde realised, once she was married and had given Philippe a son, Etienne would no longer be the heir.

Philippe was smiling at her and lowering his head for a kiss. It came as something of a shock for her to realise that her mouth was the first part of her body he had ever touched, save for her hand and her cheek. In six years. Six years in which he had watched her grow from a child into a girl. She did not suppose she was yet a woman. Her legs were too long for the rest of her body and she had very little bosom. Even Annette, a year her elder, had more. While her hips were so slender it was impossible to suppose she could ever be a mother.

But she was prepared to wait, because he knew what she would be at the end of it. Thus Jacqueline. Only another year.

His lips brushed hers, and she could no longer hold her breath. But his breath was sweet, and he was smiling into her mouth. She wondered what he was actually thinking about her. Did he love her? Was it possible to love someone more than twenty years younger? And if it was possible to love her, was it possible to love her and not wish to touch her?

But then, did she love him? It was not something she had ever considered before. One was not expected to love one's husband, only to serve him and obey him and bear him children. Thus Mama.

But it seemed such a waste, not to love a man like Philippe de Mortmain.

Philippe raised his head, holding her hand now to slip the huge sapphire ring over her finger. The ring had belonged to his mother, and was quite the most magnificent thing she had ever seen. She was afraid to look at it, much less touch it. The overseers and their wives and children cheered again. Then it was time for more congratulations from the family, more presents and glasses of ice-cold sangaree. At dinner, for the first time she sat at his right hand, turning her head to look down the sweep of the table at Aunt Marguerite, seated at the far end, some thirty feet away. From this day next year, *she* would be seated there not her aunt.

She suddenly wondered who would then sit at Philippe's right hand. And immediately, where Jacqueline might be, as she had not appeared all day.

'Why did you send Miss Fitzgerald away?' she asked.

He turned to her. 'Because you are no longer a girl,' he explained. 'To trail behind a governess. Even an Irish governess. Or to be influenced by her points of view. And now, I think you should retire early, my dear. It has been a long and exciting day for you, has it not?'

She really did not like it when he spoke like that, almost as Mama might have done, or her own father. And yet there was no question of disobeying him. She rose immediately,

110

curtsied to the table, and left the room. Was he angry with her? He had answered her question good humouredly enough. Perhaps she had not measured up to his expectations, this of all days. Did he not like her gown? But he had chosen the material himself, according to Jacqueline. It was made of straw coloured satin, with a white fichu and sleeve frills. Jacqueline had said that it should, of course, be worn with a wig, but she was too young and her own rich brown hair had been curled into ringlets which lay on her shoulders and on her bosom, because the gown carried the most daring décolletage she had ever worn – she could just imagine Lucy whispering to Françoise, 'What a waste for such a flat-chested child.'

She had supposed she looked perfectly elegant, and the ring set off the whole thing. Now she was out of the room she could hold it, and slip it up and down her finger, and take it off to look at the flickering candlelight through the translucent stone. And she was being sent to bed before anyone else. She wanted to weep.

'Well, mademoiselle?'

She checked, her foot on the first step of the great staircase, gazed at Jacqueline. A strange looking Jacqueline, for she wore a cloak with a hood, which effectively concealed her clothes, and carried another such garment over her arm. And she had never addressed her as mademoiselle before, Richilde realised.

'Jacqueline!' She ran forward, was embraced, kissed on both cheeks and then the mouth. And felt a tremendous rush of happiness. This was her friend. Perhaps her only friend, now that Henry was away across the sea. And certainly her best friend. Of course she now knew exactly what function the mulatto girl filled in the house, but she thought that only brought them closer together, in that it was a function she also would be fulfilling before too long. She had questioned Jacqueline about the duties of a mistress, which to a certain extent had to be those of a wife, and never obtained any answer other than a smile, just as Mama had always answered such queries with a frown and an admonishment that all would be revealed to her in good time. She had also asked Jacqueline what would happen to *her* after the wedding. Not that she was in any degree jealous. Rather would she have liked to think her friend would be there with her always, guiding her and advising her. And again Jacqueline had just smiled, and said, 'That must depend on how well you please the Seigneur. But you will always be my friend, won't you, Richilde?'

A promise she had been happy to make, without reservation.

Now Jacqueline gave her another squeeze. 'The day of your life. At least up to now. And I have not congratulated you.'

Richilde held her away. 'I have been sent to bed.'

'What nonsense. You have been sent to look at a bed. Today your education as a girl ends, and your education as a woman begins. But it is not something that the Seigneur would discuss before your mother or your cousins. Come.'

She held Richilde's hand. My left hand, Richilde thought, and thus she is also holding my ring, crushed against her fingers as it is crushed against mine. But she has not commented on it. No doubt she has seen it too often before. And besides, they were hurrying up the stairs and along the great gallery to the very end, then up another flight of stairs. The flight of stairs to the Seigneur's private apartments, where none of the children had ever been allowed.

Footmen opened the double doors and she entered a small withdrawing room. She was past wonder, she supposed. Because everything on Vergée d'Or was wonderful. But this was to be her very own. It adjoined a huge dressing room, and then a boudoir, looking out over the trees at the sea. And then the bedroom. It was the largest she had ever seen, just as the bed was the largest she had ever seen. She glanced at Jacqueline. Would she sleep here tonight?

Jacqueline smiled at her, able to read her thoughts. 'Come, we have a visit to make.'

'A visit?' Richilde glanced through the window; it was quite dark outside.

112

'There is someone I want you to meet,' Jacqueline said. 'Someone Philippe wants you to meet, although you must never tell him that you have done so.' She held out the cloak, wrapped Richilde in it. 'There is a private entrance at the back of the house,' she said, and smiled. 'It is the one that I use.'

Richilde's heart started to pound, even if she had no idea what she was doing, what to expect. But Jacqueline was also excited. She opened a door in the boudoir, which led into a closet, at the back of which there was another door, and this led down a staircase, unusually narrow for this vast house, and both unlit and unguarded by any blue and gold clad sentries. Jacqueline had armed herself with a candle, however, and with this she led them down the curving steps, their reflections sending great shadows guttering up the walls.

'You aren't afraid?' Jacqueline asked.

'Of course not,' Richilde said, unsure whether or not she was lying.

'There is nothing to be afraid of,' Jacqueline said, reassuringly. 'Not even Mama Céleste.'

'Mama Céleste?'

They had reached the foot of the stairs, and Jacqueline doused her candle. Now it was utterly dark and Richilde gave a little shiver. But Jacqueline knew exactly where to put her hand on the lock, and a moment later the door swung outwards to admit them into one of the exterior rose gardens. 'Quiet now,' she said. 'The white folk will still be up.'

Richilde glanced at her curiously; there was no moon but there was also no cloud; the stars were bright and she could see her friend's face. And never before had Jacqueline used such a term. Had she forgotten that she was with a white girl?

'Who is Mama Céleste?' she asked again, whispering.

Jacqueline held her hand, led her round the flower beds towards a wicket gate set in the white paling. Now the house was a blaze of light to her left, and indeed Richilde could

113

hear the voices of her cousins raised in animated conversation, coming from one of the verandahs.

They went through the gate, Jacqueline carefully closing it behind them, and then walked away from the chateau itself, towards, Richilde realised, the factory. She had never been down this path, although she had been taken for a ride round the factory in Philippe's coach.

'Mama Céleste,' Jacqueline said, speaking normally now they were away from the house. 'Is a *mamaloi*. Do you know what that means?'

Richilde frowned. 'She is a witch.'

'Not at all,' Jacqueline said, quite sharply. 'Voodoo is not witchcraft. It is a religion, just like Christianity. Mama Céleste is a priestess.'

Richilde was more confused than ever. 'You mean she lives on Vergée d'Or?'

'Of course.'

'And Philippe doesn't drive her away?'

'He doesn't drive Father Thomas away,' Jacqueline pointed out.

'Yes, but . . .'

'Black people also have their gods,' Jacqueline said. 'Their beliefs. Philippe knows that Mama Céleste is good for the plantation. She is a famous *mamaloi*, revered all over the island. Even if they have never met, he also knows that she helps him to keep his slaves in subjection.'

'They have never met?' Richilde glanced left and right, at the great trees beneath which they were hurrying. The path they were taking skirted the factory and the slave village, she realised, and headed ever inwards, towards the canefields, and beyond, the jungle.

'He cannot afford to recognise her presence,' Jacqueline explained. 'Voodoo is regarded as heresy by the Church, and is officially condemned. The practice of it is a crime. But of course everyone knows that it exists, and that without it the black people would not be so docile. So it is there, but it is not there. Do you understand?'

'Yes,' Richilde said, doubtfully. What she could not

114

understand was the idea of Philippe, so masterful, so omnipotent and so ruthlessly his own man, being bound by a situation which not even he could control.

'That is why you must never admit to him that you have visited Mama Céleste,' Jacqueline went on. 'Even though he knows that is where you are going tonight.'

'But why?' Richilde asked. 'I do not believe in voodoo. I know nothing about it. I will have to confess this visit to Father Thomas, if it is wrong.'

'You will not,' Jacqueline snapped, her voice again sharp.

'Then I must go home,' Richilde said, stopping.

Jacqueline looked at her. 'Would you disobey Philippe?'

'How can I be disobeying Philippe, when you say he will not recognise that this creature exists? I cannot believe that he does know where we are going, or that he would approve.'

'Listen to me,' Jacqueline said. 'I have not told you this before, and I would prefer not to have to tell you now. I was going to keep it until after you had met Mama Céleste. But your Philippe is not the man you think he is.'

'What are you saying?' Richilde demanded angrily.

'Listen to me. All his life he has had too much wealth, too much power, too little restraint. All his life he has been able to do exactly what he wished, as he wished it. And as a youth, perhaps, he was equally blessed with too much health, too much vigour. Thus now that he is nearing forty, he is in many ways already an old man.'

'Philippe? What nonsense. Why, he is . . .'

'Why do you suppose there are no direct heirs to the plantation?' Jacqueline asked. 'Why do you suppose he has never married? He has slept with me in his arms for the last seven years, every night, and I have never become pregnant. Can you answer that?'

Richilde stared at her. She had no real conception of what they were discussing. As Jacqueline realised.

'A man has an organ,' she said. 'With which it is necessary for him to enter the female, for the gratification of them both, and for fertilisation. But his organ must be hard, or entry cannot be attempted. You have seen them, on the slaves.'

Richilde gasped for breath; somehow she had not associated anything like that with Philippe.

'For most men, it is a simple matter,' Jacqueline continued. 'The sight of a pretty naked woman, sometimes even the thought of one, and they are ready. Poor Philippe can manage it but once a week, if then. And pleasure, the real pleasure, which they say is essential to impregnation, much less often than that. I have had him weep in my arms, because of his impotence.'

'Philippe? Weep? Now I know you are lying.'

'It is something you will see soon enough,' Jacqueline said. 'If you are unfortunate. And when he has finished weeping, his anger is terrible to behold. This is why he looks to you, of his house, but not of his blood, young enough to be his daughter, and utterly pure and sweet. He dreams, and hopes, and even prays, that with you in his bed he will find the happiness only I have ever been able to grant him. But even more, he prays that you will be able to give him the son he has always wanted. He is so desperate that he will leave no stone unturned. And he knows that someone like Mama Céleste, with the aid of her gods, will help you to be everything of which he dreams. Can you refuse to honour such a wish?'

Richilde chewed her lip. But she was already resuming her walk, reminding herself not to be afraid, or even repelled by what she had just heard. Today she was no longer a little girl, but a woman. And thus, from today, she had to act the woman's part. She followed Jacqueline down the path, round behind the negro village. A dog barked at them, and then was quiet. The breeze off the Atlantic soughed through the trees to muffle the sound of their footsteps. And the stars, gleaming through the trees wherever there was a break in the foliage, seemed to provide sufficient light for Jacqueline to know exactly where she was going.

And to raise a question which had not previously occurred to Richilde. 'Jacqueline,' she said. 'Do *you* believe in voodoo?'

Jacqueline glanced at her. 'I pray to Jesus Christ every night,' she said. 'But I pray to Ogone Badagris as well. Who is to say which of them answers my prayer?' She pointed. 'There is Mama Céleste.'

Richilde saw a little hut, snuggled in the trees. She looked over her shoulder; the negro village was perhaps half a mile away behind her, the chateau more than two miles distant. Here she was in the foreign land.

But with Jacqueline at her elbow, there was surely no cause for fear. She followed her friend forward, to stand before the hanging mat which made a door. When she would have spoken, Jacqueline shook her head, and gestured her to be quiet.

'Who seeks Céleste?' came the whisper.

'Jacqueline Chavannes,' Jacqueline said, and nodded to Richilde.

'Richilde Hamilton,' Richilde said, and wondered why she was taking part in this farce at all.

'You are expected,' said the whisper, and Jacqueline raised the mat.

Because it was a farce, Richilde reminded herself, fiercely. It had to be a farce. Of course this Céleste person would say they had been expected. Of course . . . Her breath was taken away by the stench inside the hut, a mixture of every unpleasant odour she had ever known; from human excreta to rotten meat, overlaid with the most delicious perfumes, to make her senses reel, just as the utter darkness, disturbed only by the guttering candle set in the floor, made her lose her sense of balance. She was quite happy to follow Jacqueline's example and fall to her knees, blinking, aware of the mosquitoes, where outside in the breeze they had not troubled her, and slowly identifying the crimson robe beyond the candle. But the woman had to be wearing a mask; no face could be so ancient, so gnarled, so inhuman.

'You are the one who would be mistress of Vergée d'Or?' Céleste said.

Again farce; everyone on the plantation knew that. 'I am

117

she,' Richilde said.

'And you would have your husband love you,' Céleste said, 'and be fruitful, through you?'

'I am to be his wife,' Richilde said.

'Do you suppose that alone is sufficient?' Céleste asked. 'Have you not come to me, for help?'

'I . . .' Richilde glanced at Jacqueline. But the mulatto's eyes were closed; she hardly seemed to be breathing. 'Can you help me?' Richilde asked.

'I can teach you to be a woman, such as your husband will never have known.'

'Did you not teach Jacqueline the same thing?' Richilde asked.

'Jacqueline Chavannes is one of us,' Céleste said. 'Her ability to love, through self knowledge, is expected. It is not expected in a white woman. Would you learn these things, white girl?'

Once again Richilde glanced at Jacqueline. If only her friend would wake up and come to her rescue. 'I . . . if it will make my husband love me.'

'He will love you, white girl,' Céleste said. 'If you know yourself, he will prize you above all others. He will prize you even above the brown girl. Does she know this?'

'I know this,' Jacqueline said, without opening her eyes.

'And you wish this?'

'I wish this,' Jacqueline said.

'Then it shall be so,' Céleste said. 'Stand, white girl, and take off your robe.'

Richilde stood, heart thumping, and removed her robe. She hesitated, then let it fall to the ground.

'And now your gown,' Céleste whispered.

Richilde gazed at her. She had no real objection to undressing before a black woman; she undressed before Amelia every day. But she had never undressed before Jacqueline. Besides, she did not know what would happen after that.

'Show her the way,' Céleste said.

Jacqueline also stood, shrugged her robe from her shoul-

118

ders, and Richilde discovered to her consternation that beneath the single garment her friend had been naked.

'If you will not obey me, white girl, then do you waste our time,' Céleste said.

Richilde unfastened her gown, allowed it, too, to lie on the noisome earth of the hut. Once again she seemed to have lost her mental balance, her ability to reason, before the odours with which she was surrounded, before the softly insistent whispering of the *mamaloi*.

'Now come to me,' Céleste said.

Richilde opened her eyes, stretched, sat up in utter alarm.

But she was in her own bed. She had been doing nothing more than dream. Except that her hair was still wet. With salt water. Because last night she had bathed in the sea. It had seemed the most natural thing in the world, as they had made their way home, she and Jacqueline. There had been nothing she could not do, could not say, no demand of her throbbing body she had even considered refusing. Thus to plunge into the tumbling rollers, to be knocked down by them and regain her feet in the shallows, gasping for breath and laughing, while the next wave thundered up to her and sought her out again, like an embrace, reaching into the most private recesses of her body, caressing her as she had never been caressed before. That had been no dream.

Slowly she lay down again, feather pillow clutched to her chest. Therefore nothing else had been a dream, either. She had been ... she could find no words to express her thoughts. Stroked? Manipulated? *Loved*? By a *mamaloi*. A woman of incredible age, and ugliness. But a woman who had *known*, everything there was to know, about woman.

She rolled over, on to her face, afraid to look at the light, afraid to admit what her eyes might see. Had Philippe known what would happen? According to Jacqueline he had not. But he had known what he wanted in a woman. Someone who could love, who could move, who could feel, with the rhythmic passion of a black girl, who would fear no centuries old Bible-induced inhibitions, who would understand

119

that when a woman went to a man it was not merely for the procreation of children, not merely a duty to be performed by a wife for the gratification of her husband, but a tremendous upsurge of physical joy, of sensation, of ecstacy.

Had Mama ever known such joy, with Papa? Aunt Marguerite, with Uncle Maurice? Madeleine, with her po-faced Englishman? Catherine, with François de Milot? Or Claudette, with Etienne? She could not believe it. Nor did it necessarily follow, as none of them would have known a *mamaloi*, first. And yet . . . she seized the mirror which lay on the table beside her bed, studied her face. It had not changed. No one looking at her could tell that she knew the secret of all human pleasure.

But, oh yes, they would. Because when she remembered, her nostrils dilated as she could never recall them doing before, and her lips parted, and her eyes sparkled, and she realised she was beautiful.

And her nipples ached, no less than her vagina.

Another sprawl across the bed, the mirror thrown from her hand. It was not to be confessed. Mama Céleste had insisted upon that. Not only would the priest not understand, but Ogone Badagris would be angry. Ogone Badagris was no less jealous a god than the Almighty.

But then, she had sinned. She had blasphemed, for a start. And she had worshipped a false god, momentarily, but with her entire being. And if she did not confess, she would be but compounding crime upon crime.

Jacqueline had laughed at her fears. Jacqueline found it simple, in her mixture of races, to mix her gods with a similar facility. Jacqueline was a devil from hell. Or the most adorable creature on the face of the earth. It was entirely a point of view.

But not to confess . . .? Because in her ecstacy, and at Mama Céleste's behest, she had even prayed to the Snake God, without knowing whom she sought. But she had prayed, as she prayed to God . . . for the safe homecoming of Kit and Henry, for their preservation from all the dangers implicit in being soldiers, in time of war. And for their

120

speedy and safe return. But now . . .

She burrowed into the sheets. Did she want them to return, at least, before she was married? Kit, with that pentrating gaze of his, his analytical mind, would certainly know that she had changed. And Henry . . . could she doubt that Henry knew of Ogone Badagris, had even worshipped him? And if the Snake God could do so much for a woman, what might he not be able to do for a man? Might that not explain Henry's remoteness, these past few years, even before he had departed for America? His ability to be there, and yet obviously not be there? It was a characteristic he shared with most of the blacks. It was obviously the only way they could survive their slavery and their mistreatment. But never before had she realised that they were all probably praying to their god.

She listened to an immense noise in the distance, a shouting and a cheering coupled with the rattle of hooves. Even the great gong in the downstairs hall which summoned them to dinner was being beaten. At six o'clock in the morning?

She sat up again, looked at Amelia, who was hurrying through the door, and wanted to lie down and bury her face once more. How could she look Amelia in the eye, or any black person ever again, after having knelt, naked before the shrine of Ogone Badagris and given over her body to the ministrations of his priestess?

'Mistress, mistress,' Amelia shouted. 'Mistress, them boys come home.'

'Who?' Richilde got out of bed without meaning to. 'Who has come home?'

Amelia gazed at her in surprise; her mistress had never slept naked before, to her knowlege. But she was too excited to care. She wrapped Richilde in her robe. 'Them soldier boys, mistress,' she cried. 'The war done. Them English people done beat, and the soldiers come home. Master Louis is downstairs, and . . .'

'Louis,' Richilde shrieked. She forgot her slippers, threw open the door and raced along the corridor, into the great gallery, and on to the porch, where the rest of the family was

121

already assembled, incongruous in dressing robes and night caps – even Phillippe – while at the foot of the stairs the overseers and their wives and children were gathered to greet the men who were disembarking from the coach.

'Louis!' Marguerite de Mortmain shouted, and ran down the stairs to embrace her son. 'Oh, Louis, thank God you are home.'

'Louis.' Uncle Maurice shook his head, stood back to gaze at the white uniform. 'But you look well. Well.'

'Home the victor,' Philippe said. 'You are to be congratulated boy. Boy? You are a man.' He embraced his cousin. 'You are a hero.'

'But Louis . . .' Jeanne Hamilton felt her way forward. 'Louis? Where is Kit?'

'Kit?' Louis looked embarrassed. 'Well, Aunt Jeanne . . .'

'Henry!' Richilde cried, almost tumbling down the stairs to reach the bottom, and dart into the knot of slaves to seize Henry's hand, only just stopping herself from throwing both arms about his neck. 'Henry! You're safe.'

Henry looked embarrassed and gave a hasty glance at Philippe de Mortmain. But this morning even the Seigneur was smiling.

'Yes, mistress,' Henry said. 'I am safe.'

Her prayers were answered, Richilde thought. Her prayers to whom?

'But Kit,' Jeanne Hamilton wailed. 'Where is Kit?'

'Well, Aunt Jeanne,' Louis said, going very red in the face. 'Kit decided not to come back. He has stayed in America.'

Jeanne Hamilton gave a moan of horror, and had to be supported by her sister.

'He gave me this letter,' Louis said. 'Well, it seemed the right thing to do. For him. We met his cousin, Alexander. He is doing very well for himself. He is aide-de-camp to General Washington. And he and Kit plan to go into business together. There is much business to be done in America.' He realised he was gabbling, but he could not bear to see his aunt so distressed. 'I mean, the war isn't really over, yet. We are still fighting the English. But there is a truce in North

America. The British realise that they have lost there. And Kit, well, he knows that he is not French. He has chosen to become an American, Aunt Jeanne.'

'My husband,' Jeanne Hamilton sobbed. 'And now son . . .' she gazed at Richilde as if expecting her to disappear before her eyes.

Philippe de Mortmain decided there had been enough excitement for one morning. 'I am sure Kit has made the right decision,' he said. 'As I know you will appreciate when you have read his letter, Jeanne. Marguerite, you will put Jeanne to bed, and give her a sedative, and when she awakes again she will be much happier. Louis . . .' he clapped his cousin on the shoulder. 'I am pround of you, proud to have you back. Now tell me, was Henry Christopher a good servant?'

'Indeed he was, Philippe,' Louis said, his facing shining with pride. 'Do you know, Kit invited him to stay in America, and he refused. He said his home was here.'

Philippe de Mortmain shrouded the black boy in his gaze. 'There is loyalty for you,' he remarked. 'Welcome home, Henry Christopher. Now come, gentlemen, ladies, I am sure we have displayed ourselves in our nightclothes long enough!' He turned, to Richilde 'A word with you, mademoiselle.'

She followed him, her heart pounding. Was he angry with her? It was so difficult to tell. But he was leading her into his upstairs study, while the rest of the family departed to their apartments, casting curious glances behind her. But she was his betrothed now. Would he treat her like a schoolgirl after they were married? After she was a mother?

Philippe sat behind his desk, gestured her to a chair. 'How beautiful you are,' he remarked. 'Even in déshabillé. Always so beautiful, my Richilde.'

She opened her mouth, and then closed it again. She didn't know what to say, felt the heat of her flush.

'Did you have a talk, last night, with Jacqueline?' he asked.

'Yes, monsieur.'

He gazed at her. 'Thus today you are a woman.'

Once again she did not know how to reply. How much did he know?

'I do not know what Jacqueline has told you,' he said, 'about me. Yet my plight is plain to see. I am cursed in my inability to procreate.'

Richilde waited, her heart pounding.

'Thus I must expose you to witchcraft,' he said, bitterly. 'Yet must I have an heir. Of my loins.' He smiled. 'And yours. Do you understand me, Richilde?'

'I can promise nothing, monsieur,' she said. 'Except to be your wife to the best of my ability.'

'That I understand. And that I seek. Thus I sent you to that witch. You understand that she is a witch?'

'I understand that she practises a religion at variance with our own, monsieur.'

'Yes,' he said. 'What did . . . no, I do not want to know. You must never tell me, Richilde, as you must never tell anyone, what she said to you.'

He does not know, she thought. He does not even suspect. Or he would have said, what she *did* to you.

'But you must never forget,' he went on, 'that it is a strange and different religion. It is the religion of the West African demons, and it carries with it the taint of *obeah*, and even the Africans agree that is witchcraft. It is an evil thing, by our standards. Yet do I permit it on my plantation, as it is tacitly permitted all over St Domingue, because without their religion the blacks would not be so peaceful.' He half smiled. 'That is the theory, at least. It was held by my father. Have you heard the drums?'

Richilde frowned at him. Because she had, from time to time, thought she had heard drums in the night, and rolled over with her pillows across her ears; the cadence, so regular it seemed to drive all thought from her head, to send her mind spinning through a kaleidoscope of remarkable and unspeakable dreams and desires, had been terrifying.

Then she stared at him, her mouth open. Because she realised that, after last night, her dreams could never be either remarkable or unspeakable again.

'You have,' Philippe said. 'I can see it in your face. They meet, in the bush at the rear of the plantation, and they offer the blood of a cockerel to their Snake God, and they indulge in obscene dancing and even more obscene ritual. I know of these things. I send my spies to their meetings often enough. And the Snake God tells them to fear the white man, and especially me.' Another smile. 'So we are all happy.'

Richilde's mouth slowly closed, tightly. Suddenly she understood that Philippe de Mortmain was as afraid of the black people as he claimed they were of him. Her future husband.

'So,' he said. 'We know these things, but we do not acknowledge them. Black people are creatures apart, creatures of the night, perhaps, as that is their colour. And you are now seen by all as the next mistress of Vergée d'Or. There will be no more familiarity with them. Your greeting of Henry Christopher just now was too effusive. Remember that he is your slave, not your friend. A slave cannot be your friend.'

Richilde drew a long breath; his disapproval was less severe than she had feared. 'Am I to see Mama Céleste again?'

'No. Once is sufficient. I do not know if I should have allowed it at all. But Jacqueline promised . . . once is sufficient. I would have you spend your next year preparing yourself entirely for my bed. As I will do the same. There, you have my word, and you have a pact.'

'But . . . Jacqueline . . ?'

'Has she discussed my bed with you?'

'No.' Richilde lied instinctively. 'But . . . everyone knows that . . .'

'Jacqueline has fulfilled her role.'

'You'll not send her away?' Richilde cried.

'Indeed I shall not, unless you wish it. But I swear to you that I shall not touch her again.' He got up, came round the desk, held her hands. 'From this moment, I wish to love only you, sweet Richilde.' He kissed her on the mouth.

125

It occurred to Richilde that he was not quite sane. A thought she immediately rejected. But that he was as confused and uncertain as herself, or as anyone else for that matter, seemed plain. Philippe de Mortmain, the most feared and respected *grand blanc* in all St Domingue. Why, as he had sent her out to learn from Mama Céleste, as he had turned her into a woman, had he not taken her, there and then? Why wait a whole year, and make her wait as well? If she was ever going to be a wife to him, she wanted it to be now.

Suddenly she was afraid herself, did not know what to do, only that she must find Jacqueline, and talk with her. Only Jacqueline knew her secrets as she knew Philippe's. Only Jacqueline seemed to understand them both. And only Jacqueline would know which god had answered her prayer.

As if she did not know that already. Only Christopher had come home. Kit, like Father, had gone. She supposed she would not see him again. Jacqueline would be able to tell her about these things. It did not cross her mind for a moment that Jacqueline might be angry or concerned at Philippe's vow to exclude even her from his bed, from this moment forth – from what she had said last night, the mulatto would regard that as a blessing. But Jacqueline was not to be found. 'She has gone into Cap François,' her maid said. 'Her brother has also returned from the wars. She has gone to welcome him.'

The scowling young man, Richilde remembered. How odd to think that he had spent the last three years fighting shoulder to shoulder with Kit, and with Henry Christopher, just as she had spent the last three years shoulder to shoulder with Jacqueline. She wondered how much more closely would their lives be intertwined.

'An invitation,' Françoise said. 'From Thérèse de Milot, for tea.'

Françoise sniffed, and held the envelope as if it were burning. Now indeed was the metamorphosis complete. The Mortmain girls had been invited to Rio Negro for tea often before. Never Richilde Hamilton. But now she was the betrothed of Philippe de Mortmain. She hurried off to get dressed, wildly excited. But not at the thought of sitting down to tea with Madame de Milot and Catherine. That was a bore. But to get there, she would have to ride in the carriage, with Henry Christopher. Of course Jean François would be there as well, but still, it would be an opportunity to talk . . . to disobey Philippe right away. But surely she could be permitted to ask Henry about Kit, and about America, and . . .

'Tea with Thérèse,' Philippe said, smiling at her, as she emerged on to the porch, carrying her parasol, Amelia hurrying behind. 'That is good of her. Remember that she has an aunt who is a fourth cousin of His Majesty, by marriage, and therefore regards all other human beings as inferior creatures.' He winked, his strange indecision of earlier quite vanished. 'But remember too that you are the future mistress of Vergée d'Or, and could buy her out three times over. Toussaint,' he shouted, descending the staircase beside her. 'You'll watch the weather. Those are rain clouds.'

'I will do that, monsieur,' Toussaint agreed, climbing down from his seat himself to open the door for Richilde. Because Madame de Milot had paid her the ultimate compliment of sending her own coach for her. Oh, confound it, she thought. She got in, and Philippe closed the door. Amelia climbed on to the box to sit beside Toussaint. Philippe waved. How splendid he looked, standing on the steps of his palace, lord of all he surveyed. If only she could understand. Anything, of what was happening around her.

Even the weather. They had left the plantation, heading south west, now, for Rio Negro. The Milot Plantation, was several miles further inland, away from Cap François. Thus they seemed to be moving into the shade of the huge mountains which formed a backbone to the island, each gigantic peak bigger than Mount Misery, reaching up until they seemed almost to touch the sky. Those mountains were still many miles away; no one ever went there, or knew what really existed there. They were truly the homes of devils and monsters, their lower slopes wrapped in impenetrable forest,

127

their upper peaks always lost in cloud. And today the clouds were lower than usual, forming a dense grey blanket just at the tree level, spreading across the island. As Philippe had said, it was going to rain. She hoped it would not start until after they had reached Rio Negro; she was wearing her newest silk gown, and she did not wish it to get wet.

The first drops fell, splattering on to the dust of the road almost like bullets, pounding on the roof of the coach. Suddenly the entire afternoon was dark. This was going to be a heavy storm. She tapped on the roof, recoiled as Toussaint opened the hatch and peered in; a flurry of raindrops came with him.

'Send Amelia down,' she said.

The coach pulled to a halt, and Amelia scrambled through the door, panting and already soaked. 'I thanking you, mistress,' she said. 'Aiee, but it wet.'

Now there was wind, pushing the rain before it, and the pouring water was so thick it was almost impossible to see fifty yards. The entire day smelt damp, as the overdry grass and shrubs sucked at the moisture in gratitude.

'Toussaint,' Richilde shouted, through the trap. 'Can you see?'

'I can see, mademoiselle.'

'But you must be very wet.'

'Well, I am wet, mademoiselle.'

'Then don't you think we should stop? You and the postilion can sit in here until the rain stops. It can't last long, this heavy.'

'I am thinking we should go on, mademoiselle,' Toussaint said. 'I am thinking . . . whoa, whoa.'

A jagged flash of lightning had cut across the sky, accompanied almost immediately by a roaring crash of thunder, and the horses had started to rear. Richilde hung on to the window as she listened to the crack of the whip and could imagine Toussaint slashing and straining to control the animals, even as she felt the carriage swinging sideways.

'We going capsize,' Amelia shrieked. 'I knowing this. We going capsize.'

'Nonsense,' Richilde snapped. 'Nonsense . . .' The carriage left the road, went bumping into the ditch, came to a sudden jolting stop, with a thump that threw Richilde off her seat and into Amelia's arms. They fell to the floor together, sat there for a moment, only dimly realising that the floor was covered with water which was soaking their gowns.

The door was pulled open. 'The horses have broken out,' Toussaint said. He looked like a large drowned rat. But Richilde was more concerned with what was happening behind him; the ditch had turned into a river of fast flowing water, which seemed to be rising as she looked at it.

Toussaint saw her expression. 'We can't stay here,' he agreed. 'Too much rain, too quick. You will come out, mademoiselle. It is damp.'

An understatement, she thought, as she eased herself forward, held his arm, and jumped down; the water immediately rose to her waist, even soaking the bottom of her corset.

'Ow, me God,' Amelia shrieked. She did not specify to which god she was appealing. 'Ow, me God.'

'You have to get up,' Toussaint explained.

'I'm trying,' Richilde gasped, having her legs knocked from beneath her by the force of the water, and having to clutch him to remain upright. 'On top of the coach?'

'The coach may get swept away,' Toussaint said. 'Up the hill. Come. Racine, you helping the girl?'

He clutched Richilde's arm, pushed at her thighs, got her climbing up the slope and out of the water. It was terribly difficult work with her sodden skirts wrapping themselves round and round her legs, and now one of her shoes came off; she had not worn boots but light slippers, as she had not anticipated having to do any walking, much less climbing. While the rain continued to pound on her head, plastering her hair to her scalp, cutting through the flimsy bodice of her gown to sting her back and shoulders.

'Trees,' she shouted. 'Over there.'

'No, mademoiselle,' Toussaint said.

'But . . .' she watched another vivid flash of forked lightning cut across the afternoon.

'The trees will be struck,' Toussaint said. 'This is best.' He found her a place to sit, half sheltered by an outcrop of rock, some fifteen feet above the rushing water; even as she watched, the coach trembled then fell over onto its side, the splashing crash bringing another scream from Amelia. But now she too had reached comparative safety, sitting like a rag doll with her legs thrust out in front of her, and still clutching the collapsed remains of her mistress's parasol. Racine, the postilion, sat beside her, while Toussaint stayed close to Richilde.

'Toussaint,' she said. 'Are we in any danger?'

He gave one of his quick, crooked smiles. 'You may catch cold, mademoiselle.'

'I mean really.'

'The Seigneur will send someone, soon enough,' he said.

She watched the pouring rain, still limiting visibility to less than a hundred yards, blinked at the vivid streaks of lightning, shuddered at the rumbles of thunder. Yet where she would normally have been terrified, she was reassured by the presence of the little coachman, by his own lack of fear. She glanced at him. Pierre Toussaint. A strange name, for a slave.

'Toussaint,' she said. 'May I ask you a question?'

'Mademoiselle?' He was obviously astonished that she should require permission.

'Why are you called Toussaint?'

'It is my name, mademoiselle. It was the name of the master who first owned me.'

'Yes,' she said. 'But to have a surname . . . none of the slaves on Vergée d'Or has a surname.'

'Well, mademoiselle, not many on Rio Negro either. But Madame de Milot, well, she is proud of me.' He looked embarrassed. 'I can read. My first master taught me to read. I read well, mademoiselle. So Madame de Milot lets me read all the books in her library, and then she has me read to her guests.' The embarrassed look faded into a sudden hardness. 'They find it amusing, mademoiselle, to be read to by a slave. But you see, I have to have a proper name, to recite.'

'Yes,' she said. 'Do you hate her? Madame de Milot?'

'Mademoiselle?' He looked positively alarmed.

'And me. Us. White people. For being the masters. If you are allowed to read, you must know that it was not always so.'

Toussaint brushed water from his face and hair; the dye of his green coat was starting to run beneath the flood of water rushing down his neck. She wondered if he was as aware of the absurdity of the situation as she was.

'Tell me,' she said. 'I will not repeat it. But I would like to know.'

A sidelong glance. 'Well, mademoiselle,' he said. 'As you say, when you read history, you know that things always change.'

'It is often possible to make them change,' she said, 'Would you like to do that?'

'Me? Mademoiselle, I drive a coach. And I have one leg shorter than the other. How can I make anything change?'

'You can pray to your god,' she said. 'To Ogone Badagris. Even to the god of war, Damballah Oueddo, to change them for you.'

Now he gazed straight at her.

'I know of these things,' she said. 'I have talked with Mama Céleste. Do you know Mama Céleste?'

Toussaint's face seemed to close. But she would not be distracted by his withdrawal. The rain, which had by now completely saturated her gown and was in any event pouring down her neck to leave her as wet as if she had been sitting in a bath, gave her a curious feeling of personal intimacy, awoke some of the responses that Mama Céleste had achieved, while it also seemed to isolate the pair of them from the rest of the world – even from Amelia and Racine, huddled together beneath them.

'I know you have,' she said. 'I would understand about these gods of yours. I would understand about your people.'

'Why, mademoiselle?' he asked.

'Because . . .' for the first time she was grateful to the rain,

131

which hid any suggestion of a flush. 'Because we share the same country. And because we may well still be sharing it, if there ever is a change.'

'And do you understand, mademoiselle,' he said, 'that there can only be a change, in St Domingue, by means of a war? That it would be a terrible war? The most terrible war ever fought? Because my people do hate yours.'

'I understand that,' she said. 'But I believe it is because not enough of my people care about your people, that this hatred exists.'

'And you would change that,' Toussaint said thoughtfully. 'Then would you be blessed, by Ogone Badagris. But hated by your own people. Do not share your thoughts, mademoiselle.' He half smiled. 'Do not share this conversation, either. Or they will stretch me on the wheel.'

'Did you suppose I would do that?' she asked.

He considered her for several seconds. 'No,' he said at last. 'I did not think that.'

'And when the change comes, Toussaint, and you are a great man among your people, for you will be, as you are the most learned of them, what will become of me?'

Now his eyes were fathomless pits. 'For that, mademoiselle, must you truly pray. For any promise I might make you would be meaningless. Listen.' She could hear the sound of bugles, the shouting of men. 'The Seigneur comes to find you,' Toussaint said. 'Give me your hand, mademoiselle.'

She held his hand to stand up, and for a moment his fingers squeezed hers.

But, she suddenly realised, he had not told her which god to pray to, his, or hers.

Chapter 5

THE PAPALOI

Bokman was an obeah man who appealed to all the darkest characteristics of the superstitious slaves, and [would lead] them into battle smeared with the blood of the cockerel he had just sacrificed.

'I cannot leave you for a moment,' Jacqueline said. 'And you attempt to drown yourself.' But she smiled as she spoke, smoothed the pillows beneath Richilde's head. She was the best friend in all the world, and the most reliable. Where Mama had merely thrown up her arms and swooned when the half drowned rat that was her daughter had been brought in, Jacqueline, only just returned from town and herself soaked by the sudden downpour, had taken immediate command, wrapped Richilde in blankets and had then insisted she go to bed with a glass of hot buttered rum. It was the strongest drink Richilde had ever tasted, causing the room to rotate gently around her head.

'I was in no danger,' she said, drowsily. 'Toussaint was there.'

'Toussaint?' Jacqueline was contemptuous.

'He knew exactly what to do,' Richilde said. 'And he wasn't afraid.'

'I have told you before,' Jacqueline said severely. 'Do not become involved with Toussaint. He is an evil man.'

'Toussaint?' Richilde was incredulous. 'I cannot believe that. He is unlike any other Negro I have ever met.'

'Which is why he is dangerous,' Jacqueline said. 'He dreams of freedom. That is dangerous for a slave. Madame de Milot made a mistake in allowing him the use of her library. What can he do with such knowledge, save dream? And how may he make his dreams come true, save by causing a great deal of trouble?'

Richilde attempted to think. Because undoubtedly what Jacqueline was saying was very true. And there had certainly been a hint of menace in what Toussaint had said to her. But as Jacqueline said, his dreams had to be only dreams.

And she had more important things on her mind. 'Is your brother well?' she asked, to change the subject.

'Oh, yes. He has grown up.' Jacqueline pulled a face. 'Badly. He also dreams. He always did. Just like Toussaint. But he is even more dangerous than Toussaint.' She sighed. 'Why do men have to dream about things they cannot have? Why can they not be content?'

'Jacqueline,' Richilde said. 'I must talk with you. You must explain what is happening to me.'

Jacqueline gazed at her for a moment, then she got up and shut the door which had been left open to allow the maids to pass in and out with dry towels; Amelia had also been put to bed. 'You are confused by Philippe's vow,' she said. 'You think I may be upset.'

'But . . . you know of the vow? He made it only yesterday morning.'

'I know everything about Philippe.'

'And you are not upset?'

'Why should I be? I knew it would happen. And besides,' she sat on the bed and kissed Richilde on the forehead. 'I am not terribly sorry. I have told you, he is not an easy man. Now he is your problem. But if everything happens as it should, as it must, you will be all right. I know this.'

'As it must? As you knew would happen?' Richilde clutched her friend's hand. 'That is what you must explain to me. Everyone knows what is going to happen, apparently. Except me. You must tell me how they know, and why I do not know.'

Once again Jacqueline gazed at her for some seconds. Then she said, half to herself. 'It is right that you should know, I suppose. But it is a deadly secret. It is known only to three people, and none of them, except me, of course, must ever know that I have told you. Will you swear that to me?'

'Of course.' But a great light seemed to be shining in her mind. 'And the other two people are Philippe and Mama Céleste.'

'You have a brain, behind those big amber eyes,' Jacqueline said.

'Tell me.'

Jacqueline shrugged. 'As I *have* told you, Philippe has not only never had children, he finds even the sexual act difficult, nowadays. This despite the fact that he is healthy, and certainly fond of women. That is why he took me from my father. He thought that with me . . . I do not boast, when I say there is no one more beautiful in St Domingue.'

'I know that,' Richilde said.

'Well, even with me he found it difficult. And he came close to despair. I thought he might even blow out his own brains, such was his anguish. So I took him to Mama Céleste.'

'You took Philippe de Mortmain to Mama Céleste?'

'It was his only hope.'

'But . . . you said he had never met her.'

'Well, as I have just told you, it is a secret shared only by us three. And now by us four. And Mama Céleste certainly saved his reason. She told him of you.'

'Of me?'

'Not by name. She told him that a girl would come to him, a white girl, just a child, from across the sea. Of his house, but not of his blood; of his nation but not of his nation, and that this child would make him whole again, and bear him children, and be a perfect wife to him.'

'My god,' Richilde said at last understanding everything that had happened from her very first day on the Plantation.

'But she also said that he must not touch this child until her sixteenth birthday, and that for a year before that day, he was not to touch any woman.' She smiled. 'I cannot tell you how delighted he was when you came to Vergée d'Or,

135

when I convinced him that you had to be the girl of the prophecy. That night he took me twice. He had never managed that before. Or since.' She kissed Richilde again. 'Mama Céleste is a great *mamaloi*. In her care, you have nothing to fear.'

'Jacqueline,' Richilde said. 'Have you ever been to the drums?'

Jacqueline's head turned, sharply.

'Because I would like to go,' Richilde said. 'I would like to see the ceremony. After all . . .' she attempted a smile, 'I am under their influence now, am I not? If I am ruled by Mama Céleste.'

'The drums are not for you, child,' Jacqueline said. 'They are black people's drums. For you, they would be dangerous.'

'And not for you?' Richilde asked. 'You are not black.'

'I am not white, either,' Jacqueline said. 'But you . . . the drums would consume you, white girl. They are not for you.'

On fine days, when the sun scorched down, it was difficult to accept that there were ever hurricanes, or even rainstorms for that matter. Richilde had never experienced a hurricane, although she had heard sufficient tales about the tremendous damage the winds could cause. Not that she supposed there was any force on earth could harm Vergée d'Or chateau. Because all of its old security had returned for her, and the doubts she had known for that unforgettable week had disappeared. She was a part of it, at last, a figure in a prophecy. Now she could understand Philippe, his moods and his fears, because she knew them herself. Together they trod a narrow and terrifying line between the Christianity in which they had been born and educated and in which they would be married, and the dark forces which surrounded them, physically and supernaturally, and which could not be ignored or gainsaid. But the knowledge that they shared that narrow path was all that mattered, even if she dared not tell him that she knew, could only watch him when, as she alone seemed able to discern, one of this moods of uncertainty was sweeping over him.

Yet she knew that there was more to be discovered, and perhaps even more to be shared. She put down Jacqueline's lack of co-operation to a form of jealousy. The mulatto did not mind sharing Philippe, whom she obviously loathed and feared in any event, as her owner rather than her lover; but she would not share her prerogative of being the intermediary between the white people and the black priestess – there was the source of her power. Richilde begrudged her none of it, had every intention of maintaining Jacqueline at her side for the rest of her life – she could not imagine life without the quadroon's calm presence and gentle smile, or without the utter intimacy she provided – but she also saw no reason why she should not attempt to get closer, and therefore understand more, about this strange belief that seemed to be taking over her life. And there were other roads to Rome.

She walked down by the stables, shading herself beneath her new parasol, looking in the doorway, inhaling the scent of the horses, watching Jean François standing by the forge, huge muscles rippling in his arms and shoulders as he beat at the iron horse shoes – he was naked from the waist up.

'Good morning, Jean François,' she said.

He turned his head, and a strange look flitted across his face to suggest she had interrupted some deep train of thought, but it was gone so quickly she could not decide what it was. Then he laid down his hammer. 'Mademoiselle?'

'Is Henry around?'

'I am here, mistress.' Henry had been polishing the coachwork, and now stepped round the vehicle.

'I am sure Jean François can spare you for a moment, Henry,' Richilde said, and went outside. A moment later Henry joined her. He too was naked from the waist up; his physique, for all his youth, was not greatly inferior to the big black man's. 'Yes, mistress?'

'You have not told me about the war,' she said. 'About America. About Kit.'

He grinned, his face for a moment almost recapturing the careless excitement of their games together as children. 'It was playing soldiers,' he said. 'Only with real muskets, and real bullets.'

'You have seen men killed?'

'Many men.'

'Was it not horrifying?'

He shook his head. 'I did not think so, mistress. But the uniforms, the numbers . . . There is no sight on earth like ten thousand men on the march, all wearing uniforms. That is the most beautiful thing I have ever seen, Mistress Richilde.'

She made a face. 'You should be a soldier. Henry, why did you not stay, with my brother? You might have been able to become a soldier, and wear a uniform.'

'A slave cannot be a soldier, mistress,' he said. 'And St Domingue is my home.'

'As it is the home of your gods?' she asked, her breath quickening.

His eyes narrowed.

'Henry,' she said. 'I know of them. And I have heard the drums. Henry, I wish to attend one of your prayer meetings. Will you take me?'

'I?'

'I know you believe in Ogone Badagris,' Richilde said. 'All black people do. I know you pray to him. And I know you must attend the drums. I wish you to take me with you. Just once. I shall tell no one about it. I promise you. And I shall wrap myself in my cloak, and no one will know it is me. Please, Henry, will you take me?'

'I came back,' Henry said. 'Because St Domingue is my home. And because my mummy has told me, often, that Mr Hamilton told her to raise me, to be big and strong, to take care of you, Mistress Richilde. That is my duty, she has always said. To take care of you. And I am failing in that duty. You are marrying a bad man.' He bit his lip, as if realising the enormity of what he had just said. But he would not lower his gaze. 'Now you would have me fail again. The black man's gods are not for you, Richilde. They would frighten you.' He turned, and went back into the stable.

Henry's refusal distressed her where Jacqueline's had not. She had been so sure of him.The old Henry would never have refused her anything. But Henry had changed, during his years away. He was growing up, developing a mind of his own.

And his remark about her marriage was disturbing, even if it was entirely predictable. She did not suppose there was a single black person, certainly not on Vergée d'Or, and unaware of the prophecy, who supposed she, or anyone, could possibly be happy married to Philippe de Mortmain. And to Henry there would be a deeper and more disturbing aspect of the situation; it would mean the final and irrevocable break between them. As Madame de Mortmain, mistress of Vergée d'Or, she would be required to stand always at her husband's right arm, to support him in everything he did. Henry could not see that she might hope to use that position to improve his lot, and the lot of everyone on the plantation. Certainly that she would use it to dilute her husband's more savage moods. Henry knew only that Philippe de Mortmain was the master, who ruled his empire by fear alone.

But there was nothing that either Henry, or herself, or even, she supposed, Ogone Badagris himself, could do about it now. For suddenly the wedding was rushing upon them all. It would be the greatest event to take place on Vergée d'Or within the memories of any of them, even the oldest slave: Jacques de Mortmain had married his wife in Paris. Thus the preparations – the accumulation of innumerable cases of wine, shipped especially from Bordeaux to supplement the vast stock in the chateau's cellars; but also the preparation of entire vats of sangaree and rum punch, for the celebrations would last all day; the selected breeding of all the turkeys and hens and sucking pigs which would be slaughtered for the wedding dinner; the arrangement by Lucien of all the species and herbs he would use to produce this, the greatest meal of his life; the redecoration of every inch of the chateau, the laundering of all the sheets and pillow cases in the spare bedrooms; and above all, the making of the gowns – all began to dominate the life of the plantation from the moment the 1782 grinding season was completed.

It was decided, by Mama and Aunt Marguerite, and Claudette, and Catherine, and of course, Thérèse de Milot, sitting in conference, that the three younger Mortmain girls would be the bridesmaids, with Lucy the maid of honour. This was what Richilde had always assumed would happen, and she would not understand the long discussions which preceded the decision. Granted that she and her old playmates hardly ever spoke to each other nowadays, and that Françoise was herself betrothed to a planter named de Beaudierre – a liberal, it was whispered disparagingly, whatever that meant – and that Lucy was clearly well on the way to being an old maid, and that Annette, by some way the prettiest of all the Mortmain girls, did not seem interested in any of the unmarried planters, or army officers, that her mother from time to time suggested as suitable husbands, but they were all three of them unable to resist the lure of the wedding, of the preparations, of the new clothes which would be theirs.

Even if they had to play second fiddle to their hated cousin. It took seven dressmakers, supervised and constantly scolded by Jacqueline, to make Richilde's trousseau. For however generous Philippe might have been over the past years, those were all, as Jacqueline remarked contemptuously, children's things, and now Richilde was to be a woman in every sense of the word. If the cumbersome pannier had at last gone out of fashion, much to her relief, there were sufficient other accessories to fill an entire spare room, powdered wigs, so absurd when intended to conceal her own splendid brown hair, straw hats and felt hats and silk hats, each with their accompanying ribbons and bows, ostrich feathers of frightening value, canes for walking and sticks for just holding, all inlaid with precious stones and strips of jade or ebony, boxes of rouge for her cheeks and lips, gloves and parasols, underskirts and corsets, shoes and boots, even stockings, although they were rarely used in this climate.

And of course, gowns. Satin gowns and silk gowns, taffeta gowns and linen house gowns, all dominated by the slowly maturing wedding gown of white satin, lined with white silk, and decorated with white lace ruffles. Her train was of white silk, and would lie several feet on the floor behind her, and Philippe gave her a magnificent necklace of enormous pearls, which, with her sapphire betrothal ring, was to be her only jewellery. While amazingly, she discovered, she was to be allowed to wear her own hair, as she was a bride. It would of course be powdered, and presumably it would be very difficult for anyone to tell the difference. But she would know. She was delighted.

'You are beautiful. Quite beautiful,' Aunt Marguerite said, two days before the wedding, which was to take place on Richilde's sixteenth birthday, when for the first time she was allowed to try on the complete ensemble. Because whatever her feelings on the matter, that Richilde should have gained the prize she must have felt belonged by right to one of her own, Marguerite de Mortmain knew where her prosperity, and that of her sons, lay, and was determinedly enthusiastic.

'Quite beautiful,' Mama agreed. 'Oh, if only Kit could be here to see you, my dear child. If only.'

'Kit!' Richilde cried, looking through the opened dressing room door. Because there he was.

Could it really be Kit, this tall, powerfully built, sunbrowned man, who looked much older than his nineteen years? But it had to be Kit, in his smile, his walk, the way he opened his arms for her. She gathered her skirts and raced forward, ignoring the shrieks of her aunt and the dressmakers.

Aunt Maguerite ran behind her. 'Richilde,' she shouted. 'You cannot wear that gown outside this room until the day. If Philippe were to see you it would mean terrible bad luck. Jeanne, you must stop her.'

But Jeanne Hamilton had left the rocking chair in which she spent most of her time – she had abandoned the fitting

141

and the stitching to her sister and the seamstresses – and was also rushing towards her son. Kit hugged them together.

'Oh, Kit,' Jeanne murmured, kissing his cheek. 'Oh, Kit. To have you back. You never told us you were coming.'

'I'd not let the wedding of my little sister go by,' he said. 'And as I was on passage to Kingston, in any event . . .'

'Is your ship in the harbour?' Richilde cried. Because of course he had written to tell them how his cousin Alexander had become the owner of a trading vessel, and had found Kit a berth as mate, with a master's ticket to follow just as soon as he had gained sufficient experience. 'You must take me down to see it.'

'I shall,' he promised. 'Whenever you can spare the time.'

'Oh, Kit,' Jeanne said again. 'To have you back. If only papa could be here too. What a happy family we would be.'

Kit hugged his mother closer, gazed above her head at Richilde with sombre eyes. 'Mama,' he said. 'Papa isn't coming back.'

'Of course he is,' Jeanne said. 'As soon as he has made his fortune. Now that the war is over, and like you, he can become an American, and stop being an outlaw, why, he may even get back for the wedding.'

'Mama,' Kit said. 'Papa is dead. I have spoken with a man who knew him, twenty years ago, in the Mississippi country. They lived together for a while, trapping. And this man was there when Father died, Mama. Of a fever.'

Jeanne's head jerked backwards as she stared at her son. 'I don't believe you,' she said. 'You are lying,' she shouted. 'You are a nasty, deceitful boy, and a horrid one, coming back here to spoil your sister's wedding. Go back to America, and tell your lies there. I hate you.' She pulled herself free and ran from the room.

'Your mother is not herself,' Philippe de Mortmain said. 'She is seldom herself.'

'Philippe!' Richilde squealed, gathering her gown; she hated his habit of being able to approach so quietly.

'You look simply superb, Richilde,' he said.

'Do not look at her,' Aunt Marguerite begged. 'It is ill

142

fortune. Do not look at her, Philippe.'

Philippe looked at her.

And she returned his gaze, allowing the gown to fall back into place. Because were not they superior to everyday superstitions, safe beneath the protection of their heathen gods?

'Do we believe in luck Philippe?' she asked. 'Or do we make our own.'

He laughed, and seized her fingers to kiss them. 'We make our own, sweet girl. We make our own.' He gripped Kit's hand. 'Welcome home, boy. Welcome home, brother-in-law-to-be. Now let us leave these ladies to their needles, and walk together, and you will tell me of America. Besides,' he added, 'here is Jacqueline. Who do you suppose has come home, Jacqueline? The bad penny himself.'

'Why, Kit,' Jacqueline Chavannes said. 'How splendid you look. Will you not give me a kiss? When you ran away, four years ago, without even saying goodbye, I thought you hated me.'

Kit glanced at Philippe, who did not seem to find anything exceptional in his mistress's choice of words, then kissed the quadroon on each cheek. She had not changed at all, remained exactly as he remembered her – and he had thought about her a great deal – even wore the same perfume he remembered. But, he realised, *he* had changed. He saw her differently. Still beautiful, certainly, still alluring, but with a brittle hardness in her eyes and lurking at the corners of her mouth which almost turned her beauty into ugliness.

'You have grown,' Jacqueline said, kissing him in turn. 'Why, you are a man. You must come and sit with me, and tell me of your adventures. When you can spare the time.' She stepped past him, closed the dressing room door.

'Poor Jacqueline,' Philippe de Mortmain said. 'She is about to become redundant.' He winked. 'As of the day after tomorrow. But actually, she had been so for some time now. I approach your sister as recently chaste as she herself.'

'I wonder she remains here,' Kit said. 'Madame Jacqueline, I mean.'

Philippe laughed. 'Mainly because she has nowhere else to go. What, return to that miserable shop in Cap François? Certainly she is welcome here, for as long as Richilde is content that it should be so. I would not return so old a friend to poverty, unless forced to it.'

So, Kit thought, as they walked, as he told his future brother-in-law of America, what she has feared has come to pass. And instead of being here to stand by her side, as she always hoped and intended should happen, I have taken myself off to a new life. No wonder she was angry with me.

But did that mean she was not his for the taking? If he wanted her? Because of course he did want her, at least with a part of himself. She was the only woman to whom he had ever made love, and she remained the most beautiful woman he had ever seen. He wondered what cousin Alexander, with his somewhat rigid views on colour, would say were he to appear in Virginia with a quadroon in tow. Alex would certainly disapprove. But that was something he would be prepared to face, were he sure that Jacqueline Chavannes was truly what he wanted, could be sure that she would love him, and not herself, not subject everything he might want to her own plans, her own ambitions.

'Why, Annette,' Philippe said. 'You remember Kit?'

'Of course I remember Kit,' Annette de Mortmain said. They had wandered into one of the rose gardens, and disturbed the girl, who was seated on a bench in the shade, reading a book. 'How splendid you look, Kit.'

'As do you, Annette,' he said. She had always been the prettiest of the sisters, – save only perhaps for Madeleine who was due here later on this afternoon, though her English husband had decided against making the journey – but he had never taken much notice of her before; she was only a year older than Richilde. But now she was seventeen, with long yellow hair and dark eyes, and a perfectly white complexion, and with a figure which suggested she was already a woman. He flushed at his thoughts. 'You are quite a beauty.'

'Then I will leave her to entertain you,' Philippe said, and hurried off. Clearly he had been bored, had been doing nothing more than his duty by Richilde's brother.

'Why do you not sit down,' Annette suggested, and he obeyed. 'Are you really a sailor now?' she asked.

'Indeed I am. I've always loved the sea.'

'I remember,' she said. 'I wish I could be a sailor.' Her turn to flush. 'I mean, were I a man. Sometimes I wish I *were* a man, and able to travel, as I wished, and adventure, as I wished. Instead of just sitting here on Vergée d'Or, waiting to die.'

'There's a sombre thought, for a young lady,' he remarked. 'Waiting to be married, you mean.'

She shrugged and smiled. 'If you could see some of the gentlemen Mama has produced for me to marry, you would agree with me that the two eventualities are too similar for comfort. But if I cannot adventure myself, at least I can do so at second hand.' She showed him her book, a French edition of *Hakluyt*, then laid it down and held his hand instead. 'Tell me of America, Kit. Everything you can think of.'

Kit supposed that never in the history of Vergée d'Or, perhaps even in the history of St Domingue, had there been such a glittering assembly of notables in one place, from the Governor-General, Monsieur Peynier, and all his principal officers and their wives, through almost every planter in the north of the island, and even one or two from the south, and all the leading merchants of Cap François. It was strictly a *grands blanc* gathering; he estimated he was by many degrees the lowest person present, either regarded from a financial point of view or from his birth.

But whatever his stature, he was the bride's brother, and therefore exalted. Because dominating even this magnificent assembly, dominating even the glittering wealth displayed by the Milots, was the Mortmain clan. Etienne, wearing a moustache nowadays, and somewhat plump, with his superbly lovely, auburn-haired Claudette on his arm, her babe carried behind her by a white nurse; Louis, also wearing a moustache, which grew but slowly and required continual stroking, apparently – but genuinely pleased to see again his old comrade in arms; Uncle Maurice and Aunt Marguerite, better dressed than he had ever seen them, smiling and bowing as if they were the hosts; Madeleine, tall and slender despite the three children who clung to her skirts, two of whom, the eldest boy and girl, had acted as attendants for Richilde and were clearly overwhelmed by the whole occasion; Catherine, who had allowed herself to put on weight, no doubt, he surmised, to match her husband François de Milot, who was decidedly fat; Françoise, eager to display her Ferrand de Beaudierre, a small planter whose eyes burned with some inner fire, and who seemed anxious to tell everyone how things could not continue as they were at present – without actually specifying which things he was referring to – and Lucy and Annette, splendid in pale blue and gold gowns, as they were the principal attendants of the bride. Annette had never looked lovelier, he thought. But, he had realised over the past twenty-four hours, he had been allowing himself some dangerously immoral thoughts. Annette was his first cousin.

And then, Mama, for this evening also dressed with an elegance he had never seen in her before, but catastrophically and obviously revealing her dementia for all to understand, as she wandered from guest to guest, telling each one that her husband was but delayed, and would be arriving at any moment, to give away his daughter in marriage. His fault, Kit thought, with desperate self bitterness. Better he had not returned at all.

An emotion he experienced even when he regarded the bride and groom, standing together, flanked by the Bishop and Father Thomas, as they raised their glasses and prepared to cut into the many-tiered cake. Richilde looked radiantly happy, and in her happiness she was the loveliest woman in the room. Philippe de Mortmain merely looked alert, watching always to make sure that every guest had everything he or she desired, only smiling when he caught the eye of someone who was smiling at him. But that he was more than twice Richilde's age, that he was in every sense a very mature man where she was equally in every sense a totally innocent young girl, was disturbingly obvious. And presumably not everyone present knew of the blackness which could consume him. From this moment Richilde would be at the mercy of that.

Which was a totally irrational consideration; had she not in reality been at the mercy of that for the past eight years?

The toasts were drunk, and he could legitimately leave the drawing room and wander among the servants, gathered in the great hall to watch their masters and mistresses disporting themselves. Most of them remembered him, as he remembered them, and he had not yet had the time to greet more than a few. This he now rectified as he made his way slowly to the kitchens, to congratulate Lucien on the splendour of his meal, while all the time he searched the throng . . . and at last found Henry, sitting by himself on the wall of the back patio, gazing out towards the distant beach, and the sea.

He had, of course, seen Henry earlier. But only for a brief greeting.

'Well, old friend,' he said. 'A milestone in our lives would you not say?'

'A milestone for Miss Richilde, Master Kit,' Henry said.

'Do you not feel a sense of loss?' Kit asked. 'She is your twin.'

'I lost Miss Richilde many years ago,' Henry said. 'When we came to this place, I think.'

He'd been brooding again, Kit realised. And Henry Christopher was too intelligent to be allowed to brood. Besides . . . perhaps it was un unthinkable thought, but it occurred to Kit that perhaps Henry felt more for Richilde than a slave should feel for his mistress.

'Henry,' he said. 'You know, if ever you change your mind about living here, my offer remains. You can come away with me. And I am not living in America itself, you know. Well, I suppose I am. But I have adopted the sea as a livelihood. In a year or two I shall have a master's ticket and, in any event, I sail on a vessel owned by my cousin. You remember Alexander Hamilton?'

'I remember Mr Hamilton,' Henry said.

'Well, you could sail with me. It's a good life, Henry. A free life. Even for a slave.'

Henry gazed at him.

'And then,' Kit went on, somewhat lamely. 'Well . . . I do not think you are really happy here.'

'I must stay here,' Henry said.

'Why? Because of your mother? She is old, just as my mother is old. They are going to die some time soon. And then, what will you have stayed for? While Richilde . . . Well, as of tonight, Richilde will have no more need of either of us. Not ever.'

'She will need, Master Kit,' Henry said. 'She will need, more than ever. One day.' He slipped down from the wall. 'It is for that day I must be here.'

He walked into the gloom. Kit looked past him, saw the massive figure of Jean François standing by the gate. With the big man, he could make out the smaller shape of the lame Milot coachman, Jean Pierre Toussaint. When Henry joined them, the three men walked into the darkness together.

The women clustered round the bed, smoothing pillows here, straightening the sheet here, clucking and laughing, joking and even weeping. There was an awful number of them, many people Richilde had hardly seen before this evening, but all anxious to assist the bride in preparing for the most important night of her life.

She sat up in bed, her back against the pillows, her satin and lace nightgown half concealed by the sheet which had been folded across her stomach. Her hair had been released from its various pins and curls, and was loose on her shoulders – it had been brushed time and again to rid it of most of the cloying powder. And remarkably, she was not aware of the slightest feeling of fear. She estimated that she was by some distance the calmest person in the room. The

148

amount of wine she had drunk had certainly helped, but she was more aware that she had been waiting, and preparing, for this night for seven years; that thanks to Mama Céleste, and to Jacqueline, she was in every way ready, and indeed eager, to belong to her husband, to know if, as was promised her, the touch, the feel, the love of a man was superior to any other physical sensation.

So no doubt she was the greatest sinner on the face of the earth, the most utter heretic. She was a sinner in never having confessed one part of her secret life to Father Thomas. And she was a heretic in having reserved that secret part of her life to Ogone Badagris. And she was a depraved woman, by any Christian standards, in having, so often during the past year, reawakened with her own fingers the enormous sensual pleasure first revealed to her by Mama Céleste, in having, so often, left her bedchamber in the middle of the night to walk, all by herself, on the empty beach, and plunge into the rollers, and be loved by them, because that too had been undertaken in a spirit of pure self gratification.

Thus Christian ethics. But she could always reassure herself that such behaviour was approved by the Snake God, more, was demanded by him.

And all would be expiated tonight. In the love of her husband, in her ability to welcome him, without fear and without restraint, would she atone for all of her crimes. She told herself that after tonight she would no longer even need Ogone Badagris. He would have done his duty by her, and could then be allowed to revert to his more important duties, of caring for the black people.

Why, after tonight, tomorrow morning, in fact, she could even confess the whole thing to Father Thomas. There would be nothing he could do about it then. Tomorrow morning she would awaken as Madame de Mortmain, Mistress of Vergée d'Or, and would hold his livelihood in the palm of her hand. Oh, she was a depraved creature.

'Well, my child . . .' Aunt Marguerite bent over the bed to kiss her on the forehead – her mother had long been put to bed. 'I think the time has come to leave you.' She smiled. 'In my day, the ladies of the family, at least, remained to witness the consummation. But Philippe will have none of it. So you must face him alone.'

'It will be well, Aunt Marguerite,' Richilde assured her. 'All will be well. And I must thank you, for everything.'

Marguerite ushered her daughters and all the other women through the door, turned and curtsied. 'It is we who should thank you, Madame de Mortmain,' she said. 'I will wish you a good night.'

A good night, Richilde thought. And a happy one. Because she could hear the noise now, the shouting and the laughter, the approach of the men. She hoped he would keep them outside. She had no desire to share this evening with anyone but Philippe. And perhaps . . . She turned her head as the inner door opened.

'Jacqueline,' she cried. 'Listen . . .'

'I know,' Jacqueline said. 'Those women stayed so long.' She ran across the room, took Richilde in her arms. 'Remember everything.'

Richilde nodded.

'Then be happy,' Jacqueline commanded. 'And make him happy, too.'

A quick kiss, and she ran from the room again, just as the noise reached the door. The men shouted advice and congratulations and a variety of lewd jokes, and Richilde sank beneath the covers until just her head was visible. But only Philippe came through the door, laughing and replying to the repartee, but with a touch of impatience in his voice. Then he closed the door and shot the bolt, turned to face her.

'I suppose they must have their little games,' he said.

'Perhaps they are envious of you,' she said, sitting up.

'Envious? Yes, they should be that.' He wore a nightshirt, and a cap, but this last he now threw on the floor. 'Richilde, my Richilde,' he said, sitting on the bed to take her in his arms and kiss her, again and again, sending his tongue questing into her opened mouth as she attempted to match it with her own – for how long had she dreamed of doing this – moving her body against his.

'Oh, Richilde,' he said, and at last released her, only immediately to hug her close again. 'You are everything I have dreamed of, everything I have waited for. Oh, Richilde . . .' he half threw her away from him, stood up, took off his nightshirt. Here at last was a man, a white man. She had of course during her life seen many naked slaves, of both sexes, but that had been before her awakening of this last year, and she had hardly looked at them closely any more than she ever looked closely at horses or donkeys or dogs in a state of arousal. But here was a man, and her husband, huge, magnificent, and so ready for her. Truly she had to suppose that the tales Jacqueline had told her of his impotence were no more than figments of the quadroon's imagination.

'Do I frighten you?' he asked.

'Frighten me? Oh, Philippe . . .' she reached for him, slipped her hands round his naked buttocks, brought him against her, smothered him in her embrace. She tilted her head back. 'Do you wish me to undress also?'

'Yes,' he said. 'Yes, I would look upon you, too.'

She released him, rose to her knees, lifted the nightdress over her head and threw it on the floor.

'Richilde,' he said. 'My Richilde. My marvellous little girl.'

She was on her back, with him on top of her. It was quicker than she had either expected or hoped, and certainly she was not aroused as she wanted to be, and as she was sure she would be. But of course tonight the important thing was Philippe. That he should possess her and be happy. And there it was, inside her, hard as a bone, with an ease she would not have supposed possible.

She felt almost no pain, only a delightful sensation spreading away from her groin, even as she reached for his mouth again, sent her fingers scouring up and down his back in her anxiety to hold him against her . . . and was taken completely by surprise when he suddenly pushed himself up and rolled away from her, rising to his knees at the edge of

151

the bed.

'Philippe?' She raised herself on her elbow.

'Soft,' he muttered. 'Two thrusts and then soft. Soft,' he suddenly shrieked.

She gazed at him. He was certainly incapable of entering her again, at this moment.

'Let me help you,' she said, reaching for him.

'No,' he snapped, leaping from the bed. 'It would do no good. It is the same as always. I have been betrayed. Betrayed,' he screamed, his entire body seeming to swell with fury.

She bit her lip, uncertain what he meant. 'Philippe,' she said. 'If I have in any way . . .'

'Not you' He gave her a glance then reached for his nightshirt. 'Never you, poor child. You are but an innocent pawn in this game. But that Jacqueline . . . by Christ she shall pay for this.' He picked up his riding crop, crossed the room and opened the inner door before she fully grasped his intentions. Then she leapt from the bed herself, ignoring her robe in her haste.

'Philippe,' she shouted. 'Philippe . . .'

He had already crossed the inner room, which was his own private dressing room, she realised. Somewhere she had never entered before. But now she was exploring entirely new territory, as she followed him down a brief corridor, at the end of which he threw open another door.

Jacqueline's bedroom. A place of heavy dark drapes and equally heavy perfume. And Jacqueline, sitting up in bed to stare at her master; she had not yet been to sleep – the candles still burned.

'Philippe?' she asked, and saw the riding crop. 'Philippe?'

'Bitch,' he shouted. 'Whore from the pit of hell. You and your black magic. You and your obeah.' He swung the crop, and the quadroon gave a shriek and rolled across the bed, but the leather thong caught her on the shoulder, with such force that a red weal immediately appeared, and her scream ended in a gasp of pain as she fell to the floor on the far side.

'Philippe!' Richilde shouted, trying to catch his arm, and

being thrown away by the violence of his next movement, as he stamped over the bed itself to reach his erstwhile mistress.

'I'll take the skin from your back,' he growled. 'By God, I'll see the colour of your blood. I should have done so long ago. I should have . . .'

Jacqueline gave a moan and attempted to protect her head with her arms as the whip again slashed across her shoulders.

With desperate urgency Richilde threw both arms around Philippe's right arm, hung on to it as he tried to throw her off, cut her lip on his elbow, but delayed the next blow long enough for Jacqueline to crawl to the door.

'Philippe,' she said. 'Please! It will be all right, I know it will.'

'It can never be all right as long as that witch lives in this house,' he said. 'It is she has bewitched me these past six years, all for her own purposes.' He pointed, his chest heaving. 'Get out,' he said. 'Get yourself from Vergée d'Or. So help me God, if you are seen here I again I will set the dogs on you.'

Jacqueline stared at him, then at Richilde. Richilde gave a quick nod, to try to convey to her that it would certainly be best at this moment. Slowly Jacqueline held on to the door and dragged herself to her feet, made as if to stroke her burning back, then shrugged her shoulders and tossed hair from her face – it was the first time that Richilde had ever seen her hair disordered.

Jacqueline reached into the cupboard for a valise.

'What are you doing?' Philippe demanded.

'You told me to leave, *master*,' she said.

'I did not tell you to rob me.' he said. 'Get out.'

Jacqueline hesitated.

'Please, Philippe,' Richilde begged. 'You cannot send her away, naked.'

'She came to me naked,' Philippe said. 'Let her go naked.'

Jacqueline gazed at him, her eyes black pits from the very depths of hell. Then she turned and walked through the door.

153

'Philippe,' Richilde said. 'That was cruel of you.'

'You do not know her as I do,' Philippe said. 'She is an evil creature. And I let her have the education of you.' He turned, his eyes hardly less fearful than had been Jacqueline's.

But he was her husband, and this was their wedding night. Time enough to do something about Jacqueline tomorrow.

'We will not think of her,' she promised. 'Come back to bed, Philippe. Come back to bed, and all will be well. I will make it so.'

He shook his head. 'Nothing can be all right, tonight. Perhaps never, now. I am cursed. She has cursed me. By God, I should have hanged her, rather than let her walk away from here.'

Richilde sighed, and fought to restrain the tears, the utter despair, that was threatening to overwhelm her. 'At least then, let us retire to sleep,' she said. And forced a smile. 'It has been a tiring day.'

'Aye,' he said. 'Do you go to sleep, Richilde. I will remain in here.'

'In here? But . . .' she stared at him with her mouth open.

'I will come to you when I can,' he said. 'But for this night you must sleep alone. Now leave me.'

'Madame de Mortmain,' Monsieur Chavannes said, twisting his fingers together. 'Good morning, Madame de Mortmain. What can we do for you? Some cloth? See this fine linen? May I say what a great pleasure, and an honour, it is for us to receive you in our humble shop, madame.'

You miserable old hypocrite, Richilde thought. How you must hate me, and all I stand for, yet you stand there like some obsequious eunuch, terrified of causing offence.

'I wish to speak with Jacqueline, monsieur,' she said.

'Jacqueline. Ah.' Monsieur Chavannes' eyes became opaque. 'She is not well, you understand. That is why she has returned from the plantation to stay with us. Only for a while, you understand. But of course, you know all of this.'

'Yes,' Richilde said. 'I would still like to speak with her.'

'Well, of course, madame, if that is what you wish. Will you excuse me? I will fetch her.'

He bustled out of the shop. Richilde turned, surveyed the stacked bales of cloth, twirled her parasol, looked through the outer door at the waiting carriage, and Jean François and Henry Christopher and Amelia, conferring – none of them approved of this visit, obviously, although only Amelia had ventured actually to say so.

'What, do you mean to torment her?' Jacques Chavannes asked.

She had not known he was there, concealed behind a mound of drapery at the far end of the shop. Now she could feel his dislike coming at her in waves. It was a feeling she had known the first time she had ever met him, seven years before. And if anything it had grown since his return from America. Yet Kit had told her how this man had once saved his life.

'No, monsieur,' she said. 'I do not mean to torment her. We are friends, your sister and I.'

'Bah,' he said. 'How can a mulatto be the friend of a white person? You are asking the snake and the mongoose to lie down together, madame.' He flushed, as if realising that he might have said a great deal too much, and withdrew to the far corner of the shop, as Jacqueline came through the inner door. She did not appear to have slept for the three nights since she had left Vergée d'Or – her face was drawn, and there were shadows under her eyes.

'You wish to speak with me, madame?' she asked.

'Jacqueline . . .' Richilde glanced from left to right. 'Is there somewhere we can talk in private?'

'There is here, madame.' Jacqueline said.

Richilde hesitated. But to be angry herself was utterly futile. 'I . . . I could not come before,' she explained. 'I had our guests to entertain, and to come into Cap François might have been too obvious. Philippe is very insistent that no one should know of what happened.'

'No one will know,' Jacqueline said. 'No one ever has.'

'Yes.' Richilde bit her lip. 'He still has not . . . I am not yet

155

truly his wife.'

Jacqueline shrugged. 'Then you must pray.'

'To whom should I pray, Jacqueline?'

The quadroon's eyes were dark. 'That decision you must make for yourself, madame.'

'Will you not call me Richilde? I had supposed we were friends. You knew of Philippe's moods, long before I. You will know I cannot gainsay them. At least, not until I can be a wife to him. But I can still be your friend, Jacqueline. You have but to tell me what you require, anything you require, and I shall obtain it for you. And I would be your friend, always.'

'We cannot be friends, madame,' Jacqueline said. 'Our blood makes it impossible. The mistake was mine, to suppose such a thing might be possible. Now you must go to your life, and do with it what you can. Leave me to mine.'

Richilde gazed at her. 'Hate,' she said. 'However justified you may feel it at this moment, is a wasting, hopeless, consuming emotion, Jacqueline,' she said. 'Do not waste your life hating.'

Jacqueline's smile was twisted. 'Yet is it an emotion, madame,' she said. 'And it is the only one I know. Now go to your husband, to your god, and leave me in peace.'

'Well,' Kit Hamilton said. 'I must be on my way.' He held Richilde close. 'Take care, little sister.'

And can you see into my mind, dear brother? she wondered. Can you make out the misery there?

But she smiled, and kissed him on the cheek. 'It is you who should take care, out there on the ocean. But you will remember that Vergée d'Or is always here, waiting for you, if you should choose to visit us.'

'Be sure that that will be as often as I can manage it,' he promised, and shook hands with Philippe. 'I know that Richilde is in good hands, Philippe,' he said. 'You will keep me informed as to Mama's health?'

'I shall do that, Kit,' Philippe promised. 'As I shall treasure Richilde's love above all other things.'

'I am sure of that,' Kit said, meeting his brother-in-law's gaze, before passing on to say farewell to the rest of the family.

And at the end of the row, Annette. 'I shall write to you, with your permission,' he said. 'And tell you of my adventures, supposing I have any.'

'Will you, Kit?' she asked. Her eyes shone. 'I should so like you to do that.' She blushed. 'And will you truly come to see us, often?'

'As often as I can,' he said, and bent his head to kiss her on the cheek. She wore a voluminous bonnet, and for just a moment their faces were lost to view. In that moment she half turned her head so that her lips brushed his.

Philippe watched him going down the stairs to the waiting carriage. 'I hope he does come to visit us, regularly,' he said. 'I think he may well do so.'

'Indeed?' Richilde asked.

'Have you not seen the way he looks at Annette? The warmth, indeed, with which he has just kissed her goodbye?'

'That would be impossible,' Richilde said. 'They are first cousins.'

'Who can tell what is impossible?' Philippe mused. He held her arm as they mounted the great staircase together. 'I wish to thank you, for so dissembling before him. Before everyone. It would have done credit to someone twice your age.'

She checked at the upper porch. 'But you will not remove the reason.'

His eyes gloomed at her. 'I will come to your bed, Richilde, as soon as I feel able. It . . . it is a terrible thing, for a man to admit, even to himself, such a weakness as mine.'

'I do not care for your weaknesses,' she said. 'I care only for your love. I wish to sleep beside you, nothing more than that.'

'Dear Richilde,' he said, and bent his head to kiss her. 'You shall, sleep beside me, in time. But now . . . now, when I wish to take you, and love you, and cannot, my anger grows . . . and I am afraid of harming you. I would not harm you for all the world, my Richilde.'

But you will not sleep with me, she thought bitterly, lying by herself in the centre of the huge bed. I am a bride of more than a week, and I am as virgin as the day I was born. Do you not know, you silly, proud man, so strong and imperious, that I would cheerfully exchange a few bruises to be made into your wife? Have I really lived and waited and anticipated for eight years, just to lie here all alone?

She slept, an angry, frustrated sleep, and awoke suddenly, disturbed by the silence of the night. And then realised that there was, after all, sound. The steady, distant throb of a drum. Or perhaps there was more than one, seething across the night, in their incessant rhythm dulling the senses, but beckoning at the same time. Come to me, come to me, come to me.

She got out of bed, opened the door, and listened. The house was silent. She went to the window, looked out at the ocean. There was no moon; the night was dark. And still – there was no wind to mask the throbbing of the drums.

She discovered her heart was pounding and sweat was gathering on her neck. The drums were obliterating her senses, driving the lonely resentment from her mind. Before she could reason, allow common sense and caution to come to her rescue, she had gathered her hair into a bandanna, and wrapped herself in her robe. She went down the private staircase, stood in the garden, listening. Where the drum was, there she would find Mama Céleste, surely. Hitherto she had not dared return to the *mamaloi*, however much she needed her. But tonight she could wait no longer. Not when she was being summoned by the drums.

Her bare feet scuffed the dust of the drive; she skirted the overseer's town, dark and silent, and reached the back of the slave village, heart still pounding, afraid, but determined. The throb of the drums caressed her mind, reached her belly and beyond, demanding, urging, calling. And then she discovered that she was not alone. As she approached the slave town she saw white clad figures leaving the barracoons and disappearing into the trees that lay beyond. She took her

158

place with them. No one gave her even a glance. It could not occur to a slave that a white woman, who was also the mistress of the plantation, would wish to join in their nocturnal service.

Now the darkness increased, as they entered the shade of the huge branches, and twisted vines snatched at her feet, together with scurrying lizards and the thousand and one other things that made up the night in the tropical forest. She felt no fear. She had explored the woods of St Kitts often enough as a girl, knew that the most vicious creatures in them were stinging ants, and did not suppose St Domingue was greatly different. But even had she been afraid she could not now have resisted the power of the drums.

The trees were parting again, and the white-clad figures were moving to their right around a clearing. And here there was light, provided by emptied coconut shells, cut in half and filled with oil, to burn with an eerie glow, guttering even in the windless night. And here too were six fowl cocks, tethered by their legs to sticks, eyes darting to and fro, heads jerking at the stealthy sounds around them. For the moment they occupied the clearing alone, but beginning to surround them were more and more people, kneeling and crouching in the tree fringe, men and women, and even children. Richilde knelt, well to the back of the throng, to stare at the flames and the cocks, and identifying, in the gloom beyond the helpless birds, the forms of the drummers, three of them, each controlling a different shaped instrument, each sending forth a different note, over and over again, echoing through the trees, and up and down the mountains.

She was one of the last to arrive. Only a handful of white-clad figures came behind her, to take their places in the silent assembly. But as her eyes grew accustomed to the gloom she realised that there were several thousand people present, an immense gathering. She wondered if Philippe, who claimed to know all this, had an inkling of the size of the meetings he so contemptuously permitted.

Her attention was drawn to the flickering lights in front of her, where suddenly a figure appeared beside the fowl cocks, a young man, tall and strong and gleaming in the darkness, sitting cross legged before the drummers, shoulders square and head erect. On either side of him waited a young woman, each holding a palm leaf, faces and bodies rigid with tense expectation. And the drum beat had altered, reaching ever deeper into the senses, summoning all the powers of belief it could induce.

She saw the flicker of a red robe, and raised her head expectantly: Mama Céleste. But this was not Mama Céleste. This was a man, as tall and as powerful as any Negro she had ever seen. More than that she could not tell, for the robe was across his head as well, and half concealed him. Her heart constricted. She had no idea what was about to happen. But she knew that if it was so important that it required the offices of a *papaloi* – a priest – rather than a woman, then it would be terrible indeed. And she suspected that this was no mere *papaloi*, but rather a *hougan*, a high priest of the voodoo religion.

The red robed man walked into the centre of the circle, stood next to the young man, threw his arms to the skies, and shouted, 'Hear me. O mighty one. Hear me, O Serpent, Damballah Oueddo. Hear my prayer, and promise me deliverance for my people.' He paused, and inhaled, while a moaning chant arose from the watching multitude. 'How long, great Ogone, master of all the Oceans of the World, must we wait? Hear me, O mighty lord. Speak to me, great Loco, Lord of the Trees. Grant me and my people thy sin of deliverance. Come to me gentle Ezilee, sweet *maîtresse*, and take from my mind, from my body, the very last human weakness.'

Once again he paused, and now the chant had grown louder. Richilde discovered that sweat was pouring from her body.

'Come to me, O mighty Ogone Badagris. Come to my people, O Dreadful One. Lead us to war, as is thy purpose. Grant us an end to all the white people. Grant us the mood of hate and cruelty, that their destruction may be known throughout the world, and forever. Grant us revenge, O

Dreadful One, for the wrongs that are daily committed upon us. Grant us now a sign, my lords, that our prayers are heeded.'

He stood still, his body trembling, and Richilde watched a man get up from the crowd, and hold out a machete, which the *hougan* took, slowly and reverently, testing the sharpness of the blade with his thumb. She wanted to scream. She wanted to get up and run away. But like everyone else she merely stared in horror, as the priest stood before the motionless young man, neither of them even blinking their eyes as they gazed at each other. Then the priest threw back his head and screamed to his gods in an unknown tongue, as he whirled the cutlass around his own head, and with a single unbelievable sweep of the razor sharp sword swept through the neck of his victim.

The head fell forward, and the machete had been dropped. The priest caught the head, his great hands immediately smeared with blood, while the two girls hastily fanned the still upright, blood-spouting neck with vigorous anxiety, determined to prevent a speck of dirt, a single insect from settling on the tortured flesh.

Richilde forced herself to watch. Because I am not seeing, she told herself. I am not even here. I am lying in my own bed, and dreaming. I have got to be dreaming. But the blood spurting from the severed arteries held her spellbound.

And now the *hougan* was advancing again, having held the dripping head high to present it to the worshippers. Slowly he paraded his ghastly trophy, and equally slowly he replaced the head, carefully, exactly, while in that moment another young woman threw a large piece of red cloth over the dead man.

The dead man? Within seconds his feet began to move, and then his arms, and the throbbing of the drums had resumed command over all of their senses. The young man's mask was taken away, and he was unchanged, but standing now, shuffling and posturing, exuding all the immense manhood of his naked body. Then he reached for the nearest fowl cock, and with a twist of his powerful fingers tore its

161

head from its neck.

There was a shriek from the people around Richilde, and they surged forward, holding up their hands to catch the flying blood, reaching for the quivering body to grasp it and shred it into pieces, cramming raw flesh and blood and bone into their mouths, seizing the other birds to destroy them in turn. And as they did so, the beat of the drums changed, slightly and perhaps insensibly to all but a detached observer, but the rhythm had increased, and the slaves danced, sinuously and even gracefully at first, but rapidly becoming more vigorous and forceful, while the drumbeat gradually quickened its tempo ever more. Now passion and desire and hate and fear and lust came bubbling to the surface, and turbans and gowns, cotton drawers and straw hats were discarded, flung to the edges of the clearing, while the night became a seething delirium of aroused sexuality.

Richilde knew that she must get away, if only because she was suddenly isolated, standing on the edge of the clearing. She ran into the trees, checked in horror as she came up against a large black man, gasped for breath as she recognised Jean François.

He was equally surprised, as he pulled the bandanna from her head and looked at his mistress. Immediately he drew her further into the privacy of the trees. Yet he still held her, and she felt his hands slip up to her neck, stroking across her breast as he did so, bringing her out in a rash of shivering.

'No,' Henry Christoper said.

The big man looked at him. Even at sixteen Henry was already the taller, and the broader.

'She has seen all. She will tell all,' Jean François said. 'And she must die . . .' Again his hand moved over her breast.

'You cannot kill her,' Henry said. 'And you must not touch her.'

Jean François hesitated, and Toussaint spoke. He had approached them unheard, as the four of them were quite ignored by the frenzied dancers. 'She will not betray us,' he said. 'Will you, Madame de Mortmain?'

Jean François had released her, and she could draw an

162

unhindered breath. She slipped from his grasp. 'No,' she gasped, 'No, I will not betray you.'

She looked to Henry, reached for him, felt his arm go round her shoulder.

'You can believe her?' Jean François asked. 'Married to that man?'

Toussaint looked at her, then at Jean François. 'Are you not looking at the prophecy?' he asked.

Richilde looked down at Henry's black arm resting across her white one.

'Go,' Toussaint said. 'Make haste, Madame Richilde. You should not have come here. This night your eyes have seen what no white person should ever see. Go.'

'Toussaint,' she gasped. '*Did* I see? Was that boy really ...?' she bit her lip.

Toussaint's face was as remote as that of a god itself. 'You saw, what you saw, madame,' he said. 'What your brain told you was there, was there. Now go. Henry Christopher will take you back to the chateau.'

He seized Jean François' arm, and hurried him back to the dance, speaking urgently in his ear.

'Come,' Henry said.

She realised for the first time that he was naked. She had not seen him naked before, at least since he and she had been small children together. Now she realised he was the handsomest man she had ever beheld. 'Henry ...'

He held her arm, hurried her though the trees.

'Henry,' she begged, uncertain what she was begging for, knowing only that she could still feel the touch of Jean François' hand, that she could never be the same, after this night. And that therefore he could never be the same either? Then what of all the other people? The thousands of other people who had attended the ceremony. 'Henry!'

Still he forced her on. 'What you did was madness,' he said. 'Madness, Richilde.' It was the first time he had not addressed her as mistress or madame since the day at Jean François' forge. 'And dangerous. Had you been discovered ...'

163

She dug her heels into the earth and made them stop; the lights of the chateau were in the distance. 'Henry,' she said. 'What did I see?'

'As Toussaint has said, what you think you saw, you saw.'

'Henry,' she said. 'Tell me the truth. That could not have happened. It could not.'

He looked down at her. 'The drums have a strange power over the human mind,' he agreed.

'Do you believe it?'

He hestitated. 'No,' he said. 'But I saw it. And those people back there believe it.'

'And the *papaloi*?' she said. 'Who was he?'

'So that he can be hanged?'

'Do you believe that of me, Henry?'

Another hesitation. 'No,' he said at last. 'His name is Boukman. He is a great *hougan* amongst my people.'

'He lives on Vergée d'Or?'

He shook his head. 'He has come from far away.'

'Then this was a special occasion. Why, Henry? Why? Was it to do with my marriage?'

For the first time he looked genuinely puzzled; the thought had obviously not occurred to him. 'I do not know,' he said. 'Boukman said it must be tonight. Boukman knows all things.'

'And you believe *that*?'

'It is my business to believe, for now, Madame Richilde,' he said.

For now, she thought. He was too intelligent to believe with all of his mind. Just as he was too self-possessed to continue calling her Richilde, treating her as an equal. That brief moment was past.

But she did not wish it to pass. She could not allow it to pass.

'Henry?' she asked. 'What did Toussaint mean, about a prophecy?'

'He was told a prophecy, once,' Henry said. 'He and Jean François.'

'To do with your people becoming free?'

He gazed at her.

'And it was to do with me? Or a white woman?'

'Who can tell, with a prophecy, Madame Richilde?'

'But it is to do with your freedom,' she insisted.

'A people must dream, Madame Richilde. If they cannot dream, then they are animals.' Almost he smiled. 'We are not animals, no matter what your husband may suppose. But Madame Richilde, remember your promise. If you were to break it, there would be much misery, many of us would die.'

'I will keep my promise,' she said. 'But Henry, if the prophecy were to come true, will there not be much misery then, and many deaths?'

'Prophecies are like dreams,' he said. 'They fade, when daylight comes.'

'But Henry, as we are a part of the prophecy . . .' she looked him slowly up and down. She did not wish ever to forget what he looked like. As she wished him to remember her, this night. Her fingers released the tie for her gown.

But he caught her hand. 'Tonight is also just a dream, Richilde,' he said. 'If you return to your bed now, it will not become a nightmare.'

He squeezed her hand, and disappeared into the trees, and the darkness, and the distant throb of the drums. She remained staring after him for several seconds, aware that she was till panting, that her body was still alive. Then she turned, and hurried across the lawns and up the private staircase, and into her bedroom. Her empty bedroom.

But sleeping alone, this night, was not possible. She threw her robe on the floor, made her way along the corridor into the other room. At the sound of her entry the glare of the candle, Philippe de Mortmain sat up, stared at her in total amazement. 'What the devil . . .'

Richilde knelt on the bed beside him. 'I have come,' she said. 'To make you a man. And to make me your wife.'

PART TWO
The Soldier

Caught up in the enthusiasm of Boukman's rebellion, [Toussaint] was at first employed as a doctor: already middle-aged, and wizened in appearance, he never sought to command, but before long his ability as a tactician began to be noticed and envied. He made an enemy of Jean François himself, and found it necessary to take service with the Spaniards in the other half of the island. The British invasion and the death of Jean François combined to attract him back to his native country. He took command of the black army of the north and brought men like Dessalines and Christophe out of the slave mobs and into positions of authority. He developed his own strategy to suit his brilliant tactics, and if never able to meet the British regulars on a set battlefield, he harried and outwitted them. It was during these years that he earned the nickname of L'Ouverture, from the manner in which he opened gaps in the opposing forces.

Chapter 1

THE FAILURE

The pronouncement [of 26th August 1789, 'that all men are born and continue free and equal as to their rights.'] encouraged the mulattos' wildest hopes ... and in St Domingue, both to defend their persons and to prove their re-established rights, they appeared in arms. This could be interpreted as rebellion, and they were immediately dispersed by the troops, on this occasion without undue violence. But the temper of the frightened white population was revealed by the fate of Ferrand de Beaudierre, a white man who sided with the mulattos and had the temerity to draw up a memorial claiming for his friends the full benefits of the declaration of rights. The authorities regarded this as a seditious document, and de Beaudierre was imprisoned; a white mob burst open the cell and tore him to pieces.

'Her life was not easy,' Father Thomas said. 'She had more than her share of tragedy. And her later days were clouded. And yet, in the health and prosperity of her children, the brightness of the future of her family, she must have known happiness. And now she knows the greatest happiness of all, that of being reunited with her husband, kneeling before the Lord God our Master. Jeanne Hamilton, rest in peace.'

The first clod of earth fell on the coffin with a dull thud, while the mourners waited. Only the immediate family had attended this last ceremony – Jeanne Hamilton had been socially important in St Domingue only as the mother of

Madame de Mortmain. But it was a large family, even if Kit was not here – probably did not yet know of his mother's death. Maurice de Mortmain, grey haired and stooped, was here, Marguerite at his side, also grey and old, mourning a sister who had died in truth long ago. Etienne was here, fat and florid, with his magnificent pink and white Milot wife – even after four children Claudette de Mortmain remained the most beautiful woman in St Domingue, and she had certainly assured the succession. Louis de Mortmain was here, slender and serious as ever. Catherine de Milot was here, her husband François at her side – her parents-in-law could not really be expected to attend the funeral of a woman they had despised – Catherine apparently suffered the Mortmain curse, and was childless, although she remained tall and willowy and attractively severe. Françoise de Beaudierre was here, apeing her brother Etienne in the roles of fat which she had allowed to develop, as – unlike her sister – she aped his wife in the regularity with which she produced her children, one every other year with the same precision as her parents had managed their own lives; her husband, Ferrand de Beaudierre, was as usual restless at her side, burning with an inner fire which made him wish to argue even with his illustrious host. And the unmarried girls were here: Lucy, already set to be an old maid in the tightness of her features, the way her pale hair was screwed into a chignon and her gown, even on a warm afternoon, was buttoned to the neck; and Annette, at twenty-three still in the bloom of youth and even beauty, as she was the prettiest of all the girls, and the most vivacious, when she chose to be; Annette was the toast of Cap François, but she remained a spinster. Today she had the saddest face of any of the Mortmain women. Because Kit was not here? Everyone knew they corresponded regularly, and that whenever his ship dropped anchor in Cap François he enjoyed her company more than anyone else's. Forbidden fruit, doomed to wither on the vine. However much it might amuse Philippe de Mortmain.

Who stood with his wife at the foot of the grave. The most

splendid, the most regal, the most envied couple in all St Domingue. The Seigneur in his early forties, in the very prime of his health and power. And the Madame, at twenty-two the youngest adult woman present, perhaps yielding to her cousin-in-law Claudette in sheer beauty, but still the most striking of the women, in the silk of her gown, the sparkle of her jewellery, the purity of her pearl necklace, the sheen of her golden brown hair, and above all, in the utter confidence with which she surveyed her surroundings, and with which she alone allowed herself to weep unashamedly as she watched her mother's coffin disappear.

Because I am Richilde de Mortmain, she thought. Nothing more than that need be said, or thought. I have been tried in the crucible, and not been found wanting. I have made my husband happy, which no other woman has ever accomplished. He remained cursed in his inability to have children, and that curse had naturally encompassed her. But at least they slept together, and more often than not, they made love.

What she might have to do to inspire and then consummate that love was their secret, and made their life together the more intimate, the more precious. But then, she was a woman of many secrets, as even her husband recognised, although he would never acknowledge the fact. Perhaps he even knew – certainly he suspected – where she had gone on that never to be forgotten night six years ago, when she had placed her body on his and seduced him with all the power and certainty of a *mamaloi*. But it was not a question he dared ask. As it was not a medicine she had ever dared reach for again. Now, as she looked around the mass of slaves who had also attended the funeral, she could make out the huge figures of Henry Christopher and Jean François, standing side by side, close friends these, as they worked in harness. Men who knew her secret, as she knew theirs. That had not made for intimacy. Her days for intimacy with Henry were gone forever. The intimacy that had swelled into a mad desire on that night. It had been he who had had the sense to realise the catastrophe which

170

awaited them. So he was as responsible for her marital bliss as anyone. Had he waited but a moment longer . . . but that was in the past, and she was no longer a sixteen-year-old girl. She had learned that he, like Jean François and Pierre Toussaint, and all their fellows, had their own lives to live, as she had hers. To attempt to bridge the gap between them, to consider their aspirations as a threat to herself and the society she ruled, to remember the death and rebirth of the young man as anything more than superb sleight of hand and mass delusion, could lead only to disaster, as it so nearly had done six years before. There were things which could not be explained, just as there were dreams which could never be anything more than dreams. Henry, the memory of him standing there in his naked glory beside her, was for her midnight dreams. And again, after such a dream, Philippe was the one who gained.

How incredible, she thought, that I, Richilde Hamilton, the daughter of a shipping clerk and outlaw, should have come to dominate a man like Philippe de Mortmain. And through him, perhaps, all of St Domingue. Had she been able to have a child, then her triumph would have been complete. But in that failure, and in Philippe's increasingly morose moods, was all her life at risk, all her confidence a sham.

She watched the headstone being set. It wore a very simple inscription:

JEANNE HAMILTON
WIDOW OF
RICHARD HAMILTON
1740–1789
RIP

There was really nothing else to be said about Jeanne Hamilton.

The family was already walking back towards the house. Philippe had gone with them, knowing that she would wish these five minutes alone; the slaves too, had melted away.

Except for Henry. He did not approach but remained on the far side of the grave.

'She was my mistress,' he said.

'Now I am your mistress, Henry,' she said.

He nodded, thoughtfully. 'She going see my mummy, in heaven, madame?'

It was the first time such a subject had been broached between them for six years.

'If there is but one heaven, Henry,' Richilde said. 'As I am sure there is, then they will see each other.' she gazed at him for a moment, but he had nothing more to say. So she turned away, and walked after her family.

The horses swept up to the grandstand. There were six of them in the race, but only the two Mortmain stallions were in the running – Diable and Vitesse. Each of the Mortmains had his favourite and shouted vociferously. And now the roars of the competing parties seemed to raise the very heavens. It was four in the afternoon, and this was the last event of the Cap François races, as it was the main event of the day, and the very sun, now beginning its stately decline in the west, seemed to be gathering itself for a last burning effort, as it bore down on the flying dust, the sweating horses, the straining Negro jockeys and their vari-coloured silk shirts, the stand, crowded with everyone who was anyone in either Cap François or Port-au-Prince, a kaleidoscope of pale greens, pinks and blues of the ladies, the sombre browns and blacks of the gentlemen's coats, dotted with the brilliant blue of the officers of the garrison, and then the slaves themselves, for race day at Cap François was a holiday, gathered in a vast crowd, several thousand strong, all in clean white cottons, in the cleared area beyond the paddock.

And now the horses were past, and the dust filtered slowly through the still air, coating faces and arms and expensive gowns, causing the onlookers to cough and sneeze.

'Diable,' Philippe said. 'Now there, Maurice, is a horse for you.'

Etienne de Mortmain nodded. 'Only a short head, though.'

'Enough,' Louis grumbled. 'That is fifteen hundred livres.'

'My God,' Etienne said. 'I shall have to whip that jockey.'

'You may owe it to me,' Philippe said, magnanimously. 'Now let us get home before the crowd blocks the roads. Ah, Ferrand. I trust you backed Diable?'

Ferrand de Beaudierre had Françoise clinging to his arm, as usual, and looked wildly angry, as usual. 'Horse races,' he said. 'At a time like this.'

'My dear Ferrand,' Robert said. 'The Cap François Races have been held every year for the past fifty, to my certain knowledge. Even in time of war. Do you suppose we are going to cancel them because of some absurd upheaval in Paris? There are always being absurd upheavals in Paris.'

'This, monsieur, is not an upheaval,' Beaudierre insisted. 'It is the dawn of a new age.'

'Then I tell you what we shall do,' Philippe said. 'As I have just had a most successful day, I invite you and Françoise to return to Vergée d'Or with us, and we will drink to this new day. Is that not to your taste?'

'Oh, yes, Philippe,' Françoise said. 'Come along, do, Ferrand.'

But he suspected he was being made a fool of, arrived at the château even more excited than usual, took his place in the centre of the downstairs drawing room, left hand thrust into the front of his vest, like an orator.

'I tell you, messieurs, mesdames,' he proclaimed. 'That the Third Estate is the true voice of France.'

Philippe smiled at Richilde, lazily. 'You do not suppose that the Paris scum should have been greeted by cannon and bayonets, instead of abject surrender? They would have been met differently had I been there and in command.'

Beaudierre was not to be browbeaten, even by his wealthy cousin-in-law. 'Then would you have been wrong, Philippe,' he insisted. 'You would have been attempting to hold back the tide of history. And you would suffer the inevitable fate of the royal party.'

173

'We'll have no treason spoken here, Ferrand,' Maurice de Mortmain said.

'Nor do I intend any, father-in-law. I spoke of a party, not a king. But the King, God bless him, has for too long been pulled and prodded by this faction or that, by Necker and Calonne. Were he but to commence to rule, with the aid of the people, the true people of France, then things would be different. The Fall of the Bastille will go down in history as the moment the French people asserted themselves, and became a nation of free men.'

'I hope you are right, Ferrand.' Philippe said, drily. 'I can but see it as a lot of louts seizing the opportunity to wreak a bit of mayhem. And what of the crew of the *Leopard* in Cap François, declaring for Liberty, Equality and Fraternity, and refusing to obey their officers?'

'Monsieur Peynier has managed to settle that matter,' Beaudierre said.

'Oh, indeed, by turning the guns of the fort on them. As I have said, there was the way to settle the entire matter. Had the King sufficient gumption.'

'That would lead to civil war if it were practised against a lawful assembly,' Beaudierre pointed out.

'Which I think is an extremely likely outcome of this business in any event,' Philippe said.

'What disgusts me,' Claudette de Mortmain said, 'is the way all the people here, and in Guadeloupe and Martinique, are so anxious to crawl to this ridiculous National Assembly. Sending deputies back to France, indeed.'

'They were invited to do so, Claudette,' Françoise pointed out, deciding to take her husband's side.

'They were invited to send six deputies,' Annette said, making the discussion general. 'Not more than twenty. And making some of them mulattos! They have made the entire French Antilles look ridiculous.'

'On the contrary,' Beaudierre said. 'It will show those in Paris that we, too, are anxious to play our part in making France a nation more worthy of her great traditions. A country where all men can be free, and equal before the law.

A place . . .'

'Now that sort of statement is typical of you political dreamers,' Philippe said. 'A country where all men can be free, indeed. And equal. That is exactly what those madmen in Paris are preaching. How can all men be equal, when they are manifestly unequal? And how can all men be free, when it is obviously necessary for some of them to be enslaved? What do you suppose would happen to St Domingue were all men declared free and equal, regardless of colour?'

'Well . . .' Beaudierre flushed. 'Obviously there would have to be exceptions. Black people, well, they are slaves, and there is an end to the matter. I am sure the Third Estate did not mean to deprive us of our slaves. But that apart . . .'

'You'll be giving the mulattos equal rights, next,' Etienne said.

'That, monsieur, is certainly something to be accomplished.'

'What?'

'Why else should the National Assembly have insisted that our representatives be drawn from all sections of the free community, regardless of colour? It is grossly unfair that because of a touch of black blood a man should forever be regarded as an inferior being,' Beaudierre declared. 'Or a woman. I am sure you agree with me, Philippe?'

Philippe de Mortmain stared at him for several seconds, then he got up. 'I agree with Etienne,' he said. 'That you are talking the most absolute rubbish, Beaudierre. And the most dangerous, seditious rubbish. You would do well to watch your tongue.' He stalked from the room.

Saturday morning was market day in Cap François. It was thus a slave holiday, in order that the more industrious of them could go into the town and sell the produce of their vegetable gardens and, with the proceeds, buy small luxuries for themselves. It was a great occasion, when the city seemed to boil with colourful, excited humanity; naturally it was most certainly not a holiday for the garrison, who were on duty on every street corner, not in anticipation of any

175

violence, but to arrest any black man, or woman, who had the temerity to purchase alcohol with their profits.

It was a day when most white women stayed away, but Richilde always went into town on a Saturday morning. She enjoyed being a part of the bustle and the enthusiasm, she enjoyed being able to smile at Toussaint across a crowded square, and receive in reply his grave nod, and she enjoyed being able to walk through the market stalls, Jean François and Amelia attentive at her heels, shaded beneath an enormous parasol held by Henry Christopher, to see and to purchase some of the Negro goods – for they not only sold market produce, but also carved wooden ornaments, some knives and bows or canoes filled with surprisingly accurately delineated figures, and some strange gods and enormous curving snakes. She flattered herself that she was the only white woman in St Domingue who understood what these images really represented, and had already bought several for her boudoir. Philippe was quite prepared to indulge her in what he described as her hobby of exploring the Negro 'culture', just as he indulged her visits to town, although he seldom accompanied her.

Today she was officially in the care of Etienne, because a slave ship was due in from the Benin coast, and Etienne was the slave master of the plantation.

Thus, when her basket was sufficiently full, she walked down to the docks to watch a different sort of hustle and bustle, for there were two ships apparently just making port from the blue wastes of the Atlantic, and being warped alongside the docks.

The slave ship was secured first, her gangway run out, and the cargo led ashore. Richilde had witnessed the landing of slaves before, and reached into her reticule to hold a perfume soaked handkerchief to her nostrils; the ship had spent several months at sea. As could be seen by the men and women who stumbled on to the shore, many falling over from lack of balance, combined with weakness, for they were all terribly emaciated, while their uncertainty was aided by inebriation, for again as she knew, they would all

176

have been given a tot of rum to inspire them with some animation as they landed – the auction normally took place almost the moment they came ashore.

She glanced at her slaves to see what they thought. Both Henry and Amelia had been born in the West Indies, but they would have heard sufficient tales of the horrors of the Middle Passage. Jean François had actually made such a passage, as a boy, some twenty years before. Now his face remained expressionless, however much the sight of the new arrivals must have evoked memories of his boyhood in Africa, of the Arab slaving gangs who had blown his tribal armies to pieces with their gunpowder and then shackled the surviving men and women together for the march to the coast, of the steaming hot weeks spent in the Gulf of Guinea, trapped in the foetid bowels of the slave ship, until her complement was full, of the endless days crossing an ocean not knowing if there was another side, with the bodies of his comrades in distress being fed to the sharks as they daily died, until he had arrived in St Domingue, and been delivered over to the tender mercies of Jacques de Mortmain, who from all accounts had had his son's sternness, and none of his self doubts.

But Jean François had survived and prospered. And so, she supposed, like most human beings, he was prepared merely to be contemptuous of those who had not yet succeeded in achieving his stature.

'By God, what a sorry looking lot.' Etienne strolled along the dock, accompanied by Monsieur Dessalines, another planter, tall, lean and malaria-visaged, who raised his hat to Richilde.

'Madame de Mortmain, your cousin is in a pessimistic mood.'

'Bah,' Etienne said. 'Who would not be pessimistic at the news from France? No one there appears to be capable of taking control. This Mirabeau seems an utter charlatan. Come along, Richilde, let us go home. To buy one of that lot would be to insult Philippe.

'Oh, come now, Etienne,' Dessalines objected. 'You do

177

not look closely enough. What of that fellow?'

He pointed with his cane, where a yoke of Negroes had just reached the dock. Three of the men staggered and all but fell, but were kept from doing so by the strength and balance of the fourth. This man was not tall, but was built like a bull, with immense strength of shoulder and thigh, rippling muscles in his chest and abdomen and down his legs.

And he was neither dejected nor afraid, but looked around like an angry bull, meeting the eye of anyone, black, brown and even white.

'A good investment, I think,' Dessalines remarked.

'A very bad investment, monsieur,' Etienne objected. 'The fellow has scoundrel written all over him. You'll get nothing but mutiny from such a rogue.'

Monsieur Dessalines smiled. 'There is no such thing as a slave which cannot be broken, Etienne,' he said. 'I shall have that fellow. And some of these others.'

'And we shall go home.' Etienne took Richilde's arm, and they strolled further along the dock towards the waiting carriage, escaping the stench of the slave ship, and watching the second vessel being made fast in her berth. She was direct from Nantes, and her decks were filled with excited male passengers, who could hardly wait for the gangway to be run out before hurrying down. They were dressed in the height of fashion, wore swords on their hips and tricolour cockades in their bicorne hats. But their skins were brown.

Richilde caught her breath, and looked at Etienne, who was frowning. And then back at the men again, one of whom had stepped away from his fellows, thumbs tucked into the lapels of his vest. 'Friends,' he shouted. 'Citizens. We are returned. Back, from the National Assembly. Back to tell you . . .'

'James Ogé,' Etienne muttered. 'James Ogé, by God,' he shouted, and hurried forward.

'Etienne,' Richilde begged. 'Please. There will surely be a scene . . .'

'You, wretch,' Etienne shouted. 'Ogé. Discard that sword,

178

monsieur. You are not fit to wear it.'

Ogé turned, and also frowned. 'Are you addressing me, monsieur?' he demanded, his hand dropping to his sword hilt. 'Why,' he said with mock alarm. 'It is Monsieur de Mortmain. One of the Citizens Mortmain, my friends. See how he struts? He thinks himself better than us. He thinks . . .' His words ended in a gasp as Etienne struck him across the face with his cane, so hard he almost fell.

'Oh, my God,' Richilde cried. 'Henry, stop them.'

Henry hurried forward, and just in time, for Ogé had recovered himself and drawn his sword.

'There,' Etienne shouted. 'A mulatto, by God, and drawing on me. Soldiers, seize that fellow. Seize them all.'

For the soldiers on duty at the docks had drawn closer to discover the cause of the tumult.

'Master,' Henry said, touching Etienne on the shoulder.

'Attacked,' Etienne shouted, and turned, cane slicing through the air again, catching Henry across the face and sending him staggering.

''Tienne!' Richilde screamed, being jostled sideways by the crowd of people which was suddenly rushing forward.

And pausing in horror as she realised that Henry, in falling, had instinctively swept his hand round and torn the cane from Etienne's grasp.

Instantly armed guards surrounded the black man, pulling him to his feet.

'It is all right,' Richilde said. 'Henry is my personal slave.'

'It is not all right,' Etienne said, apparently very angry. 'He assaulted me. For too long he has been an arrogant scoundrel. I will make an example of him, by God. Bind him and put him in my slave cart. As for Ogé . . .' he swung round to face the mulatto and his friends, who were entirely surrounded by soldiers.

'You cannot arrest us,' Ogé was protesting. 'We come from the National Assembly. We come . . .'

'Bearing arms,' the captain of the guard said. 'That is against the law for you, Monsieur Ogé, and you know that.'

'Law,' the young man shouted. 'There are new laws, my

179

friend. Laws you break at your peril.'

'There are no new laws in Cap François, monsieur,' the soldier said. 'You are under arrest.'

Richilde grasped Etienne's arm. ''Tienne,' she said. 'You cannot be serious about Henry.'

'Would you quarrel with me in public?' he demanded. 'And over a slave?'

She bit her lip, looked around at the interested watchers and listeners. Here was source for next week's gossip, quite apart from the excitement of Ogé's arrest. Still shouting, the mulatto was being marched down the street.

In a turmoil of uncertainty, she looked the other way, to find Henry. He was being loaded into the slave cart, his wrists bound behind his back. He made no effort to resist his captors, but he turned his head to look at her, expectantly. He had no fear, while she protected him.

'Philippe,' she said, bursting into his office. 'Philippe. 'Tienne has quite lost his head . . .'

'I have heard,' Philippe said, putting down his pen and leaning back. 'And I do not think he lost his head at all. I have never doubted that these mulattos were going to cause us trouble, one day. The sooner their ideas of equality are nipped in the bud the better. They are conspirators, all of them. And filled with heady ideas, inspired by people like Beaudierre.'

'I am not talking about Ogé's arrest,' she said. 'I know nothing of politics. But I feared for 'Tienne, as he was unarmed, and sent Henry to stop the fight. And 'Tienne thought Henry was assaulting him, and had him bound and returned here. He has ordered a flogging. That is quite absurd.'

Philippe gazed at her. 'Because you choose to call him your twin?'

She flushed. 'Of course not. Because he was doing what I had told him to. Philippe, you must order his release.'

'You are asking me to override an order given by my own slave master, who also happens to be my cousin and my heir? Do you suppose, if I were to do that, 'Tienne could ever expect to be obeyed again?'

She stared at him in horror. 'You . . . you will let the punishment stand?'

'I must. As you must understand.'

'You . . . you have been waiting for an opportunity to flog Henry,' she accused. 'Ever since he came to Vergée d'Or.'

'Now you are being childish. Do you really suppose I would not have had him flogged, whenever I chose?'

'You . . . you are playing the tyrant,' she stormed at him. 'Well, I . . .'

'Will do nothing,' he said. 'Understand me well, Richilde. I have never failed to humour all of your eccentricities, from the day of your arrival here, and I am more aware of them than you suppose. This absurd friendship for a nigger boy is but one of them. But I will not have you, or anyone, interfering in the management of my plantation, the authority of my overseers. I will have a word with Etienne, as you are so upset, but as the punishment was ordered in public, so it will stand.'

She stared at him, feeling the anger burning red spots in her cheeks. It was the first time they had ever really quarrelled, and the dispute had arisen over the subject she had always known it must, one day.

'I should go to you room,' Philippe suggested. 'And lie down for a while. When you awake, it will all be over, and forgotten. Believe me, a few strokes of the lash are not going to hurt a great buck nigger like Henry.'

She left the office, climbed the stairs to her room, threw herself across the bed. How she wanted to get up again, and storm down to the compound, and command Henry's release. She was Madame de Mortmain. These people were bound to do her will . . . but only as long as that will coincided with that of the Seigneur.

Amelia brought her a glass of coconut water. 'You going change for dinner, mistress?'

'No,' Richilde said. 'No, I will not come down to dinner. Amelia . . .'

181

'It done finish, mistress,' Amelia said. 'He is take down.'

'How . . . how many?'

'Well, I think it is twenty-five, mistress.'

'Twenty-five lashes?' Richilde sat up. 'Oh, my God! Is he badly hurt?'

'Well, I ain't see he,' Amelia said. 'But he must be cut up. Twenty-five lashes . . . oh, he must be going cut up.'

Richilde got out of bed. 'I must go to him.'

'You, mistress?'

'Yes.' Richilde pulled on her pelisse. 'You will accompany me.'

'Me, mistress? But the master . . .'

'You are my maid, Amelia,' Richilde pointed out. 'Where I go, you go. You will come with me to see Henry Christopher. Now.'

Amelia rolled her eyes, but there was no way she could refuse a direct command. 'He does be in the dispensary,' she said, sadly.

Richilde possessed her own pony and trap for riding about the estate, and this they used, and for the first time in her life she directed it towards the slave compound. It was now late in the afternoon, and the work gangs were on their way back from the fields. They stopped to stare in amazement at the Seigneur's wife driving towards their village, while the white overseers accompanying them scratched their heads in equal surprise, and one at least hastily rode off towards the chateau.

She flicked her whip in the air to increase the pony's speed, rode past the now empty triangles with a shudder and through the gate to the slave compound. 'Where is the dispensary?'

Amelia pointed, looking about her with terrified eyes. Like most of the domestic slaves, she was as afraid of the field slaves as any white person.

'You,' Richilde said to one of the crowd of young black men who had gathered round the trap. 'Hold the reins.' She tossed them to him, stepped down, and went towards the large building which was apparently the sickhouse.

182

'Mistress?' An elderly black man stood in the doorway.

'Who are you?' she asked.

'My name is Oliver, mistress,' he said.

'And you are the doctor?'

'I does dispense the medicine,' he said.

'I wish to see Henry Christopher.'

'He is inside, mistress.'

She felt like stamping her foot with impatience. 'I know that, Oliver. Open the door.'

He hesitated, looked past her at the spectators, steadily growing in numbers, then opened the door, and she stepped into the gloom. It was a noisome gloom, for although the interior of the hut had been carefully washed with lime, the smell of human sweat, and human excrement, and human suffering, could not be excluded. As her eyes became accustomed to the sudden absence of sunshine, she could see that there were perhaps a score of people in here, men and women, lying on pallets of straw on the floor, most trying to raise themselves on their elbows as their mistress came in, but several unable to muster even that much strength.

'What . . . what do they suffer from?' she asked Oliver.

The dispenser shrugged. 'They got many things, mistress. Some get bite in the fields, by insect and things. Some cut theyselves with their machete. Others got the fever. And some . . . they just swell up.'

He indicated one young man, hardly more than a boy, whose right leg was swollen to twice the size of his left.

Hastily she looked away. 'And they lie here . . .' she was going to say, in this airless filth, but changed her mind. 'Until they get better?'

'Or until they die, mistress.'

My God, she thought, carefully making her way down the row of bodies to the pallet at the end, and Henry Christopher. He lay on his face, his back a criss-cross of cuts and gashes. These had been smothered in some white substance, but they still oozed blood.

'Is he all right?' she asked, in a whisper.

'Oh, he will be all right, mistress,' Oliver said.

'But . . . what is that you have put on the cuts?'

'Salt, mistress.'

'Salt?' she could not stop her voice from rising.

'It is the best thing, mistress. That way the cuts do heal up quick.'

'But . . . was it not agony for him?'

Oliver grinned. 'You don't feel no agony, mistress, after the lash.'

She stared at him, then realised that Henry had raised his head.

'Henry,' she said, stooping beside him. 'I am sorry. Very, very sorry. Do you believe me?'

His eyes were dark pits of hell. 'I know you are sorry, Mistress Richilde,' he said.

'Can you ever forgive me?'

He gazed at her for several seconds. 'I can forgive *you*, mistress,' he said.

She stopped the trap at the foot of the great staircase, threw the reins to the waiting groom. It was already quite dark, and she frowned with impatience at the sight of the carriage waiting further down the drive. It belonged to Ferrand de Beaudierre, and undoubtedly meant that Françoise had come to call. She really was not in the mood for Françoise this evening.

'You'll draw me a bath, Amelia,' she commanded, and went up the stairs.

'Madame.'

She checked, half turned her head. Philippe stood on the lower verandah.

Amelia hastily scuttled into the gloom.

'Can you spare me a moment?' Philippe asked.

She hesitated, then turned and went back down the stairs.

'Does he live?' Philippe asked.

'Yes,' she said.

'You know, of course, that the slave compound is not the place for any white woman to visit, much less the mistress of the plantation. As for the dispensary . . .'

184

Richilde tossed her head. 'I do not agree with you, monsieur. If I am your wife, then your slaves are as much my concern as they are yours. I do not seek to interfere, believe me, only to complement your authority. I should have visited the slave compound long ago. I would say that I have grievously neglected my duties and my responsibilities. As for the dispensary, it is quite the most disgusting place I have ever seen.'

'Which is why it is no place for a white woman.'

'It is no place for a black woman, either,' she said. 'Or a black man. I am not speaking of their illnesses, which for God's sake are ghastly enough. I am speaking of the conditions in which you force them to exist. For heaven's sake, Philippe, these people represent a large part of your wealth. Are they not worth caring for? You care more for your dogs and horses than for your slaves.'

He stared at her, a frown gathering between his eyes.

'I would like your permission,' she said. 'To visit your slave compound as and when I choose.'

He continued to study her for several seconds longer. Then he said, 'I shall not give you my *permission*, Richilde. As you are so concerned, and as undoubtedly there is some truth in what you say, I shall give you my express *command*, as of this moment, that you will visit the slave compound at least twice a week, to see to the needs of your black-skinned friends.'

'Thank you,' she said. 'I would also like to rebuild the dispensary.'

'Rebuild whatever you like,' he said. 'Now come inside, and attempt to do something with your cousin. She is having hysterics.'

Richilde's turn to frown, as she gathered her skirts and hurried behind him. 'Whatever is the matter?'

'Her irrational husband appears to have got himself into some sort of trouble,' Philippe said. 'I knew it had to happen, with that hothead. She is in the small drawing room.'

Richilde went in, found Françoise seated on the sofa

Lucy on one side of her and Aunt Marguerite on the other. Françoise was weeping noisily, and at the sight of Richilde gave another great shriek. 'Richilde, oh Richilde . . .'

'Whatever is the matter?' Richilde demanded, somewhat irritably.

'Oh, Richilde. Oh . . .'

'Ferrand has been arrested,' Lucy said.

'Ferrand? Whatever for?'

'He was so angry,' Françoise wailed. 'When he heard that those coloured men had been locked up. He wrote out a denunciation of what Etienne and the soldiers had done, and went into town to nail it to the door of the Hotel de Ville. And they arrested him, and locked him up too. Oh, the disgrace of it. They say he will be tried for sedition and conspiracy. He could be hanged.'

'And quite right, too,' Philippe said

Françoise gave another shriek, and once more collapsed into tears.

'You must help him, Philippe,' Richilde said.

'Me? I think he has at last got his just deserts.'

'Nevertheless, we cannot leave one of the family locked up in the common jail. You must get him out. And for God's sake stop that snivelling, Françoise. Of course he is not going to be hanged. How can anyone hang Philippe de Mortmain's cousin-in-law? Philippe . . .'

'You have become quite the little avenging angel,' he remarked.

'You made me understand, this afternoon, the importance of the family. Whether you like him or not, Ferrand is now a member of the family. If you will not help him, then I will.'

He gazed at her for a moment, then to her surprise, picked up her hand and kissed it. 'I like avenging angels,' he said. 'We will go together, and assail Peynier, and return in triumph, with Beaudierre. Françoise, have yourself a glass of wine, and do try to stop crying.' He rang the bell. 'Have Jean François bring round the carriage,' he told Bartholemew the butler. 'Marguerite, supper may be a little late tonight, but it will be a celebratory occasion, I do promise you.'

He himself fetched Richilde's wrap, sat beside her and squeezed her hand as the carriage rumbled down the road towards Cap François; she had not dared look Jean François in the face. But Jean François would undoubtedly regard Henry's flogging as he regarded everything else – with contempt so long as he was not involved.

'I did not mean to upset you, Philippe,' she said. 'But I really cannot consider poor Ferrand left in jail all night, with a lot of coloured men.'

'Who are his friends,' he reminded her. 'But I agree with you. And you did not upset me. Rather did you excite me. As you have not excited me for years.'

She turned her head to peer at him in the gloom.

'I had forgot,' he said. 'That I had you trained, and educated, to be my wife.'

'Then the fault is surely mine, monsieur,' she said. 'For not having played the part sooner.'

'But you will play it now,' he said. 'To have a woman, strong and forceful, ever at my side, ever in my bed . . . will you do me the honour this night, madame?'

She laughed with pleasure at their little game. 'I shall be happy to do so, monsieur.'

'Then let us make all possible haste.' He opened the trap. 'Can you drive no faster, you black devil?'

'Is a fact there does be crowds, master,' Jean Francois said.

Philippe peered from his window, Richilde from the other. They were amongst the houses of Cap François by now, and undoubtedly there were a great number of people on the streets, standing in groups on street corners, muttering to each other, and insensibly moving towards the town centre, where the jail was situated. And from where there was coming a great deal of noise.

'Use your whip,' Philippe commanded. 'Drive through them if you have to. Take me to the Governor-General's house.'

Jean François cracked his whip over the horses' heads, but their progress was still very slow. Most of the crowd recognised the Mortmain crest, and the carriage attracted a considerable amount of comment, but it was difficult to decide whether it was mainly good or bad.

'I doubt you should have come,' Philippe said. 'This has the makings of a mob.'

'Nonsense,' she said. 'The soldiers will disperse these people if they get out of hand.'

'Then where are they?' he muttered.

'There,' she said, as they debouched into the square to find themselves upon the outskirts of an enormous crowd, which constantly swelled. But these were mainly white people – *petit blancs* rather than planters, with a scattering of mulattos. She wondered if the Chavannes were here. How could they not be? She had not laid eyes on Jacqueline for seven years. She had ceased to patronise Monsieur Chavannes' shop, at Philippe's request.

The soldiers, and there was a large number of them, were grouped on the far side of the square, before the Hotel de Ville, watching the mob, but making no attempt to interfere with it.

'They should be at the prison,' Philippe muttered, half to himself.

'At the prison?' Richilde looked through the window again. The carriage had by now been brought to a complete stop, so dense was the crowd. But they were not more than a hundred yards from the prison. It was there that the greatest number of people were congregated, surging against the door, and chanting. And now she could hear what they were saying.

'We want Beaudierre,' they were shouting. 'Give us Beaudierre.'

'They will have him out of there for us,' she said.

Philippe glanced at her. 'I do not think they mean to rescue him, Richilde.'

'Not to . . .' she stared at him, her belly seeming to fill with lead.

'There is no time to see Peynier,' he decided. 'I must get to those soldiers. You stay here. Jean François, you will take care of your mistress.'

'But Philippe,' she protested, too late, He had already opened the door and stepped down, to vanish into the mob.

'Jean François,' she called through the trap.

'Nobody is going trouble you, mistress,' the big coachman said.

'I must get to the prison,' she said.

'But mistress . . .'

'Come with me,' she opened the door, and stepped down, was instantly surrounded by people, odorous bodies pressing close. Hands slapped her shoulders and pummelled her back, and she lost her hat together with her breath. But she pushed forward with determination, aware that Jean François was immediately behind her, having the utmost confidence in his ability to protect her from assault. Because he loved her. All the slaves did. But he more than any other, because he had once, briefly, held her in his arms. She was aware of a remarkable feeling of exhilaration, which rose above even her apprehension, at being able to stand astride two such different worlds, at thus being able to rely on Jean François' strength and loyalty against these people, as she would be able to rely on these people against the blacks, should the occasion ever arise, should the dream shared by Jean François, and Toussaint, and Henry Christopher, ever come true.

'Richilde!' Louis de Mortmain struggled towards her. 'What are you doing here?'

'I wish to rescue Ferrand from this mob,' she gasped.

'You?' Louis looked past her at Jean François. 'And him?'

'Oh, Philippe is here somewhere. He is trying to arouse the gendarmerie. Louis . . .' her head twisted at the sound of splintering wood. Now the crowd had at last surged against the doors of the prison itself, and were hacking at the lock. A jailer's terrified face appeared at the barred window for a moment, and then disappeared again. 'Come on,' Richilde shouted.

She pushed her way forward, and was knocked from her feet by the surging bodies, who seemed unaware of who she was, or even that she was a woman. For a moment she debated identifying herself as the mistress of Vergée d'Or, and then decided against it – these people would know that she was related to Beaudierre. She thought she would be trampled, and discovered she did not even have the breath to scream, then Louis seized one arm and Jean François the other, and between them they set her on her feet again.

'We must get she out of here, master,' Jean François said.

'Yes,' Louis agreed. 'Yes, you are right. You will be hurt, Richilde. And there is nothing we can do. Philippe, and the soldiers . . .'

The crowd began to bay, and Richilde almost climbed into Jean François' arms to see what was happening. The prison doors had now been torn from their hinges, and the crowd were penetrating the interior, urged on by the yells of their supporters in the square. Dimly Richilde became aware that Louis and Jean François were pulling her back towards the waiting carriage. She tried to fight them, but remained staring at the shattered doorway, watched Ferrand de Beaudierre appear there, his arms held by two of the mob, being pushed forward, his face flushed, but his eyes blazing with anger rather than fear.

'Scum,' he bawled, his voice rising even above the hubbub. 'Would you defy your government? Your lawful government? Those men in there are free. They bring a message from France. They . . .' he gasped as he was pushed forward and tripped and fell down the steps. Instantly the mob surged over him, yelling and screaming.

'Oh, God,' Richilde said. 'Oh, God!'

She realised that Louis was no longer holding her arm. He, too, was overcome by the horror in front of him.

They saw Ferrand de Beaudierre once more, being raised in the air, arms and legs flying, face already a bloodied mass, mouth opening for a last scream of pain and terror, and despair, as he realised what was happening to him, and then he disappeared again, and the mob roared.

'You must come away, mistress,' Jean François said, and dragged her to the carriage. She realised tears were streaming down her face and she knew she was going to be sick. She fell to her knees beside the carriage and vomited, while Jean François stood beside her, unsure what to do. She saw other feet, and raised her head, looked at Pierre Toussaint.

She sucked air into her lungs. 'Is this a part of your prophesy, also, Toussaint?' she asked.

He gazed at her for a moment, then at Jean François, and turned, and vanished into the crowd.

Chapter 2

THE DAY

The opposing sides had now for two years confounded the colony with their disputes, while the slaves, in whose future neither whites nor browns had shown the slightest interest, had continued to perform their duties. Now, on 23rd August 1791, the Negroes in the northern half of the island revolted. The planters and their families and their overseers, and those of their servants who remained loyal, were murdered, not in their scores, but in their hundreds. Women were violated and disembowelled; men were sawn in half; the glare from hundreds of burning plantations and the incoherent gasps of the first refugees to stagger into the towns spread the panic like the plague itself – over-night a country the size of Ireland became a no-man's land of hatred and violence.

'No, no, no,' Richilde saud. 'I want the walls green, the roof white. You will have to change that, Oliver.'

'Yes, mistress,' Oliver said with a happy smile. He didn't mind having his people scrape off all the white paint they had inadvertently put on the walls. Painting, and scraping the paint off again, was a game. Compared with working in the fields.

While Richilde sighed; unless she was down here every moment of the day something always went wrong. But it was an artificial sigh. She enjoyed being down here every moment of the day, even if it was merely to see her slaves happy. They liked working for the mistress, because her work was so different, and interesting. They had fallen to with a will to destroy the old dispensary, while she had transferred the sick up to one of the stables by the chateau, over the frowns and mutterings of Lucien the cook and Bartholemew the butler, and of Jean François, the head coachman, who had growled about his clean horses being messed up with a load of sick people. While Henry Christopher had stood and watched in amazement. But he had found time to say, 'Now you are an angel, madame.' Which was the most important praise she had received, far better than Philippe's pat on the back. It made her feel that one day, perhaps, she and Henry could again be friends, despite the flogging. When they were old together.

But now the new dispensary was almost complete, four times the size of the old building, with jalousie windows to let in the air while keeping out the glare, with clean straw on the floor, and orders that it was to be renewed every day, with fresh paint being lavished everywhere . . . a colossal preoccupation of so many field hands, Fedon grumbled. But Philippe merely smiled and let her have her own way. He was a far more sensitive man than he sometimes appeared, and he could understand just how difficult she had found it ever to regard the chateau as her own. She had come to it as a little girl, had grown up in it, surrounded by the housekeepers – the genuine housekeepers – Negresses who had spent their lives in domestic service with the Mortmains, who knew every sheet and every pillowcase amongst all the hundreds that were laundered every week, and who would have been amazed and distressed had their new mistress attempted to interfere with their management of the house and the staff, just as Lucien would have been had she suddenly announced that she wished to cook a meal – or even plan a menu.

But the new dispensary was hers, her concept and her design and her ambition. Besides, its construction was occupying the minds of the blacks, and that was very important right now, with all of St Domingue a seething mass of incipient revolt.

It was difficult to grasp, Richilde thought, as she turned

the trap and walked the pony through the slave compound gateway and on to the drive leading up to the chateau, greeted as always by the black women she passed on their way to the fields. Certainly here on Vergée d'Or, and she had not been off Vergée d'Or for several months, not since that fiery young man James Ogé, on his release from jail following the tragedy of Ferrand de Beaudierre – and while Monsieur Peynier had written post haste to Paris to discover whether or not the mulattos *had* been granted full equality with the whites – had promptly raised the flag of revolt in the name of the National Assembly. He had, apparently, been widely supported, and had formed an armed camp outside Cap François, from whence his followers had fired upon and killed an emissary sent by the Governor-General to parley. Naturally such an act of open rebellion had not been countenanced. Peynier had called up the troops – who were white and certainly prepared to obey him against coloured rebels – and the mulattos had been dispersed. Ogé had fled across the border into the Spanish half of the island. But the whole colony remained in such a ferment it had not been considered safe for ladies to ride abroad, except under considerable escort.

Not that she had any desire to ride abroad in any event. That night in Cap François had been the most terrible she had ever known. The city she had always loved, the people she had always delighted to be amongst, had suddenly revealed a very ugly face, had discovered a savagery she would not have supposed any Frenchmen capable of possessing, and especially those who prided themselves on inhabiting the Paris of the Western Hemisphere, Vergée d'Or had become the only truly secure place on the island, just as the vast mass of the black people, proceeding about their appointed tasks, smiling at her and touching their foreheads as she rode by, had become the most reassuring of human factors. She wondered what they thought of it all, whether they understood anything of the immense upheaval which was taking place in France itself, and which was sending its blood-streaked tentacles all the way across the

194

ocean to affect their lives. Probably only a very few of them, like Toussaint, thought of it at all.

The white gate to the chateau paddock was opened for her by a waiting slave, and she threw Henry her reins as she stepped down. 'He is thirsty,' she said. 'Make sure he gets a good drink, Henry.'

'Yes, mistress,' he said.

She smiled at him, was disappointed not to receive a smile in return. But he had his moods. He had always had his moods of introspection, suggesting some apparently inner conflict. She blamed his gods. In their gloomy possession of all the bestial instincts in humanity she thought they were responsible for many of the ills suffered by the black people, though they might also grant them the occasional relief of orgy. She was happy to be done with them. They had served her well, when she had needed them. Now she no longer did so. She could only hope their worship would never lead Henry into an absurdity, like conceiving it might be possible to escape to the forests and mountains, to starve if he was not hunted down like a wild beast.

She walked towards the house itself, long strides fluttering the divided skirt of her habit, taking off her tricorne to fan herself, looking forward to an ice cold glass of sangaree. Despite all the tragedy which seemed to have filled these last two years, she supposed that she had never been so happy. She was growing into her role. It had taken a long time. Eight years. In the beginning she had required all her mental energy, her physical strength, just to maintain herself as Philippe's wife, and even after she had become sure of her success there, she had then devoted herself to becoming pregnant, while the constant worry for, and care of, her mother had further encroached upon her personality. In many ways Mama's death had been a release. As in many ways Henry's flogging, that dreadful day last year, had jerked her to her senses. She had at last realised that she could not spend her life merely moving from Philippe's bed to his table and back again, and expect to have any part in the life of her people. Because they were her people. Only by making sure everyone, from Philippe down, understood that all the time, could she ever hope to control events, to help the black people achieve some measure of contentment.

As she had obviously developed herself. Kit had noticed it, when he had arrived for Christmas, and to look at Mama's grave. 'You have become a woman, Richilde,' he said. 'But more than that, you have become Madame de Mortmain.'

Poor Kit. He had come, also, to see Annette. Because now that their cousin Alexander was high in the United States Government – he had recently been made Secretary of the Treasury by his friend George Washington, who had been chosen president of the fledgling republic – the shipping line had prospered, and Kit with it. He was now the master of their finest vessel, and could call on Cap François whenever he wished. Thus he was also ready for marriage, and had broached the subject with Uncle Maurice.

And been turned away. There was no one in the world that Maurice de Mortmain would rather have had his youngest daughter marry – had Kit not been her first cousin. But there it was. And having come out into the open, Kit had had no alternative but to leave – their surreptitious but well-known meetings and loving handclasps were no longer possible. Annette had wept for two days, and had then declared that she would never marry, but would join Lucy in her steadfast chastity. While Richilde had accepted the fact that she might not see her brother again for years.

But, she thought as she approached the house, perhaps Annette was the lucky one, at that, in avoiding the tragedies as well as with the triumphs of matrimony. For on the lower verandah, Françoise de Beaudierre slowly rocked herself to and fro. Her hair was uncombed, and although it was nearly lunchtime she still wore her undressing robe. Françoise had not dressed in six months, since Ferrand's death, just as she had hardly spoken in that time, even to her children. She merely sat, and rocked, and stared into space, and occasionally wept, silently and copiously. And she hated. That much was very evident. She hated all humanity. But

196

she hated Richilde and Philippe the most of any, because they had set off so confidently to bring Ferrand home, and had failed. Besides, undoubtedly the lynch mob, a white mob, had been whipped up by the planters' agents. Françoise could not be convinced of Philippe's innocence in the matter, however much the rest of the family assured her of it.

That he had not been involved was as certain as anything on earth, Richilde knew, but she could not blame her cousin for feeling so bitter; she avoided the front verandah, went to the back of the house, and the private staircase to her apartment, where Amelia would have her bath waiting for her.

'Madame.'

She checked, and turned, frowning even as her heart did a surge up and down her chest. It was nearly eight years since she had heard that voice. 'Jacqueline? Jacqueline Chavannes?'

The quadroon stepped from the rose bushes, pulled her cloak back from her head. Certainly it was Jacqueline Chavannes, and certainly Jacqueline had to be about thirty years of age. But this woman looked much older than that. And she too had recently been weeping. There was a complete absence of the elegant demoiselle Richilde remembered, in the shabby clothes and undressed hair of this distraught creature.

'Whatever are you doing here?' Richilde asked.

'I wish to speak with you, madame.'

Richilde hesitated. 'Then you'd best come upstairs,' she said. 'If Philippe were to discover you . . .' She opened the door, led her old friend inside. 'You'll see I use the private staircase just as often as you ever did,' she said, attempting to lighten the atmosphere.

'Yes, madame,' Jacqueline said.

They reached the top, and Richilde showed her into the bedroom. Amelia was already there, with the tub, but Richilde dismissed her with a wave of the hand. Amelia cast a curious and disapproving glance at the mulatto woman as

197

she left the room.

'Will she not tell . . . your husband, that I am here?' Jacqueline asked.

'She is my servant, not his,' Richilde said. 'She is not likely to forget that.'

Jacqueline sat down, head bowed, hands on lap. 'You have succeeded in everything, where I failed.'

'I am not yet a mother.' Richilde sat down beside her. 'What has happened? What do you wish of me?'

'I need your help, madame,' Jacqueline said. 'I know that it is presumptuous of me, after all that has passed between us, but . . .'

'If you need my help, Jacqueline, then you must call me Richilde.'

Jacqueline raised her head. Her eyes were filled with tears. 'You mean you *will* help me?'

'If it is in my power to do so, certainly. And if you will tell me what it is you require.'

Suddenly the huge dark eyes overflowed, and the tears rolled freely down those once lovely cheeks. Jacqueline slipped from the bed and knelt before Richilde. 'It is my brother . . .'

'Jacques? He is in trouble?'

'He was with Ogé.'

'My God,' Richilde exclaimed

'And now they have been captured together. But you must know of this.'

'No,' Richilde said. 'No. I did not know. I understood the rebels had fled into the Spanish colony.'

'They did so, Richilde. But the Spanish authorities have arrested them and returned them to Cap François. How can you not know of this?'

'I suppose because I did not enquire,' Richilde said. 'Go on.'

'They arrived two days ago, and were tried immediately, and sentenced to death.'

'Oh, my God,' Richilde said. 'But . . . can Monsieur Peynier *do* that?'

'He has done it, madame. Richilde. Twenty-two of them. Not one of them older than I.'

Richilde stared at her, aghast.

'They are to be executed the day after tomorrow,' Jacqueline said.

'But . . . if he *was* rebelling, and Monsieur Peynier supposes that he has the power . . . I will do what I can, of course, Jacqueline. Believe me. But I cannot promise anything.'

'I do not expect you to intercede for my brother's life, Richilde,' Jacqueline said. 'I know that is forfeit, by the reason of his rebellion. I am here to beg for your help in securing him a decent death.'

Richilde frowned at her. 'I do not understand you. A decent death? What is to happen to him?'

'Twenty of them are to be hanged, as rebels,' Jacqueline said, her voice faltering. 'But the Governor General is determined to make an example of Ogé, and his closest associate. Because Jacques was taken when in Ogé's company, it is supposed he shares the responsibility for the revolt with him. Richilde, they are to be broken on the wheel.'

Richilde stood before her husband's desk. 'You did not tell me Ogé had been taken.'

He raised his eyebrows. 'I did not know that you were interested.'

'And with him, Jacques Chavannes?'

He frowned. 'Now, who told you that? Louis? I told him not to speak of it, the wretch. I knew it would upset you.'

She sat down. 'Does it matter who told me? Philippe . . . is it true they have been sentenced to death?'

'They are rebels in arms against the government of the colony, Richilde. There can only be one punishment for such as them.'

'But . . . the National Assembly . . .'

'Has turned out to be a more sensible body than we had hoped it could possibly be. Peynier has received a letter from

199

it informing us that it was never intended that any resolution passed in Paris should alter the laws or the way of life we have practised here for centuries, and which may be regarded as essential to our security. That in effect gave us carte blanche to deal with these upstarts as we thought fit.'

'We?'

'I am consulted by the Governor-General in matters of security, as you well know.'

'And you approve of sentencing twenty-two young men to death?'

'You speak as if they were young gentlemen. They are young scoundrels. Besides, these are unusual circumstances. You must understand, Richilde. Whatever is truly happening in France, whatever is the eventual outcome of all these meetings and assemblies and speeches and pronunciamentos and riots, it is obvious that there is a great upheaval going on over there, and that Paris, all of France, is going to be entirely preoccupied with its own affairs for some time to come. Thus we are left entirely to our own resources. We, no more than a few thousand whites, with a few hundred soldiers, must hold down several hundred thousand blacks and, alas, because of our parents' casual lusts, several thousand mulattos, without the supporting power of France. Thus it is absolutely essential that we show the people of St Domingue, of whatever colour, that we mean to continue our rule – we, the planters – and that we will make a most condign example of those who attempt to rebel against us.'

She supposed he had just repeated part of the speech he had made to the Governor-General, and sighed. 'An example. To be hanged, in public. But Philippe . . . I am told that Ogé and Chavannes are to be broken on the wheel.'

'They were the ringleaders. It is fitting that they should suffer the most severely.'

'I don't even know what breaking on the wheel means. Is it very painful?'

'Painful?' he smiled. 'I would describe it as the most terrible form of execution ever devised. It is far worse than

200

being burned alive. The culprit is stripped and then spreadeagled on a carriage wheel, arranged so that everyone watching can see his suffering. The executioner, using an iron bar, then taps his bones, one after the other, starting with the smallest of course. Each tap breaks a bone.'

Richilde clasped both hands around her throat.

'Obviously,' Philippe went on, 'no one dies from merely breaking a bone, especially wrists and ankles and ribs and such like. Or even all of those. A skilful executioner can reduce his victim to an absolute jelly before he permits death. Of course, no one knows for sure whether or not Pallot is skilful – he has never done it before.' He smiled again. 'But I am told that he is feverishly reading books on anatomy.'

'You . . . you can sit there, and discuss something so . . . so barbaric, with a smile?'

'They will suffer horribly,' he acknowledged. 'But that is necessary, don't you see? We want their deaths never to be forgotten, so that every scoundrel who considers rebellion will have to stop and think that he too might wind up on the wheel, like Ogé and Chavannes. You must understand that, Richilde.'

'I don't know,' she said. 'I wish I did understand why it is necessary to make a man suffer when he is going to die anyway. But Philippe, Ogé led the revolt. Jacques Chavannes didn't.'

'We can't make an example of just the leader. Believe me, there were those wished to have them all die on the wheel. I argued against that. I do not think the spectators would have been able to accept that.'

'The spectators . . . my God. But Philippe, you know Jacques. He's just a confused young man. Surely one of the other twenty is more guilty than he.'

He frowned at her. 'Who have you been talking to?'

'Nobody. But . . . he saved Kit's life, once, in America.'

'Perhaps he did. But it was the sort of instinctive thing that soldiers do. And it was a long time ago.'

'Philippe, please. I'm not asking for his life. I know that

isn't possible. But let him be hanged, like the other men. Please, Philippe. If you were to speak with Peynier . . .'

His frown deepened. 'You've seen Jacqueline.'

'Well . . .' She flushed.

'And I know you haven't been off the plantation in weeks. You mean she came here?'

'Well . . .'

'After I told her never to set foot on Vergée d'Or again? You should have thrown her out.'

'She was distraught, Philippe. This is her brother, we're talking about. Her only brother.'

'The sentence cannot be changed now.'

'Because it would show weakness,' she said bitterly. 'I know. Or do you just hate him, that much. Because of her?'

'Yes,' he said. 'I hate him. Because of her. Because of all the humiliation she caused me, for so long, when I thought I could not do without her. But that has nothing to do with his fate. He has committed armed rebellion against the government of the colony. He has to die. And he has been chosen as one of those of whom an example will be made. There is an end of the matter.' He leaned back. 'Would you like to attend the execution?'

'Me?'

'Don't sound so shocked. It will be quite an occasion.Claudette is going. And Catherine, and Thérèse de Milot.'

'To watch two young men being broken into pieces?'

'I am told it is a sight never to be forgotten. I have never seen a proper execution. I was in Paris when they executed Damiens for attempting the life of Louis XV, but Aunt Aimée would not let me go. She went. They tore him into four pieces with horses. She never tired of telling me of it. One should try to experience most things in this brief life of ours. I think you should come. Madame Peynier is attending. And so will most of the ladies in Cap François.'

He was being his most hateful, arrogant, baiting self. But she was not going to lose her temper. 'I think that is too horrible for words,' she said, quietly. And raised her head.

'Are you going?'

'Of course.'

She stood up. 'I'm sure you will enjoy yourself,' she said, and left the room.

Rio Negro Great House blazed with light. It was a small party – for their thirtieth wedding anniversary Thomas and Thérèse de Milot chose to entertain only their immediate family. But it was a large family, for now it included the Mortmain clan, even if only half of them had actually decided to attend.

But like all Milot parties, it was a lavish affair. They played at bowls on the lawn, and drank iced sangaree. They dined on turtle steaks and crayfish tails, fresh salads and ripe fruits, and drank claret. They sat on the patio to watch the August sun disappearing into the mountains, to fan themselves even as they felt the sweat trickling down their backs and soaking their corsets, and drank iced champagne.

'I think we will have a hurricane this year,' Thérèse de Milot declared. 'I can feel it in the air.'

'You can always feel hurricanes in the air, in the summer,' Etienne said. 'But they never actually happen.'

Thérèse gave her son-in-law a disapproving look. 'They do. These things go in cycles. When I was a girl we had hurricanes here three years in succession. Do you remember that, Thomas? We were newly weds.'

'Too long ago,' Thomas de Milot said, and raised a laugh. 'Richilde, my dear girl, you were not at the execution.'

Richilde caught her breath. She had made Philippe promise not to mention the execution. But in her heart she had known there was no way it could be avoided. It remained the most exciting thing that had happened in Cap François for years – and at least, she supposed, it meant that everyone no longer discussed poor Ferrand de Beaudierre.

'No,' she said. 'I do not find executions my favourite form of entertainment.'

'But it was splendid, Richilde,' Catherine de Milot said. 'So dramatic. There is something utterly memorable, about twenty-two young men, being led out to die. Oh, I nearly wept.'

'They were weeping too,' Etienne said, with a laugh.

François de Milot pulled his moustache. ''Tienne and I were having a wager on which of them would break down completely. I must say, I never expected it to be Ogée himself. The confounded fellow cost me twelve crowns.'

'That really was quite disgusting,' Thérèse de Milot declared. 'He is supposed to have been the leader of these people. And then to start screaming and shouting and begging. Really!'

'He actually offered to give us lists of everyone else who had been a party to his revolt, if we'd let him be hanged,' Philippe said.

'And did you see ... well ...' Claudette de Mortmain flushed.

Etienne gave a shout of laughter. 'I thought that was what you were looking at. Anatomical studies. Did you know, dear Mama, that fright can make a fellow ... well, I mean ... talk about ramrods.'

'I really think that is unsuitable conversation for mixed company,' Marguerite de Mortmain protested mildly.

'I don't think this entire conversation is suitable for any occasion or company,' Richilde declared. 'I think the whole thing was too horrible for words. And actually to go and watch it ...'

They looked at her in amazement.

'You don't have to get upset, Richilde,' Etienne said. 'Your friend Chavannes died like a gentleman. Do you know, he never uttered a sound? And it took him over two hours to die. I thought he was never going to make it. I had visions of this dreadful jellylike creature rolling about the streets of Cap François, making himself a general nuisance.'

Richilde glared at him, trying to convey her utter loathing in her expression.

'Everyone is soft, nowadays,' Thomas de Milot said, into his champagne. And belched. 'When I was a boy ...'

His son raised his eyebrows, and sighed, loudly. But his

father ignored him.

'We had executions like that every week. We were used to them. And here on the plantations, too. Do you remember that time a dozen Negroes escaped Rio Negro, and went into the hills? Philippe? No, I suppose you were too young.'

'I remember, Thomas,' Philippe said. 'Even though I was only a boy.'

'And we went after them. Your father, and mine, and myself, and about twenty overseers. We caught them, too, and brought them back. And papa decided to make an example of *them*. Do you know what he did, Richilde?'

'I don't want to know,' she said, hopelessly.

'It was that very lawn out there,' Thomas de Milot said. 'Where we played bowls before supper. We played bowls then, too. Only Papa had pits dug, into which he placed these scoundrels, buried them up to their necks so that only their heads were showing, and *then* we played bowls. Only instead of knocking over a pin, you see, you had actually to kill a man. Or knock out his eye, or something. Papa worked it all out. A very complicated set of rules. But he was good at that sort of thing. I won, as I remember.' He sighed. 'I was much stronger then.'

Richilde got up. 'If you'll excuse me, Thérèse, I really think I must be going.'

'Going, Richilde? It's not yet midnight.'

'I'm sorry. I don't feel very well.'

Thérêsè looked at Philippe, who also got up.

'I must apologise for spoiling your party,' he said. 'But if Richilde isn't well . . .'

'Weak stomachs,' Thomas de Milot said. 'People nowadays have weak stomachs.'

'Ring for Charles, will you, Catherine?' Thérèse' said.

Catherine got up, slowly and resentfully; her mother-in-law had this habit of using her as an extra maid.

'I shall say goodnight, Thérèse, Thomas,' Richilde said. 'Thank you for a most delicious meal.' She looked past them, over the gardens and the stables, in the direction of the white township. 'Where is that fire, do you suppose?'

Thomas de Milot merely turned his head, but François got up. 'Must be a canefield,' he said. 'When the weather gets this hot fires are liable to start anywhere. Would you like me to ride out there, Papa?'

'The butler can see to it,' Thomas said. 'Sit down and have some more champagne.'

'Where the devil is that Romerre?' Thérèse de Milot enquired. 'Catherine, did you ring the bell?'

'Of course I did, Mama,' Catherine said.

'No doubt he will be along directly,' Richilde said. 'Good night.'

She went through the open glass doors into the large drawing room, and thence into the hall. Philippe hurried behind her. 'Richilde,' he said. 'You really are being rude.'

'I consider they were rude to me,' she said. 'Teasing me like that, and about something so ghastly!'

'Old Thomas is right. You really should not be so soft centred. Life is a cruel business.' He stood in the great hall, hands on hips, looking right and left. The hall was deserted. 'I must say, though, Milot seems to be losing his grip. This place is going downhill.'

Richilde went to the huge front doors, made of cedar reinforced with iron bars, and thence on to the front porch. Normally there would always be half-a-dozen liveried grooms waiting here, as well as their own coachmen. The coaches waited in a line, horses patiently munching at their nosebags. But there was no one in sight.

'The scoundrels have run off to see what's happening,' Philippe said. 'My God, I'll have them at the end of a whip.'

'How very odd,' Richilde said. 'Listen.'

Because suddenly she heard the sound of drums, and conch shells, and then a great deal of confused sound, punctuated by a pistol shot. While the whole night sky to the west had started to glow.

She gazed at Philippe with her mouth open.

'By Christ,' he said, and left her to run back into the house.

'Etienne,' he bellowed. 'Louis. Get up. Get to the

206

coaches. Thomas, there is trouble out there. You have a slave revolt on your hands.'

Richilde stood alone on the front porch, staring into the darkness. A slave revolt? That was impossible. There had never been a slave revolt in St Domingue. At least, not for a hundred years. There had not been a slave revolt anywhere this century, save for the Dutch colony of Berbice, and that was nearly thirty years ago. And everyone agreed that that had been caused by a panic on the part of the planters.

And Henry Christopher and Jean François had run off to join it? Oh, my God, she thought. Henry, broken on the wheel. Oh, my God!

'Hurry.' Louis ran outside, catching her arm as he did so. He was herding his mother and Claudette as well. 'Philippe wants us back to Vergée d'Or as rapidly as possible.'

'But . . . Philippe . . .?'

'He will follow on horseback, as soon as he has discovered what is happening here.' Louis half pushed her down the steps, and into the first coach, where Marguerite and Claudette were already seated; the three younger Mortmain girls had remained at home.

'Wait for your father,' Marguerite said, as Maurice de Mortmain appeared in the doorway. 'Do hurry, Maurice.'

Thérèse de Milot and Catherine stood above them. 'Take care, Louis,' Thérèse shouted. 'Do not stop for *anything*.'

'Why do you not come with us?' Marguerite asked.

'Come with you?' Thérèse enquired.

'Oh, yes, Mama. I think that would be a very good idea,' Catherine said. 'If you will wait just five minutes I will fetch the children, and . . .'

'Stuff and nonsense,' Thérèse de Milot declared. 'This is my home. *Your* home, Catherine. And you wish to abandon it? Shame on you, girl. Shame on you. Now come and help me, and we will close these doors.'

'Wait for your father,' Marguerite said, as Maurice de Mortmain on the box, the three women inside, peering out of their windows at the darkness, looking back at the flames.

'It will be nothing,' Marguerite de Mortmain said,

reassuringly. 'It will have been some kind of a riot, caused by the fire. The overseers will stamp it out.'

'No one will ever riot on Vergée d'Or, anyway,' Claudette said.

Richilde chewed her lip. She did not suppose they would ever riot on Vergée d'Or either. But Henry and Jean François had run off. Of course they would not wish to take part in anything so dangerously stupid as a slave revolt, it must have been sheer curiosity. But at the very least it would mean another flogging for Henry and, as Philippe himself was involved, it would be a far more serious one than the first. She blamed Toussaint. They were too friendly with the lame old coachman, and undoubtedly had gone to find him, and discover what was happening. Oh, if only she had not decided to go home early, their absence might not have been discovered.

Vergée d'Or lay bathed in moonlight, silent and quiet. It was not quite two in the morning.

The carriage rumbled up to the front porch, and sleepy grooms hurried forward to take the bridles – but how reassuring their presence was.

'I will rouse Fedon, and the town,' Louis said, jumping down and running to the stables for a horse. 'I will send the messenger to Cap François, as well.'

'Fedon? Cap François?' Marguerite asked.

'This is what Philippe has instructed us to do,' Maurice de Mortmain said, handing them down himself. 'Ah, Bartholemew. I wish the doors closed and the shutters raised. Haste, man.'

The Negro butler stared at the old man in amazement, then looked past him for Henry Christopher and Jean François. He scratched his head. 'They got hurricane, master?'

'Just do as I say.'

Richilde followed them up the stairs. 'I'm sure that if we were just to go to bed it would be best,' she said. 'This way we are creating a crisis where there may not be one.'

'I am doing what Philippe told me to do,' Maurice

explained, patiently.

'Well, I think the storm shutters are a good idea,' Claudette said. 'My God, the children. I must wake the children.'

'But why?' Richilde asked.

'Because . . . because I must.'

Richilde went up the inner staircase, encountered a sleepy Amelia.

'Eh-eh, mistress, but you home early. Them boys saying we got storm.'

'Yes,' Richilde said. 'There is a rumour of one.'

'You going to bed, mistress?'

Richilde stood at the foot of the staircase to her apartment, biting her lip irresolutely. Of course she could not just go to bed, if everyone else was staying up. She turned her head, as there came a hubbub from the front drive, and her heart gave a curious leap. But those weren't black voices. She hurried back along the great gallery, stood at the top of the stairs, watched the white women and children flooding into the downstairs hall. 'What on earth is . . .?'

'Orders from Monsieur Louis,' explained old d'Albret the chemist, who appeared to be in charge of them. 'We are truly sorry to invade your home, madame, but Monsieur Louis said we must all come up here.'

'Yes,' Richilde said, absently. 'Yes, Amelia, find Rosamund and tell her I wish bedding brought downstairs. Everything we have, for these people. You are welcome, to be sure, Monsieur d'Albret. Perhaps you will arrange them in families.' She gathered her skirts and went down the stairs, watched Fedon and Maurice de Mortmain organising the white men, handing out muskets and pistols, barricading the windows and doors and making loopholes for their weapons, while Bartholemew and the footmen stared at them in bemusement. 'Uncle Maurice,' she said urgently. 'I am sure we are doing the wrong thing, anticipating trouble where there is none.'

He ignored her. She felt like stamping her foot, and shouting at them all to listen to her. Instead she went outside on to the front verandah, stood in the cool of the dawn, gazing down the drive. The white township was alive with lights as the last of the overseers gathered their families and their most precious belongings to take to the safety of the chateau. But now the slave village was awake too; she could see lights flickering down there. And they were being treated as enemies already, while they still obviously knew nothing of what was happening. Equally obviously, they had to be told something to reassure them and to keep them quiet.

She went down the steps, turned towards the stables and her pony and trap, and paused in horror – almost the entire western sky had turned brilliant red with the blaze – clearly all of Rio Negro's canefields were burning. But was it just the canefields?

While she hesitated, there was a drumming of hooves, and a horse dashed up the drive, to come to a steaming halt beside her, while Etienne de Mortmain half fell from the saddle. 'A drink,' he gasped. 'For God's sake get me a drink.'

'Bartholemew,' Richilde snapped, and the butler hurried off to his pantry.

''Tienne, you're hurt.' Claudette almost tumbled down the stairs, her eldest child, Felicité, a girl of nine, running at her heels.

He shook his head, drank the brandy brought to him by Bartholemew. 'Not me. But it is hell out there. Thousands of them. They tried to stop me on the road, but I got through. You're barricaded here? That is good. Have you sent into Cap François for troops?'

'Yes,' Louis said. 'I have sent a messenger.'

'One messenger?' Etienne shook his head at his brother. 'Not sufficient. They are on the roads, I tell you. I will go myself. Fetch me a fresh horse, Bartholemew.'

'Into Cap François?' Claudette cried. 'Oh, 'Tienne, take me with you. I'm so afraid.'

Etienne hesitated, glanced from face to face. 'It would not

be safe for you,' he said. 'The roads are dangerous. Can't you understand that? You are better off here.'

His terror was frightening to watch.

'Where is Philippe,' Richilde asked, trying to keep her voice calm.

'I don't know. I know nothing, save that the overseers were routed by a charge of the blacks; the fools would try to fight them in the open. Then they retreated to the chateau. I happened to be mounted, and thought I had best ride over here to warn you. Now I will go to Cap François. They must be told.'

'You rode off and left Philippe?'

'And your sister? And the little ones?' Marguerite de Mortmain cried.

'For God's sake, did you wish me to stay and be killed?' he shouted. 'I did not know where they were. Anyway, Catherine is a Milot now. It was her business to stay. Mine was . . . to come here,' he said lamely, obviously deciding against proclaiming that his place was with his family. 'And now I must warn Cap François. That is my duty. I will be back in the morning, with the soldiers.' He mounted the fresh horse, kicked it in the ribs, and galloped down the drive.

Claudette burst into tears. The Mortmains looked at each other. Then they looked at Richilde.

Because, she realised, in Philippe's absence, she was the one to whom they had to turn. She was the mistress of Vergée d'Or.

'Well,' she said. 'I am sure he is doing the right thing. As he says, he will be back in the morning, with the soldiers. It really would be far too exhausting and dangerous a ride for you, Claudette. Now, let me see . . .' She went back up the stairs, her intended mission to the black people forgotten, looked at the huge grandfather clock in the hall. The time was just past three. 'I think,' she decided, 'as obviously no one is going to sleep tonight, that we shall all have a cup of chocolate. Batholemew . . .' she looked left and right, but after delivering the horse for Etienne, the butler had dis-

211

appeared. 'Do ring the bell, would you, Lucy.' She frowned at her cousin, who was just coming down the stairs, followed by Annette – both wore their nightclothes. 'And then,' she said. 'I think it would be a good idea for you to get dressed. We have guests in the hall.' She paused, uncertainly, amazed at the way they were hanging on her every word. Because they were terrified, needed to be reassured, and told what to do. And did she not need to be told what to do?

Fedon came hurrying through from the back of the house. 'Those black bastards have gone.' He checked, and flushed, at the sight of the group of gentlewomen. 'I beg your pardon, madame, mademoiselles But your servants appear to have fled the house. Even Bartholemew. They left the back doors open, too.'

'Then have them closed,' Richilde said, and tried to ignore the dreadful pounding of her heart, the sick feeling which was spreading away from her stomach. 'Please attend to that, Monsieur Fedon. And we shall have to make our own chocolate. Aunt Marguerite, will you take charge of that? I'm sure some of the ladies from the township will wish to help you. Lucy, perhaps you would help Aunt Marguerite too. Annette, be a dear and wake Françoise, and help her to dress. Claudette, as you suggested earlier, you had better get up the other little ones, Françoise's as well, and make sure they are dressed.' She rubbed Felicité's head. 'You can help your mama. Uncle Maurice, Louis . . .' she walked away from the throng, was joined by the two men.

'I can only apologise for my son,' Maurice de Mortmain said.

'He was always a coward,' Louis said, bitterly.

'If he brings the soldiers,' Richilde said. 'I will forgive him everything.' Even having Henry Christopher flogged, she thought. Or sneering at Jacques Chavannes dying. All factors in causing tonight's horror, surely.

'But if he is right about what is happening at Rio Negro,' she said in a low voice. 'Then it may well be that we shall have to fight here on Vergée d'Or. I would have liked to have spoken to our blacks, have reassured them. But if the

212

domestics have gone down there it may be too late. So we must prepare to stand a siege, at least until the soldiers get here. How long will that be, Louis, do you think?'

'They should be here by lunch time, Richilde,' Louis said. 'But . . .'

'If only Philippe were here,' Maurice de Mortmain muttered. 'If only.'

'He will be here,' Richilde said, almost angrily. 'And when he arrives he must find that we have anticipated his dispositions, as far as we can. Now then, Louis, will you take command of the front of the house, with half of the men? Appoint Monsieur Fedon to command the rear, with the other half. Less twenty. Uncle Maurice, I would like you to take twenty men, and maintain a sort of mobile reserve, able to go to the assistance of whichever part of the house is most threatened.'

They stared at her.

'It's what Frederick the Great would have done,' she insisted. 'Or Kit, had he been here.' Oh, God, she thought, to have Kit here, with his confidence and his decision, and his courage. 'And it is what Philippe certainly would wish.'

'Of course you are right,' Louis said. 'I am a fool not to have considered the situation from a military point of view.' He smiled, and kissed Richilde on the cheek. 'Don't worry, Richilde. No one is going to burn *your* house.'

My house, she thought, retreating to the stairs the better to survey the ordered chaos which was spreading about her. She had never thought of it as *her* house, before. Oh, God she thought, let Philippe come. Please let him come.

She went upstairs, hunted through the various bedrooms, gathered Annette and a sleepy, complaining Françoise and the various children together, and made them go up to the master apartments at the top of the house.

'If the blacks have overrun Rio Negro,' Annette said, thoughtfully. 'What has happened to Catherine and the children?'

Richilde caught her breath. No one had up to now dared put that question into words. 'We do not know that the blacks have overrun Rio Negro,' she pointed out. 'Only that the overseers have retreated to the chateau, which they are undoubtedly holding, as we shall hold Vergée d'Or, if we have to. Anyway, if there was to be a disaster there, you may be quite sure the women would have been got away. Philippe would have seen to that. Now, children, I want you to stay in here with Tante Françoise and Tante Annette.'

'Here?' Annette whispered. 'But suppose the house catches fire? We will be trapped.'

'Here you will be safe from bullets,' Richilde said. 'And Annette, if the house catches fire it will be because it has fallen. Would you not rather die of suffocation, or even burning, than fall into the hands of the slaves, alive?'

Annette stared at her, mouth slowly sagging, tales of what had happened in Berbice filtering back to her through the mists of memory.

Where, oh where, was Philippe?

She encountered Aunt Marguerite in the great gallery. 'All the woman must have pistols, Richilde,' Marguerite said. 'And an extra charge for each of the children, so that they may . . .' she hesitated, unable to speak the dread words.

'Of course, Aunt Marguerite,' Richilde said. 'Will you see to that?' She opened the door, went out on to the upper porch. Here four men had been stationed, clutching their muskets, peering into the gloom. Because it was no more than a gloom now, with the western sky such a sheet of pink flame, and the dawn rapidly approaching. The dawn, she thought. Everything would be better in daylight. And by dawn the troops would have left Cap François, and be marching to their help.

'There they go,' one of the men said.

She stared down the hill at the slave village, at the flaring torches, listened to the hubbub, the raised voices. Still enquiring. Still wanting to know what had happened. It could have been averted, she thought. If we had just come back here, sent a messenger into town, certainly, but had not panicked, like those Dutchmen in Berbice, not . . .

'Listen,' said another man.

A huge noise was swelling towards them, a shouting and screaming, a whistling of conch shells, coming out of the west.

Louis stood beside her. 'They will be here in half an hour,' he said. 'You will retire inside and barricade this door if they appear on the drive,' he told the men.

They nodded.

'Louis . . .' she bit her lip; her voice had trembled.

'Yes, I'm afraid,' he said. 'You're always afraid, just before a battle, Richilde. But when it actually starts you don't have time.'

'A battle?' she asked. 'Or a massacre?'

He shrugged. 'Battles have been won at greater odds, eh? I remember my Frederick too. Do you think Henry is out there?'

'I don't know where he is,' she said.

He smiled at her. 'Because I was wondering if he remembers his Frederick as well.' He squeezed her hand. 'We'll hold them, Richilde. I promise you.'

'If only Philippe were here,' she said, and gazed down the drive, into the first pale fingers of the dawn, suddenly rendered brighter than she had ever known it by a myriad flood of torches, held high and waving to and fro. Held by people. More people than she had ever seen before in one place in her life, thousand upon thousand of them, and they were all black, and constantly being reinforced as she saw men and women pouring from the slave village to swell their ranks, to join the thunderous clamour as they poured up the drive. Some had already diverted to the white township, in search of liquor or loot, and she could see flashes of flame rising from there as well to indicate that that too would soon be reduced to ashes.

But her attention was taken by the mass coming up the drive, headed by a huge figure, who did not march so much as leap and twist, dance and jump, his red robe swirling through the air.

'Boukman,' she muttered. 'Boukman. Oh, if you can bring

him down, the day is ours.'

She bit her lip. Never before had she asked for the life of a man.

And would his death make any difference, to those shrieking legions behind him, advancing towards her, their banners streaming in the dawn breeze . . . their banners? Her stomach did a complete roll as she blinked to clear her eyes, saw the ghastly, hate and pain and terror filled features of Thérèse de Milot and Catherine de Milot, and at least two of Catherine's little girls, their heads stuck on the end of poles, their long hair straggling behind them, while there was a fifth pole, carried in the centre, on which the lower half of a woman's body was impaled, the legs flopping to either side. The lower half?

She had a sudden, irrelevant ghastly thought: Thérèse's dead mouth was frozen open. Had she, like poor Ogé screamed and begged, or had she died as a Milot should, with stoic courage?

And how should a Mortmain die?

'Don't look, madame,' one of the men begged, and another grasped her arm to urge her inside. 'Don't look.'

But Richilde resisted him, checked herself in the doorway, to look. Because Philippe de Mortmain had, at last, returned to his plantation.

Amazingly, he appeared to be unhurt, although he had been stripped of all his clothing save for his boots. He was being half marched, half carried in the front ranks of the slaves, and these now halted, just beyond musket shot from the chateau, while Boukman in turn stopped his gyrations. Even the noise seemed to settle, as they gazed at their prey.

Richilde stared at her husband. He was attempting to move, and she was sure he was shouting something. Was he afraid? Who could not be afraid, in such a situation? And Philippe could be in no doubt as to how much he was hated by his slaves. It was a hatred he had arrogantly cultivated.

Just as she was in no doubt that he had always been afraid of them. And now they were about to kill him. She knew that, and he undoubtedly knew that too, just as he must know that she was looking at him now.

Did she love him? Had she ever loved him? Or had she just always envied his power and his wealth, even as she had feared them, had wanted to share in them, had never hesitated for a moment when offered that prize?

Just as now she must share in the terrible agony of having it ripped from her grasp.

Fedon panted up the stairs to stand beside her. 'They want to parley, I should say,' he said. 'Don't you think they want to parley, madame?'

Louis de Mortmain stood beside him, his face grim, because he too had recognised the remains of his sister, and his nieces. 'Of course they wish to parley,' he said. 'They are offering Philippe's life, against our surrender.'

'It is a chance, madame,' Fedon said. 'If they would agree to let us go into Cap François . . . Say the word, madame, and I will speak with them myself.'

Richilde was hardly breathing, as she watched her husband being marched out in front of the procession by four of the black men. One of them she recognised: Jean François. She could not make out Henry Christopher. To parley she remembered what they had heard of the slave revolt in Berbice. The planters had all congregated with their wives and families, in one strong house, and there they had resisted all the efforts of the slaves to break in. Until, after twenty-four hours, water had run short, and the slaves had offered to parley, offered to let the white people gain their boats and go down river to safety. The white people had agreed, and had left the security of their fortress – and had been cut to pieces. The lucky ones, that is.

'He is saying something,' Lucy de Mortmain had come to stand with them. 'Oh, my God, poor Philippe. The humiliation of it.'

Richilde continued to gaze at him. He had been forced to his knees by the men holding him, his body grotesquely white in the dawn, while Jean François stood beside him, a sharp-bladed knife in his hands. The humiliation of it. But Lucy had put her finger on the truth. Philippe de Mortmain was already dead. After today, he would never be able to look a black man in the face again.

'We cannot parley,' she said.

'But madame . . .' Fedon protested.

'Philippe knows that as well as we do,' she said. 'If he is speaking, he is begging us not to be tricked. We cannot parley.'

Louis stared at her in horror.

'My God,' one of the men whispered. 'Do not look, madame, I beg of you.'

Richilde's nostrils dilated. Because they had not meant to parley, after all. They had only, with demoniac patience, wished to save their master's ultimate degradation until it could be overlooked by the whites. For now Philippe was stretched on his back on the earth, and they could hear his shriek of pain and misery and shame even above the chanting of the crowd, and a moment later Jean François held aloft his bleeding trophy, waving it at the horror stricken defenders of the chateau.

Jean François. The man she had thought she could trust with her life. The man who had once held her in his arms. The man who *loved* her.

Lucy fell to her knees, and began to pray. Richilde realised she was in pain; her fists were so tightly clenched the nails had bitten into her palms.

Because, she thought, she *could* have loved Philippe, given only a few more years.

The only sound in the chateau was that of Marguerite de Mortmain weeping, from the downstairs hall.

'Now we know we have to fight, or die,' she said, in a low voice, and watched her husband being dragged away, writhing and screaming while blood streamed down his legs. Surely he would soon be dead and out of his agony. 'Go to your posts, messieurs,' she said.

She wanted to be sick. She did not seem to have any control over her stomach. But she was the mistress of Vergée d'Or, and, she realised, her determination was the only thing that stood between them all and a similar fate,

218

just as the constant awareness of her position was the only thing that stopped her from collapsing on the floor in screaming hysterics. She walked through the house, speaking with every man, making sure they had sufficient ammunition, smiling at the women, reminding them of the strength of the chateau, pausing to stand by the weeping Marguerite de Mortmain, unable to say a word of comfort to her, and being brought to a horrified stop by a scream which came up the hill, the most unearthly wail she had ever heard.

She ran to the window, stood beside Louis. The wind had dropped, and the night was still. The scream had come from a long way off, and now, too, seeping up the hill, they could hear the slow clank of machinery.

'Oh, my God,' Louis said. 'Oh, my God.'

Richilde understood that the slaves were feeding Philippe through his own cane crushers. Her knees seemed to have lost their strength and she all but fell. But there had been only one scream. He was dead, or beyond feeling. Now he had to be forgotten, as she concentrated upon saving the lives of the living. If she could.

'They are coming, madame,' Fedon said.

She looked in the direction of his pointing finger, saw the dark mass moving once again up the drive, Boukman to the fore.

'That man,' she said. 'Wearing the red robe. He is their leader. Bring him down, and they may well withdraw.'

'You hear that?' Fedon told his overseers. 'Bring down the *hougan*.'

Once again the slaves halted, perhaps two hundred yards from the chateau, and Boukman harangued them. She could not make out what he was saying. But she recognised Jean François at his side. Jean François. He at the least had to be killed, and Philippe's death avenged.

She was amazed at the intensity of her own thoughts, how filled with hatred, when for so long she had been sympathetic towards these people, had endeavoured to understand them, had wanted only to improve their lot.

And had the evidence of her own ears and eyes that

219

nothing they could do could truly atone for the hundred years and more that the planters had tortured and exploited them.

Boukman waved his stick, and the mass moved forward.

'Steady now,' Fedon said.

'Take aim,' Louis said, walking up and down behind the men at the windows. 'Choose your targets carefully. Wait for the command.'

'Fire,' Fedon shouted, and the sound of muskets ripped through the rooms and along the corridors of the huge house, while the air became filled with acrid white smoke. From the downstairs hall a woman started screaming in a high-pitched wail, but the men were cheering, for the Negroes had been halted, and were indeed in full retreat down the drive.

'Well done, lads, oh, well done,' Louis de Mortmain shouted.

'Recharge your pieces,' Fedon command. 'Quickly now, they may come again.'

'Not them,' Louis said. 'Not for an hour at the least. By then the soldiers will be nearly here. We'll hold them, Richilde. We'll hold them.'

Richilde looked down the drive. The sun had risen now, and its first beams were playing over the plantation, shining upon the score or so of bodies which lay scattered on the drive and in the flower beds, some lying still, other writhing in agony. And then upon the black mass gathered further down the hill, sullenly waving machetes and home-made spears, and even some muskets they had obviously obtained at Rio Negro, and which they did not know how to use.

And still, miraculously, Boukman stood before them, unhurt. Once again he was gesticulating and shouting, but this time without any immediate response – Jean François was no longer to be seen. Perhaps, she thought, he is amongst the dead.

She did not wish to think of Henry Christopher. And it was terribly important not to think of Philippe, of the way he had died, or of what tomorrow might bring. Tomorrow had

220

first to be reached.

'Lucy,' she said. 'While there is a lull in the fighting, I think we should prepare some breakfast. We may be here for some hours yet. Madame Fedon, will you help us? Madame d'Albret?' She led the ladies into the kitchen. 'I'm sure the men would appreciate something to eat,' she said, smiling at them reassuringly. And then left them and went to find her uncle. He sat on the bottom step of the great staircase, shoulders bowed, overwhelmed by the catastrophe of his daughter.

'Uncle Maurice,' she said, and sat beside him. 'I think you should take Aunt Marguerite upstairs and put her to bed.'

He raised his head. 'Yes,' he said. 'Yes, I must do that. I . . .' he just ceased speaking. His eyes had a faraway look. She kissed him on the cheek and hurried off to speak with Father Thomas.

'Perhaps you could lead the ladies in morning prayer, Father,' she said. 'I'm afraid the men will have to stay at their posts, but it will be a great comfort to them all, surely.'

'Of course, madame. Madame . . .' he was interrupted in his attempt to offer sympathy.

'Here they come again,' someone shouted from the front of the house. Richilde gathered her skirts and ran through the hall to stand beside Louis, and watch the dark mass again surging up the hill, led this time not by Boukman but by a single huge man, young and strong, and brave, as he ran with his machete pointed straight at the front door of the chateau.

Henry Christopher.

'Him, at the least,' Louis muttered, and levelled his musket. Richilde opened her mouth and then closed it again. Of course he had to die. He and all the others had to die, that *they* might live. There was no alternative.

But she closed her eyes as the musket exploded, opened them again, and saw Henry still running, and now at the very foot of the patio steps, while behind him the huge mass had also surged across the lawns and flowerbeds, not checking this time as the musket balls tore through them, yelling their

221

paean of hate and revenge.

She looked left and right, at the men feverishly reloading their pieces, listened to the splintering of glass and the crashing of timbers, from the library. 'Uncle Maurice,' she shouted. 'Your reserve. To the west wing.'

But Maucice de Mortmain had gone upstairs with his wife; the men he had been appointed to command were standing around irresolutely.

'In there,' she shouted, pointing – and then watching the defenders of the west wing come retreating through the hallway, several having discarded their weapons.

'Don't retreat,' she shrieked. 'Stand and fight. For God's sake . . .'

There were black men in the library, and swarming through the small drawing room. At the sound of their shouts the white men at the eastern windows turned back from their posts to face this new threat. Richilde watched in horror as Fedon himself turned, and was struck down from behind by a machete thrust through a broken window. She realised in that instant that the house had fallen. The unimaginable had happened, and they were all going to die.

She stood on the bottom step of the great staircase, and stared at the white women and children, huddled in front of her, at Father Thomas, looking utterly bewildered as he held his crucifix above his head, obviously unable to understand why his payers were not being answered. She looked beyond them, at Lucy, running in from the kitchen, a black man behind her, reaching out to catch her by the hair and bring her tumbling to the floor, screaming her terror in heart-breaking shrieks. And remembered that she held a pistol in her hand. She levelled it, as the man bent over her cousin, tearing the clothes from her back, and squeezed the trigger. She did not suppose she hit him – she was blinded by the powder smoke – but he jerked away, and Lucy, her gown in ribbons, regained her feet and came staggering towards the stairs.

Then the entire hallway was filled with black men, and machetes. An enormous wail arose from the white women and children, as an enormous snarl rose from the black throats. Lucy brushed past Richilde and ran up the stairs, panting and screaming, a horrifying sound. Richilde reached for breath, and then ran behind her, hating herself for a coward, for seeking just a final few minutes of life, her ears filled with the ghastly sounds coming from behind her.

She gained the great gallery, an utterly empty great gallery at the moment; the little knot of men on the upper porch still fired down into the mass below them, unaware that their battle was lost. But there was nothing she could do about them. There was nothing she could do about anything. Like them, she could only prepare to die. She looked at the portraits of all the past Mortmains staring down at her from the wall, at her own portrait, added there four years before, the alert amber eyes, the half smile, so confident, the pointed chin, the wealth of golden brown hair . . . That was what the man who killed her would see, just before he cut off her head to mount on a stick, save that the mouth would be wide open, screaming its terror. Unless she anticipated them.

She looked down at the pistol in her hand. But it was empty. She dropped it and ran along the corridor, gasping for breath, thence up the stairs to her bedroom, burst open the door, stopped in consternation. She had forgotten her earlier dispositions. But here were Françoise, lying on the bed and howling, Felicité, staring at her with wide eyes, Claudette, seated on the bed with her arm round her daughter's shoulders, Annette, standing by the window to look out, but turning to gaze at her cousin, the other six children huddled in a corner in mutual terror – and Lucy, sprawled on the floor, still shrieking between repulsive gulps for air.

'They are inside,' Richilde said. 'They are inside. Oh, God, they are inside.'

Annette pushed past her, closed the door, turned the key. 'Where is Mama?'

'I don't know, Richilde said. 'She went to her room, with your father. Oh, my God.' She leaned against the door, listened to the screams and the howls from outside, the bestial baying of men who were avenging every terrible ill done them for so long.

'We must kill ourselves,' Annette said.

They gazed at her.

'We must,' she shouted. 'Have you any *idea*? Didn't you see Catherine . . .' Great tears rolled out of her eyes and down her cheeks. 'At least the children,' she begged. 'Claudette . . .'

Claudette held Felicité tighter, while one of the smaller children began to cry.

'Wait,' Richilde said, heart pounding at the thought of escape. 'The private staircase. If we can reach the garden . . .' She ran into her dressing room, pulled open the door, the others crowding behind her, gazed down the stairwell in stupefaction at the black men coming up towards her, turned to push her cousins back into the bedroom, watched the door come crashing down, gazed at Henry Christopher.

He was naked from the waist up, and there was blood staining his machete and his right arm, and also splashed across his chest. But it was not his blood, from the vigour of his movements. Behind him was a crowd of eager slaves.

Annette fell to her knees. 'Henry,' she begged.

For a moment he filled the doorway, taking long breaths, discovering just who had so far survived. 'I can save one,' he said, speaking English.

They stared at him, and then Claudette, without speaking, held up Felicité.

But Henry had found the one he wanted. Richilde thought she was going to choke, with relief, with self horror that she might survive where her cousins could not, with an utterly breathless feeling of helplessness as she understood that her life could only be saved in one fashion.

Henry pushed Annette out of the way, stepped towards her. 'No, Henry,' she gasped. 'Not me. One of the others. The child . . .'

He lowered his shoulder, and thrust it into her midriff, closed his hands on her thighs, one of them still grasping the machete, and lifted her bodily from the floor, draped across him like a sack. The impact knocked all the breath from her body, and before she could regain it her head was hit a sickening blow on the door frame as she was carried through, and down the corridor, and into Jacqueline Chavannes' old room, there to be thrown across the bed.

She raised herself on her elbow as he dropped his pants. 'Henry,' she said. 'One of the children. Please . . .'

'You are my twin,' he said.

She watched the door open, other people come in. They had come to watch their mistress being raped. The ultimate humiliation. But nothing she could suffer could equal what Philippe had suffered. She fell backwards as he knelt above her, huge and demanding, his face twisted with a mixture of passion and lust – and also distress and even tenderness. She was suddenly no longer aware of fear, because he would save her, and because she had always known that what was about to happen would happen, one day. She had known that from her very earliest childhood, without being prepared to accept the fact.

He split her gown from her bodice to her knees in a single tear, ripped her petticoats with no more effort, paused in amazement at her corset – she realised that he knew nothing of white women's clothes. She brought her arms around in front, thinking vaguely that she might assist him, and he supposed she was fighting him, thrust them back again, and pinned them there with his own as he lowered his body on to hers, was inside her with a gigantic thrust which seemed to impale her against the bed. Her ears were filled with a tremendous drumming, above which she could hear the most heart rending screams. Her own screams? But they were coming from the next room.

He lay on her, crushing her with his weight, while dark faces surged about her, pulled at her legs and her hair, tried to thrust hands between their heaving bodies to reach her breasts and her crotch. Presumably they were people she knew, people who had helped her build the new dispensary, who had touched their hats as she had passed them yesterday morning, had smiled at her and pretended she was their friend. She did not wish to look at them, but she could not move, pinned as she was to the bed by Henry's weight, while he lay still. She could feel him breathing, against her neck, but he would not raise his head. Out of remorse, inability to meet her eyes – or because he knew that to move would be to relinquish possession of her, mean that he would have to hand her over to the eager mob?

She wondered if he was still inside her. She could feel nothing. It occurred to her that she had felt nothing after the entry. She had been too numbed, her brain too dull with shock after shock, too unable to contemplate what was actually happening about her . . . and she was obsessed with a sense of utter failure. Madame de Mortmain, who had been going to defend her chateau to the last, or at least die in the breach.

She stared past Henry at Jean François, standing above the bed, huge and bloodstained. Some of that blood would be Philippe's. And smiling at her, mouth a wide cavern of dark desire.

'There she is,' he said. 'Man, Henry, if you knew how I been looking for this one.'

Richilde realised that her ams had folded themselves over Henry's back, holding him tightly, crushing him against her. He was her shield. Her only possible shield.

But now he was pushing himself up, rolling away from her to sit beside her. Jean François dropped his pants. 'I knew you would be having her,' he said. 'But she is sweetness, eh?' he knelt above her, reached for her sweat wet hair, while she shivered, desperate to bring up her knees and curl herself into a ball, too afraid to move.

'No,' Henry said.

Jean François turned his head, looked at the machete. 'You gone mad, boy, or what?'

'She is mine,' Henry said. 'She has always been mine. You know that, Jean.'

Jean François laughed, and seemed to pick up one of Richilde's breasts, pulling her from the bed. 'I know you did

226

always dream of she,' he said. 'But I did dream too. you know I ain't never think she had bubbies like this? How we going get this thing off?' He thrust his fingers into the top of the corset and attempted, futilely, to peal it down. Richilde's head flopped backwards and she stared at the ceiling. Let him lose his temper and kill me, she prayed. Oh, let him.

'She is mine,' Henry said again, standing above his friend. 'I led the assault. Without me, you wouldn't be here now. She is my reward.'

Jean François let her go; she hit the bed with a thump. He turned to face the younger man. 'You want a reward? I am the general. We agreed so.'

'Boukman is the general,' Henry said.

They stared at each other, and Richilde held her breath, unable to decide what she really wanted to happen . . . and had her nostrils suddenly assailed by the acrid smell of burning wood.

'Fire,' came the yell from outside.

'Fire!' It was taken up from down the stairs.

'We are at the top,' Jean François ran for the door.

'Henry,' Richilde gasped, unsure whether she was asking to be saved, at least temporarily, or whether she was asking him to leave her to die.

He picked her up as if she had been a toy, hesitated for a moment, and then plucked the sheet also from the bed and wrapped her in it, ran through the door. Dimly she could see that they were passing through her bedroom, a place of blood and scattered bodies, then they were running down the stairs, to pause at the head of the great gallery, watching the flames sweeping up the grand staircase, sending billowing clouds of smoke in front of them.

Henry hesitated; he had never been inside the chateau before.

'Down there,' she gasped.

He ran in the direction she had indicated, while she hated herself for having spoken. They would have died instantly if they had waited a moment longer, and inhaled the smoke. But now they were hurrying towards the back of the house,

227

and survival. Brushing shoulders with other Negroes now, all fleeing the holocaust they had ignited, bursting into the morning. She had forgotten it was broad daylight. She twisted her head as they ran towards the stables, looked back at the chateau, at the flames billowing from the upstairs windows, listened to them crackling and to the boom of collapsing timbers. It would be destroyed, together with its ghastly secrets.

The black people stared too, unable to believe that such a symbol of white supremacy was crumbling into dust before their eyes. Why, Richilde thought, that smoke, reaching higher than the factory smoke had ever done during grinding, must be visible in Cap François itself.

Conch shells were wailing, and her heart constricted as she saw the leaping figure of Boukman, red robe flapping, coming down the drive, waving his stick. 'You all stand here,' he shouted. 'You think it is done? It ain't yet begun. We have to fight the soldiers. We have to beat the soldiers. We have to march on Cap François . . . It ain't done until Cap François burning just like that. Follow me. To Cap François.'

She looked up at Henry. And he looked down at her. It was the first time he had looked at her since the rape.

'I must go,' he said.

She waited, afraid to think, and he licked his lips. 'Nobody ain't looking at you now,' he said. 'Crawl into them bushes, and wait, until they is all gone. It ain't going be long. Then . . .' he faltered, drew a long breath. 'There got to be somewhere you can go, Richilde. Somewhere.'

He set her on the ground, rolled her into the bushes. Still wrapped in her sheet, she looked like a corpse, she supposed. Then he turned his back on her, and strode off behind the black army.

Chapter 3

THE TERROR

The mulattos hesitated but an instant, and then joined the blacks, hoping no doubt to be able to control events. They were mistaken. Boukman himself was taken in one of the early skirmishes with the regular soldiers, and promptly executed, but a new general was found in the Negro Jean François, and as the National Assembly had appeared to favour the planters, the Negro army marched into battle wearing the white cockade of the royalist party.

Richilde was aware of tremendous thirst. But no hunger. She did not suppose she would ever wish to eat again. She realised she was still lying where Henry had left her, behind the wall of the stable, still half wrapped in her sheet, with the whalebone of her corset eating into her thighs and ribs, and bathed in a most tremendous heat, partly from the still burning building, and partly from the sun, which was low in the western sky, and shining full upon her. She supposed it must be about five in the afternoon. Only twenty-four hours ago she had been dressing to attend the Milots' wedding anniversary party, afraid, rightly, that the conversation might be too disgusting to stomach. The conversation!

The chateau still glowed. The upper storey had by now completely fallen in, but the lower floor had accepted the blazing timbers early, while every so often a wine barrel in the cellars flared up, to send flames leaping up the stairwells, following the undispersed immense smoke cloud which hung above the plantation.

She had to have water, and she remembered that there was a pump behind the stable. Once she had drunk, she would be able to decide what to do. Henry had said there must be somewhere she could go. But the only place she could think of was Cap François, and presumably the blacks lay between her and the city.

And anyway, how could she, Richilde de Mortmain, consider walking to Cap François – much less walking there when wearing only a sheet and a corset?

But first, water. It was very necessary to plan, to proceed step by step, and not to think about last night, about any member of her family, about Philippe. Or about herself.

She dragged herself to her feet, let the sheet fall. It did not seem particularly relevant. She walked around the building – the horses had all been released and it was empty. She worked the pump, allowed the stream of water to flood over her hair and shoulders while she lapped at it like a dog, and seemed to freeze as she heard voices.

'Eh-eh,' Amelia said. 'But look at she.'

Richilde turned, slowly, gazed at the women. There were perhaps a dozen of them, and behind them there were others again. And children, and dogs. The inhabitants of the slave compound, come up the hill to gaze at what was left of the chateau.

'Amelia,' she gasped. 'Oh, thank God, Amelia.'

'Man, mistress,' one of the other women said. 'You ain't know your tail is bare?'

'Mistress?' Amelia gave a shriek of laughter. 'She ain't no mistress no more. She is a slave, now. We are the mistress.'

Richilde knew her lips were trembling; they had always been friends. Such intimates, in their shared experiences. 'Amelia,' she said.

'You call me mistress, girl,' Amelia said. 'Mistress. And you ain't looking at me when you speak.'

'Why should you hate me?' Richilde asked. 'I have always been kind to you.'

'She ain't calling you mistress,' one of the women pointed

out.

Amelia thrust her forefinger at Richilde. 'You,' she said. 'I sentencing you.'

'Let we cut off her bubbies,' said another of the women. 'Like we did with that red hair one. I ain't never hear screeching like that. And she fighting so. That was sport.'

Richilde's stomach did a complete roll, and her knees gave way. To her horror she discovered herself kneeling before them.

'We going do that later,' Amelia decided. 'But first we going play with she a little. I sentencing you,' she said again. 'To twenty-five lashes. Take she down to the triangle.'

They gave a shriek of delighted approbation, and surged forward. Richilde turned on her knees, reached her feet in an endeavour to flee, and had her arms gripped. She tried to fight them, and was kicked and punched, her hair seized to pull her head backwards until she thought her neck would break and her eyes start from her head. Now quite a crowd had gathered, everyone seeking to grasp some part of her body, and she was being thrust forward, facing Amelia, who was walking backwards, laughing at her, and snapping her fingers in her face. Then she tripped over a dead body, realised with a gasp of horror that it had been a white man. She half fell, was pulled back to her feet, and again forced on her way. Her head sagged, and she stopped fighting, understanding something of the terrifying horror that Philippe must have known this morning. But would her fate be any different? Only in degree.

Her bare toes were paining and bleeding from being dragged over the stones. Her flesh was burning from exposure to the sun and aching with the many fingers tearing at it. She only dimly understood where she was when they halted, and her head was jerked back, so that she could look up at the triangle above her head. Oh, Christ, she thought. But she could not possibly survive twenty-five lashes. She did not think she could survive one.

A rope was looped round her wrists, suspended from the apex of the triangle, and she was pulled upright, while the crowd of women and children leapt and laughed about her, poking her body with sticks to see it writhe, tugging her hair. Then other ropes were brought out from the uprights, and secured to her ankles and drawn tight, until she was held fast, her feet a few inches from the ground, all her weight being taken on her already agonisingly painful wrists, trussed as she had seen many a black man, or woman, trussed in her time, with never more than a faint awareness of revulsion.

Fingers were dragging at the cords for her corset, and a moment later it fell from her body. That at least was some relief. But only momentarily.

She found herself staring at Oliver the dispenser. 'Oliver,' she begged. 'Oh, Oliver . . .' because he surely had to be on her side.

'Well, is a fact I ain't never know white woman had legs,' he remarked. 'And hams. And . . .' he put his hand between her thighs, and she could not even squirm. 'You all give her to me,' he said. 'I got for study this.'

'You go study one of them dead ones,' Amelia said. 'They is all the same, old man. This one getting flog.'

'But he can have she after,' said someone else.

'After,' Oliver agreed eagerly. 'Make haste with that whip.'

Richilde opened her mouth to speak to him again, to remind him of the way they had built the dispensary together, had laughed and talked together . . . and felt herself cut in two, from right shoulder to left buttock. For a moment that was all the feeling she possessed, that her legs had no relation to the rest of her body, then the searing agony raced through her system to expel a voice cracking scream from her lungs. Dimly she was aware that she was twisting and attempting to kick even when the ropes would not let her move an inch, that she could not breathe, that she could not see, that her tongue was lolling out of her mouth and in danger of being bitten . . . and that there were twenty-four more such agonising blows to be survived, before her real death could commence.

Just as she thought she would choke, she managed to get some air into her lungs. Her eyes flopped open, even as she endeavoured to tense herself against the next blow . . . and she gazed at Pierre Toussaint.

'Move, nuh,' Amelia shouted. 'Move, old man. You want to get strike by the lash?'

'Toussaint,' Richilde begged. 'Please kill me. *Please*.'

'You all crazy?' Toussaint demanded, and stepped round her.

'You moving?' Amelia shouted.

'I am moving *you*,' he said. 'This is all you have to do?'

They backed away from him, cowed by his utter confidence in his own authority.

'She white,' someone said. 'You ain't seeing that, old man? Boukman say all the white people must die, and must holler while they doing it.'

'Boukman is a madman,' Toussaint said.

'He is a god,' they insisted. 'You ain't see he walking against them white people musket, and nothing hitting he? He is a god.'

'Then I am his prophet,' Toussaint said. 'Them boys will return here soon enough, and they ain't going be happy with what they find. They going want food, and drink, not dead bodies and chopped up women. You had best prepare those things, or *you* will be flogged.'

Richilde heard them muttering, but the sound was fading. She could not believe it. Nor did she want it to happen. A few more blows of the whip and she would have died. She knew this. Toussaint could only wish her in order to inflict some other terrible torment on her. His skin was black.

'You help me,' Toussaint commanded.

She felt hands on her legs, and tensed her muscles for some fresh outrage, but the hands were only releasing her ankles.

'She is one good-looking woman,' Oliver said. 'You know I never realise that before, Toussaint, what with all them clothes and thing? When you done with she, I can have she?'

'Hold her,' Toussaint commanded, and she felt Oliver's

arms go around her waist. Her back was against him, and she moaned in agony, and then cried out as a moment later Toussaint cut the bonds suspending her wrists and she slid down the dispenser's body.

'I said, hold her,' Toussaint snapped, and pulled her away from Oliver, lowering his left shoulder to catch her as Henry had done. She was surprised by his strength, even as she lost her breath. Her head flopped against his back, and she realised she was being carried into the slave compound. There were people all around her, talking and laughing, one or two grabbing at her trailing hair, but she could not hear what they were saying because of the drumming in her ears.

Then she entered gloom, realised she was inside the dispensary. Her dispensary. And being laid on straw on the floor, very carefully, on her face. But it could only be because he wanted her body.

'I got salt,' Oliver said.

'You mad, or what?' Toussaint asked. 'This is a white woman. Salt would kill her. I will use ointment.'

A finger touched her cut, and her head jerked in agony.

'Easy, madame, easy,' Toussaint said. And she realised the pain was starting to fade. 'There is only one cut,' he said. 'It will soon heal. In six months time you will not even have a scar.'

Six months time? How could anyone consider so long a period of time, without going mad? But incredibly, she felt her muscles starting to relax beneath his gentle massaging. Yet was it not equally incredible that she, Richilde de Mortmain, mistress of Vergée d'Or, should be lying on a wooden floor, beneath a black man, and not fighting or screaming, or wishing to die? Because that urge, too, was fading with her fear.

'She will be thirsty,' Toussaint said. 'Fetch some water, old man.'

The fingers were gone. She raised herself on her elbow, and Oliver held a cup of water to her lips. It was lukewarm, but tasted like nectar.

'How long them boys gone?' Toussaint asked, slipping

234

naturally into the careless grammar of the slaves.

'Nine, ten hours,' Oliver said.

'To fight the soldiers,' Toussaint said, contemptuously. 'They will soon be back.'

'They going burn Cap François,' Oliver said. 'That is what Boukman tell them they must do.'

'Burn Cap Francois?' Toussaint's contempt grew.

'They done burn here,' Oliver reminded him. 'And they burn Rio Negro. At least, they saying so.'

Toussaint nodded. 'I was there. Tell me how they took this place.'

Oliver shrugged. 'They rush it, Toussaint. That crazy boy, Henry, he just rush it.'

'Henry Christopher,' Toussaint said, thoughtfully, and looked at Richilde. 'You couldn't stop them, madame? There must have been more than a hundred men at your command. With muskets.'

She inhaled. 'I did not know how to command them. They were afraid.'

Toussaint studied her for several seconds. Then he nodded. 'And now they think they can just rush an army, a walled town, and still win. As I say, they will soon be back. Maybe with the soldiers behind them. He smiled at her. 'You will be rescued, madame. If we can keep you alive that long.'

'You . . . you wish to help me? Don't you want to beat the soldiers?'

'I have to want that, madame. But this is a business for men, and guns, and swords. It is not a business for torturing and killing women. Especially you, madame. Of all white women, my people should least wish to kill you. They will understand that, soon enough.'

She did not understand. Despite their conversations together, despite her belief that he was basically a good and honest man . . . 'You were at Rio Negro,' she said.

He nodded. 'They followed Boukman there, as here. And men, who are roused as he can rouse them, are capable of any atrocity. White men can be roused too, madame. You saw them once, in Cap François. It must be my job to remind my people that they *are* men, and not animals.' Again the smile, but this time it was sad. 'If Boukman will ever let them stay still long enough for my lame leg to catch up with them. But Henry . . . he was splendid, eh? Are you not proud of him, madame, even if he is now an enemy?'

She frowned. Proud of Henry? But it had been a proud thing. 'He . . .' she bit her lip.

Toussaint nodded his understanding of what she could not put into words. 'He is a man. And he loves you, madame. He has often said so. Had he *not* taken you, there would have been the unnatural act. And you are a beautiful woman.'

Henry, loving her? But she had always known that. And now Toussaint . . . she looked down at herself, and then at the little old man.

This time Toussaint laughed. 'Me? I have not just fought a battle, madame. Nor do I think I would wish to, even if I had. I have a wife, madame, and children. I am content.'

She wanted to scratch her head, to try to arrange her thoughts, which were suddenly so calm, where only a few minutes ago they had been tortured emissions of emotion. And then she heard a scream, and her head jerked. The terror was beginning all over again, somewhere close.

'Oh, please,' the voice wailed. 'Please don't hurt me. *Please.*'

'Annette,' she gasped. 'Oh, Annette.'

Toussaint got up, and ran outside. 'What you doing?' It was amazing how his voice could change from a gentle monotone into a brittle rasp.

'You ain't wanting this one as well?' a woman demanded. 'Man, you too old. You can't manage more than one.'

'Please,' Annette begged. 'Oh, please.'

'Give her here,' Toussaint commanded.

'Man, you spoiling all our sweetness.'

'Go play with the dead,' Toussaint said, and a moment later emerged into the dispensary, Annette half draped across his arm. Like herself, Richilde realised, Annette was naked, and smeared in dust, her golden hair plastered to her shoulders, her eyes dull with horror.

'Richilde,' she whispered. 'Oh, Richilde.'

Richilde took her in her arms, winced when one of Annette's hands flopped over her shoulder to touch her weal.

Toussaint held a cup of water, but the French girl shrank away from him.

'He wishes to help us,' Richilde said. 'Drink.'

Annette gulped, greedily. 'They will kill us,' she said. 'I know they will. They will cut us, like they did Claudette.'

Richilde stroked her hair. She felt like a grandmother, although Annette was a year the elder. 'How did you escape the house?' she asked.

'They held me down,' Annette said. 'Twelve of them, one after the other. They held me down, and . . .'

'They are gone now,' Richilde said, staring at Toussaint with tragic eyes. 'Tell me how you escaped.'

Annette sucked air into her lungs noisily. 'I got down the private stairs, when they ran out because of the fire. Claudette came with me, and Felicité. They had . . . they had assaulted them too. Even Felicité. A child of nine. But they came with me. Only at the bottom, there were more of them, waiting for us. They dragged us into the bushes. They cut off Felicité's head. Her head,' she screamed.

Richilde held her closer.

'Let her speak of it,' Toussaint said. 'It will be better.'

'And then they took Claudette,' Annette said. 'And they cut off her breasts. Before her own eyes, they cut off . . . she screamed . . . oh, God, how she screamed.' She began to weep.

'That is best,' Toussaint said.

'But you got away,' Richilde said, stroking her hair.

'They forgot about me,' Annette whispered. 'I crawled into the bushes and lay down. But then they found me again, just now. They were going to feed me through the rollers. They took me to the factory, to show me Philippe. Oh, God, they showed me Philippe.'

Richilde gazed at Toussaint. 'Can you defend them?' she

asked. 'Can you possibly defend them?'

His eyes were solemn. 'Look at the history of your own people, madame,' he said. 'Not just here in the Antilles. Everywhere. And then you defend *them*.'

They stared at each other, and turned their heads together, to look at the doorway, and listen to the noise. The Negro army was returning.

'Oh, God,' Annette whimpered. 'They'll kill us. I know they will. They'll kill us, Richilde. They'll cut us up, as they did Claudette.'

Richilde hugged her close, and gazed at Toussaint. And then at the doorway, and Jean François.

A weary Jean François, droping with exhaustion. And more than that. A dispirited and wounded Jean François – blood trickled down his right arm.

'You were beaten,' Toussaint said.

'We didn't take the town,' Jean François said, and sat against the wall. 'You going treat this arm?'

Toussaint snapped his fingers at Oliver. 'Bring water.' He knelt beside the big man. 'You reached the town?' he asked. 'So what happen to the soldiers?'

Jean François shrugged his massive shoulders. 'They were in the town. They waited for us, in the town.'

'In the town?' Richilde cried, without meaning to. 'They weren't coming?'

Jean François turned his head, to grin at her. 'They weren't coming,' he said. 'They more afraid of we than we of them. Ow, man, what you doing?'

Toussaint removed a sliver of lead, cleaned the gash. 'You won't die,' he said, perhaps regretfully. 'So you just walked up to the walls and charged them.'

Oliver had brought water, and Jean François drank deeply. 'What else we going do?' he asked.

'You could think,' Toussaint suggested. 'You got brains? Boukman got brains?

Another grin . . . 'Not any more.'

'He is dead?'

'They took he. He fell, and they dragged him in through

238

the gate. He must be dead by now.'

'So they stopped believing he is immortal,' Toussaint said. 'And you ran away.' He applied some of his ointment to the wound to stop the bleeding.

Jean François scowled at him. 'We come home, to rest, and eat. And get some sweetness.' He rose to his knees. 'That one.'

Toussaint stood in front of him. 'Who told them to come home?'

Jean François got up. He towered above the little man. 'Me,' he shouted. 'Me, nuh? I is the general. Everyone does know that. Boukman was the *hougan*. I is the general. I saying, go home, and rest, and eat, and sleep. We can go back tomorrow. We can't fight in the dark.'

'You think the white men sleeping?' Toussaint asked.

Jean François' scowl deepened.

'You are the general,' Toussaint said. 'And you have been beaten. You watch, by tomorrow morning you ain't even going have an army. Them boys ain't going stop around here until the white soldiers come. And what of them other boys? You knowing anything about them? All the other plantations? You knowing what is happening there?'

'How I going know that?' Jean François demanded. 'I got eyes can see a hundred miles? And how I going keep them boys here, if they wanting to leave?'

'You are the general,' Toussaint said. 'Then be like a general. Send messengers. Send men to all the plantations, and where those boys have got free. Put your men on horseback, and tell them ride hard, to tell all the black people to concentrate, here on Vergée d'Or.'

'Concentrate?'

Toussaint sighed. 'Gather. Here. Tell them you will organise them into an army, and lead them against the white men. And then you must tell your own people the same thing. Tell them tomorrow you will attack Cap François again.'

Jean François shook his head. 'We can't take Cap François,' he said.

'You will take it,' Toussaint said. 'Or you will chase the white people out, which is the same thing. But you must *make* these things happen. You must lead, if you are the general.'

Jean François grinned. 'You right. I am the general. I going lead. After I have had that woman, and after I have slept.'

Toussaint shook his head. 'Generals have no time for women, or for sleep. You must lead now, while your people resting. Or you ain't never going to lead at all.'

Jean François chewed his lip, gazed at Richilde, and then stepped outside. Toussaint also gazed at Richilde, and she almost thought he winked. Then he followed his general.

'He going come back,' Oliver said. 'But I going have you first.'

'You and who else, old man?' Henry Christopher asked.

Richilde's heart leapt. She had been afraid to ask after him, had expected him to have been killed, like Boukman. Because he would have led the charge. But now he filled the doorway, as he had filled her bedroom doorway this morning, tall, and strong – and unharmed.

'Outside,' he ordered Oliver, and knelt beside them.

'He's going to kill us,' Annette whispered, nails biting into Richilde's shoulders.

'I told you to get away,' Henry said.

'I was captured by the women.'

He frowned at her, moved Annette, gently, looked at her back. 'Who did this? Which one?'

'It does not matter,' she said. 'Toussaint took care of me. Henry . . .'

'You heard Jean François,' he said. 'We got beat.'

'But you will go on fighting?'

'We have to do that, now,' he said. 'Or the white people will kill us all. You hungry?'

She shook her head. 'Henry, could I have some water, to wash?'

He frowned at her. 'You think you can wash me away?'

'I didn't mean that.'

240

His shoulders slumped. 'You should. You can bathe in the sea.'

'Could I?' she scrambled to her feet. 'Annette . . .'

'They'll kill us,' Annette said. 'If we go out there they'll cut us up, like they cut Claudette.'

'Leave her,' Henry said. 'Toussaint will care for her. Come with me.'

She hesitated, looked down at herself. Henry smiled at her. 'I like you better this way. Always, you wore too many clothes.'

She got up, followed him from the back door of the dispensary, and into the trees; although it was nearly dark he would not risk taking her through the village. This must be a dream, she thought. The strangest nightmare I have ever known, that I should be walking naked through a wood behind a black man, who held me on a bed and raped me, scarcely twelve hours ago.

But this was Henry Christopher, her twin. And he had saved her life. When everyone else was dead. Everyone else in her entire family . . . save only for Annette, and Kit. And Etienne, who had run away.

'Henry?' she asked. 'Is it true that all the plantations have risen?'

'We believe so,' he said.

'But . . . how?'

'Boukman knew. Boukman fixed the day. Boukman has spoken of the day for a long time. When the prophecy was true.'

'The prophecy,' she said. 'Was I part of the prophecy, Henry?'

He checked, looked down at her. 'I believe so,' he said.

'And now Boukman is dead. Did he prophecy his own death?'

'No,' Henry said. 'But I think he knew he would die. Richilde . . . you know I had to do it. If it hadn't been me, it would have been somebody else. More than one, maybe. And after . . . they would have killed you.'

Now it was her turn to walk away from him. 'Yes,' she

said.

'But I would have done it anyway,' he said. 'I wanted to mount you, for too long.'

'Yes,' she said, staring at the beach and the Atlantic rollers, just coming into sight beyond the trees.

'You hate me bad?'

She ran away from him, toes digging into the sand, stumbling through the shallows, throwing herself into the first of the rollers, feeling herself being smothered in the waves, feeling the water fill every nook and cranny of her body, every crevice. She had not done this since her marriage. That was too long ago.

She regained the surface, stood up to her neck, shaking water from her hair, watched him standing on the edge of the beach. 'It cools the blood,' she said.

He hesitated, then waded towards her.

'You ain't saying,' he said.

You have murdered my family, she thought. It was you, because you led the attack, so bravely, and without you the chateau would not have fallen. It was you, Henry Christopher, risen out of the dark mists of slavery and savagery that people like me and my ancestors have inflicted upon you for a hundred years; you who seized the whole rotten edifice and brought it tumbling down, in squealing, terrified agony. It was you that your people saw as Damballah Oueddo, brought to life to lead them . . . where? But as they all recognised, there could be no going back now.

'No,' she said. 'I can't hate you bad, Henry. You are my twin.'

When she awoke, it was broad daylight, and more, noon; the sun seemed to hang immediately above her head. And she was hungry, and so thirsty . . . but while she had been sleeping Henry had returned to the plantation, and had brought food, and water – and even a gown for her to wear. It was a slave gown, and had no doubt belonged to a black woman. But it was his gift to her.

And she was rested. And different. For the first time she realised that she no longer wore any of her rings. She could not remember them being torn from her fingers, but it must have been one of the women. Amelia? Yet she felt no resentment. The rings had been symbols of what had been, but what she had always felt to be a sham. Now she lived in a real world. And in the strangest of fashions, all the horrors had receded, and only lurked at the back of her mind. It was the present which mattered. And the future.

'Annette?' she asked.

'She is all right,' Henry said. 'Toussaint is caring for her.' He smiled. 'He is keeping Jean François too busy.'

She went down to the sea, to bathe, came slowly back up the beach towards him; he sat with his back against a coconut tree to watch her. She had never felt like this before. Always, when she had approached Philippe, it had been with apprehension, uncertainty, an awareness that there was no telling his mood, or his manhood. That she was taking part in a lottery, which she *must* win, every time. There had been no time for her to feel pleasure herself, or even remotely relaxed. Her life had been a constant chase, from one aspect of Philippe to the next. A constant worry, about the next time.

She did not think Henry had changed, in any way, from the boy who had played at soldiers with her beyond the orchard at Marigot. Even the hero who had led the charge so recklessly was the same Henry.

She sat beside him, water dripping from her hair. 'What is going to happen?'

His face was sombre. 'We got ten, twelve thousand people in Vergée d'Or,' he said. 'They coming all the time. There can't be a black man in St Domingue not fighting with us, or wanting to fight with us.'

'But you are not sure you can win,' she said.

'Those white men have discipline,' he said. 'And plans. I have seen the white men fight. I saw them in America. And they have uniforms,' he added, darkly.

'And you know you will not beat them by merely

charging,' Richilde said.

'Maybe not. But Jean François don't know any other way. And he is the general.'

'He has not sufficient intelligence to be your general,' she said. 'Why do you not make Toussaint your general?'

He frowned at her. 'Toussaint? He is old, and he has a short leg.'

'Does that matter? Do you suppose Frederick the Great personally led his men into battle? Or that he was the biggest and strongest of them? If that were the criterion, *you* should be the general, Henry. But a general must direct. He must work out strategy, and tactics. Make those plans of which you spoke. Toussaint can do those things.'

His frown deepened. 'You wish us to win?'

She sighed, and lay down. 'I do not wish you to be killed. Leading mad charges.'

'Well . . .' he smiled. 'Maybe two are enough. But the white men have ships, too. They can bring more men. We have no ships. I do not know that we can beat them. But I don't think they can beat us, either.'

'So you will just fight, and fight, for the rest of your lives? Is that what you want to do, Henry? Do you suppose Frederick just fought, and fought? He also built cities, and fine palaces, cared for his people, made them work to achieve prosperity, entertained writers and poets, and thinkers. That is what life is all about, Henry. Not just fighting and killing.'

'You must have peace for that,' Henry said.

She shook her head. 'He did it while almost continually at war. You must remember that those are the things you are fighting for, even in the midst of battle. If you could do that, the white men might be willing to treat with you as equals.'

'After what happened here?' He sighed, and lay down beside her, and suddenly laughed. 'You just want to see Vergée d'Or rebuilt.'

'It is my home,' she agreed. 'But it will never be a chateau again.'

'Not even if I build it for you?' He saw the expression on

her face, and looked away. 'Yeah,' he said. 'Now ain't the time for dreaming. I have to get you out of here,' he said. 'As soon as it is dark. It is a long walk to Cap François, but you cannot stay here.'

'I cannot leave Annette, either,' she said.

'I know that. We will fetch her too.'

She raised herself on her elbow. 'Henry, those things that happened at the house . . . did you wish them to happen?'

His eyes opened. 'I don't know, and that is a fact. But I wanted you.'

'And now you want to send me away,' she said.

His fingers sliding up and down her back, hurt her wound. But she refused to cry out, because to cry out might make him feel she did not wish what was happening. She had never lain on a man before – Philippe had never been able to sustain that kind of an erection. But it was magnificent, because she was able to control her movements to her own satisfaction. The wildest of thoughts tore through her mind as her passion grew, and for the first time in her life too she had some inkling of the power of lust, of the grip of the sexual passion which would drive a man into a frenzy. Or a woman.

But it was not the first time, she remembered, as she lay on his chest, and gasped. She had known it the night she had first seen Boukman. And had repressed it, because she was a white lady, and the mistress of Vergée d'or. How long ago that seemed.

'Nobody must know,' he said, stroking her hair.

'Annette will know.'

'That I have taken you,' he smiled. 'Not that you have taken me. None of your people would understand that. Now come.'

She put on the slave gown. He wanted her to go into Cap François, where she would be an object of universal pity, and universal curiosity, too. And where she would be alone, even when in Annette's company, because no one would ever understand what she had truly experienced. And from where she would never see him again, unless he was brought

245

in to be hanged, or broken on the wheel.

'Henry,' she said. 'if you came with us, escorted us into Cap François, you would be a hero to the white people as well.'

He gazed at her.

'I would see to that,' she promised.

'I am returning you to your people,' he said. 'How can you ask me to leave mine?'

'Then let me leave mine,' she said. 'Why cannot I stay with you?'

'Because this is going to be a terrible war,' he said. 'And my people will do many terrible things, and if you stay, you will become a savage, like me.'

She followed him into the trees, back towards the plantation, a humming glow of a plantation, where there were a thousand camp fires, as the slaves who had been gathering from every part of the colony cooked their meals and sharpened their swords – and who the white soldiers in Cap François were apparently afraid to attack, or even reconnoitre.

They met a group of black men, marching through the trees. 'We seek Boukman,' their leader said. He was a squat heavy shouldered man, not tall, but suggesting the immense strength of a rampant bull.

'Boukman is dead,' Henry said. 'Now you seek Jean François. What is your name?'

'Jean Jacques . . .' the big man hesitated, then shrugged. 'Dessalines.'

'Why not?' Henry asked. 'And Dessalines?'

The big man grinned. 'We sawed Dessalines in half.'

Henry pointed. 'You will find Jean François through there.'

The black men hurried off; they had ignored Richilde – in the gloom she was just another woman. She clutched Henry's arm. 'I remember him. He was landed from the slave ship on that day last year . . .' she bit her lip.

'The day I was flogged,' Henry said.

'What would you have done, had you taken Etienne, when

246

the chateau fell?'

Henry turned away from her. 'I would have killed him slowly, Richilde. That is why you must leave here.'

More people. Amazingly, these were horsemen, perhaps a hundred of them, well dressed, and armed with swords and pistols. White people? She stared into the darkness. But their skins were brown.

'We seek Jean François,' their leader said, drawing rein. 'We have heard he commands, since Boukman's death.'

'You will find him at the plantation,' Henry said. 'But what do you seek with us, monsieur?'

'A common cause, my friend,' the man said. He was in his middle thirties, Richilde estimated, wore a little moustache. At his side rode a young man, hardly more than a boy, handsome in an excited fashion. 'I am André Rigaud.' The man indicated the boy. 'This is my lieutenant, Alexandre Petion. We have many men, who wish to fight the white people. With you.'

'Who comes?'

Richilde looked up at the walls of the city, the gate rising above the roadway. She had not noticed them before. They had walked through the night, and now it was all but dawn. Her feet were swollen. Agonisingly painful.

'Annette,' she said. 'We have reached Cap François.'

Annette fell to her knees. She had fallen several times during the night, and always Richilde had helped her to her feet. This time she let her stay, kneeling.

'It is two women,' the sergeant of the guard said, and she watched the gate slowly swinging open.

'Two white women, by God,' the officer said, hurrying forward. And stopping when within a few feet of Richilde. 'Madame de *Mortmain*? My God.' He peered at Annette. 'Mademoiselle?'

Richilde started to cry, and she had not actually wept throughout the entire holocaust. But as Henry had said, these were her people. She was finished with murder and revenge, surely. She could close her eyes, and know that she

247

would awaken, safe and warm . . . She was surrounded by people, men as well as women, half carrying her. There were carriages, and there were stairs, and there was a bedchamber. Then there were only women, undressing her and sponging her, whispering to themselves, exclaiming at the great weal across her back, at the sun reddened skin and the bruised toes, muttering, smothering her in eau de cologne . . . and then most of the women were gone, and there was Dr Laval, apologising as he peered at her, and clucking his tongue.

There were glasses of cooling sangaree, and broth for her to drink. She had never felt so exhausted in her life. She wanted only to sleep, and hopefully not to dream, for weeks on end. But first of all there were questions to be answered.

Etienne stood by her bed. 'Richilde,' he said. 'My God, Richilde. But what *happened*?'

'You did not come back,' she said, hating him as she had never hated anyone in her life before. 'You did not come back.'

He licked his lips, looked across the bed at the Governor-General. 'There were less than a thousand soldiers fit for duty in Cap François,' he said. 'Monsieur Peynier decided his first duty was to defend the city. I cannot blame him for that decision. No one can.'

'You did not come back,' she whispered. 'You left us, to die.'

'I . . . what good could I have done? By myself?'

She raised herself on her elbow. 'You could have *died*,' she shouted. 'Like Philippe. You could have died with your wife and children. You could have died like a *man*.'

'Madame, madame,' Dr Laval gently eased her back on to the pillows. 'You must not excite yourself.'

She sighed, and closed her eyes. She did not wish to have to look at her cousin.

'Richilde,' Peynier said, his voice close as he leaned across her. 'It was my decision. It was a painful one, believe me. The most painful decision I have ever had to make in my life. But I have several thousand French people here. Can you imagine what would have happened to them had my soldiers been defeated by the blacks in the open? Or even had been outmanoeuvred? My task must be to end this revolt as quickly as possible.'

She opened her eyes. 'You intend to do that by sitting behind a wall, monsieur?'

'I will do that by accumulating sufficient men to defeat the blacks in battle,' he said. 'I have already sent for reinforcements. And I will do that by learning of their dispositions. I must ask you, madame. Will you answer me?'

He was a stranger to her. As Etienne was a hateful stranger to her. Had Henry allowed her, she would have stayed with him. When he had refused to let her stay, as she had known he would and must, because it was the only sensible decision he could make, for her, she had determined to abide by it, to remember that the white people were her folk, and that she had no substance away from them. She had come here in that mood, to find strangers.

And yet she must help them, as much as she could, to destroy Henry, and all he stood for. Because they were her folk? Or because she knew that, for all his admirable qualities, he stood for nothing, save destruction, and savage grandeur?

She sighed. 'There are upwards of twelve thousand blacks encamped on Vergée d'Or, monsieur. And more are joining them all the time. And they have also been joined by some mulattos. Led by a man called Rigaud.'

'The devil,' Peynier said. 'He is the one we failed to catch after Ogé's revolt. He has some military experience. But what of the mood of the blacks? I believe we may have taken their holy man.'

'Yes,' Richilde said. 'Boukman. What have you done with him?'

'We have hanged him,' Etienne said. 'High above the battlements. He will stay there until he rots. Or until the revolt is over.'

Richilde turned her head away from him.

Peynier sighed. 'Have the blacks another such as he?

Who will lead them now?'

'A man called Jean François.'

'Jean François?' Etienne cried. 'But . . .'

'Yes,' Richilde said. 'He was Philippe's coachman.'

'Would he be the one who led the assault on the city?' Peynier asked. 'A very big man? But young.'

'No,' she said, 'that was my other coachman, Henry Christopher.'

'Henry,' Etienne said. 'By God, Henry. I should have hanged him long ago. When I get my hands on him . . .'

'You had better pray, cousin,' she said. 'That he does not get his hands on *you*.'

Peynier frowned at her. 'You have spoken with this man?'

'How else do you suppose I am here, monsieur?'

'But . . . will you tell us what happened? Exactly?'

'There is nothing to tell,' she shouted. 'They overran the chateau, just as they overran Rio Negro, or Monsieur Dessalines' plantation, or any of the other plantations. They tortured and they killed and they burned the place down. They fed my husband through his own cane mill. They destroyed us. They . . . they avenged their wrongs.'

'And then they let you go?' He was incredulous. 'And Mademoiselle Annette?'

She gazed at him. 'Yes, monsieur. We happened to survive the fire, and then passions died. And so they let us go.' She turned her gaze on Etienne. 'Henry let us go.'

'Unharmed,' Peynier said, and scratched his head, displacing his wig. 'There was a miracle.'

'Unharmed, monsieur?' she asked. 'Unharmed. Why do you not ask Annette if she is unharmed? She was raped by twelve men, one after the other. Ask her, if she is unharmed.'

Peynier flushed. 'And . . .'

'Oh, yes, monsieur,' she said. 'Me too.' For is that not what you really wanted to discover, she thought?

'Kit!' Etienne de Mortmain was on the dock to greet his cousin as he stepped from the boat, shook hands and then kissed him on each cheek. 'I came as soon as your ship was signalled.'

Kit Hamilton looked left and right at the evidences of siege which clung even to the harbour of Cap François, at the absence of Negroes working on the docks, and at the row of gallows, every one carrying a ghastly dark burden, which lined the sea front. He inhaled the sour stench of untreated sewage, gazed at the unswept streets. Cap François had suddenly become a dirty, frightened place – he could almost smell the fear.

Tall, and wind bronzed, carefully dressed in his blue jacket and wearing a new tricorne, exuding the confidence of the professional seaman, he seemed to dominate the nervous Frenchmen who surrounded him. 'I have heard the wildest rumours,' he said.

Etienne showed him to the waiting gig, which he would drive himself. 'All true, I am afraid. The blacks control the entire country. Save for the towns, of course. The coastal towns, anyway.'

'And no campaign has been launched against them?'

'There are perhaps a hundred thousand Negroes under arms out there,' Etienne explained. 'We await reinforcements from France.'

Kit sat beside him, looked up at the tricolour, drooping on the flagpole. 'Republican France? You, Etienne?'

'It is still France,' he grinned. 'The blacks, poor fools, because we fly that flag, march beneath the fleur de lys. They are convinced the King will intercede on their behalf, after they are defeated. After our reinforcements arrive.'

'Do you really suppose you will obtain any? France does not know what she is.'

'Then we shall have to wait until she finds out. We will hold the city. But to think of all that wealth, all that sugar, trampled by the blacks . . .'

'Yes.' Kit gazed at the houses they were passing, the shuttered windows and doors, the closed shops.

Etienne sighed. 'Of course there have been those who have simply packed up and fled.'

251

'I have spoken with them, in Jamaica,' Kit said. 'It was they who first told me what had happened. Now tell me of Richilde.'

'She is far better than could be expected. As I told you in my letter, she is pregnant. This is in my opinion the saving of her sanity. Annette . . .' he sighed.

'Yes?' Kit's voice was sharp.

'She had not the . . . well, the experience of marriage.' He glanced at Kit. 'You understand me?'

'I should like to see her,' Kit said

Etienne shrugged. 'Of course.'

'What are you going to do?' Kit asked.

'I have told you,' Etienne said. 'When the reinforcements arrive from France . . .'

'I meant you, personally. Where are you going to go? My ship is at your disposal.'

Etienne frowned at him. 'Go? I am not going anywhere, Kit. St Domingue is my home. Vergée d'Or is mine, now that poor Philippe is dead. Well, it is actually Richilde's child's. But she will need me to manage it for her, for very many years. I am not going anywhere.'

'And the girls?'

'This is their home, too. I have written to Madeleine, asking her to come and help me, at least with Annette. But this is their home, too, Kit. To run away would be to abandon Vergée d'Or. We cannot possibly do that.'

The carriage was stopping, and Kit was shown into a house in the very centre of the city. It was not a large house, by the standards of the Mortmains, but it looked comfortable enough. 'Madame Ramile has very kindly offered us accommodation, for the time being,' Etienne said. 'Her husband owns the dry goods store by the harbour. Madame,' he said. 'This is my cousin, Christopher, from America.'

Kit kissed her hand. She wore a distinct moustache.

'And this is Louise.'

The girl, she was only a child, although a pretty one, gave a simpering smile at Etienne patted her bottom. It occurred to Kit that his cousin had managed to recover from the terrible tragedy of his family, and his wife and children, with amazing rapidity.

'You will wish to see your sister, Monsieur Hamilton,' Madame Ramlie said, and led him up the stairs. 'She is as well as we could possibly expect. A strong woman, Madame de Mortmain. A strong woman.'

She knocked on the bedroom door. 'Madame? Your brother is here.'

'Kit? Oh, Kit.' Richilde hurried to the door to greet him. A strange Richilde, both because of the poor quality and cut of her gown, and because the slender, elegant creature he recalled was swollen with her pregnancy. 'Oh, Kit.' She was in his arms. He heard the door close, but realised that Etienne was still in the room. 'Do you suppose we could be alone, 'Tienne?' Richilde asked. Her voice was cold.

'Of course,' Etienne hesitated. 'I will wait for you outside, Kit. And remember, Richilde has suffered a great deal.'

Kit held her away from him, to look at her, while the door closed again.

'He is afraid I will tell you how he ran away and left us all to die,' she said.

'Did he do that?'

'Yes.' She released him, sat down her hands on her lap. 'Have you seen Annette yet?'

He shook his head, sat beside her.

'Poor Annette,' she said. 'She suffered far more than I. I . . .' she glanced at him, her cheeks pink. 'I suffered only Henry.'

'Henry Christopher? The black bastard. And he always swore he would look after you.'

'He saved my life,' she said, softly. 'It was the only way he could do it.'

'And he did not enjoy it,' Kit said bitterly.

'He enjoyed it.' She seemed as if she would have said something more, but changed her mind. 'Will you take me away from here, Kit?'

'Away? Away from St Domingue?'

'Yes,' she said.

'But . . . what of Vergée d'Or? Etienne is sure the blacks are going to be defeated, eventually, and you will be able to regain the plantation.'

'Perhaps he is right. Everyone here thinks like that.' She gave a twisted smile. 'Madame Ramlie permits us to live off her charity, because she is sure it will all be repaid, with interest, in due course. But that is a long time in the future. I wish to leave now. I cannot remain here. Don't you understand, Kit? I cannot have my child in Cap François.'

His brows slowly drew together into a frown. 'You can't be serious? You cannot know.'

'I was married to Philippe for eight years, Kit. Eight years. In which time I never even had a miscarriage, did not miss a single menstruation. How can I not know? But I cannot have Henry's child, here in Cap François. These people hate, and fear. They are rabid with fear.'

'And you do not hate, and fear? You *want* this child?'

She met his gaze. 'Yes,' she said. 'I want this child.'

'They held her down,' Annette said, staring out of the window. 'They held her arms and legs, Kit, and they tore off her clothes, and they cut into her, so slowly. They laughed while they cut, and she screamed, oh, how she screamed.'

Kit gazed over her head at Etienne, who lifted his eyebrows.

He squeezed her hand. 'Annette, would you like to leave here? To go to Madeleine in St Kitts?'

Annette seemed to awake from a deep sleep. 'Leave Cap François? Leave St Domingue? It is my home.'

'Yes, but . . .'

'I cannot leave here, Kit.' She might have been speaking to a rather backward child. 'Don't you understand? I want to see them hang. I want to see every black person in St Domingue, hanging.'

Etienne sighed, as they walked down the stairs together. 'I suppose, in many ways, she is mad. We must hope she will get over it, in time. But you cannot blame her. She saw these terrible things happen, while things almost as terrible were

254

happening to herself. And it is my wife she is talking about. My wife, and my daughter. My God, Kit, I sometimes think I am going mad myself.'

'Yes,' Kit said.

'Richilde condemns me,' Etienne said. 'For not staying, and dying. I did what I thought was best. I swear it to you, Kit. I did not know the Governor-General would decide not to send out the troops. I did what I thought was best.'

'I am sure you did,' Kit said. They walked the empty streets, and he had instinctively led them down the lane towards Monsieur Chavannes' haberdashery. But the shop was empty, its windows broken, the interior gutted. Mulattos were no more popular in Cap François than blacks.

But why had he come down here? Because the continuous tales of rape and mayhem had made him want a woman, and the only woman he knew who might accommodate him was Jacqueline Chavannes? Or because he needed help, desperately, and it was only from her wisdom that he was likely to obtain that help? The second was the more noble motive, however it might not be the most honest one.

'What happened to Jacqueline?'

Etienne shrugged. 'I have no idea. No one knows where most people are, nowadays, unless they are here in Cap François. She is probably dead. Kit, it is your decision, whether Richilde leaves or stays. I feel that her duty is here, as the mistress of Vergée d'Or, to show an example, a determination to remain, and eventually conquer. But if you feel . . .'

Kit walked away from him. Etienne was afraid to let Richilde out of his sight, because her son, or daughter, was his passport to wealth and power – when the blacks were crushed. It did not seem to have occurred to him that there was a possibility the child might not be Philippe's.

Or *had* that occurred to him, and were his thoughts and plans even more tortuous than normal?

And what am I to do, Kit thought? Is Richilde any less demented at this moment than Annette? She too was held down and raped, and by a man she must have trusted. She

255

had managed to convince herself that he had actually been trying to help her. But did that not have to be merely an aspect of her madness? She had seen the same horrible sights as Annette, and heard the same nightmare sounds. So she was far stronger, far more able to subdue her nightmares, to pretend they were not there. But did they not *have* to be there?

Her madness was exemplified by her decision to have this child, even knowing, as she supposed, that it must be Henry's. How could any sane woman possibly contemplate such a step? For the Madame de Mortmain to produce a mulatto child, anywhere in the world, would be to damn her to total social obliteration. To have it here in St Domingue, where the only acceptable emotions were hatred and fear of anyone whose skin was even a sunburned shade darker than your own . . . except that there, in St Domingue, they would know what to do.

What a terrible thought. What a terrible decision to have to make. But how could he made any other? He would never be able to do away with his sister's child. By his own weakness he would be damning her to a lifetime of infamy. Kit Hamilton, he thought bitterly . . . a coward at the end of the day. Certainly a moral one.

Or would it not be true moral courage, to take that decision, knowing that it had to be in Richilde's best interest . . . and knowing too the horror that nothing could be done until after the delivery, just in case by some happy miracle, the child *was* Philippe's.

'Kit?' Etienne stood at her shoulder.

Kit gazed into his cousin's eyes. 'I think you are probably right. 'Tienne,' he said. 'But I make you this charge. Her life, her health, and her sanity, are in your hands. Fail me in that, 'Tienne, and by God I will kill you.'

Is he not come? Look again, Madame Ramlie, I beg of you. He said he would be here.' For all of her bulk, Richilde attempted to push herself up the bed, to look out of the window.

'I will certainly check again, madame,' Madame Ramlie said, gazing across the bed at Madeleine Jarrold.

'A sailor, at the mercy of the wind and the sea . . .' Madeleine sighed, and smoothed the sweat damp hair from Richilde's brow. 'He will come, if he can. But you are in good hands, here. Annette, fetch some lemonade for Richilde.'

She exuded calm. She was, Richilde calculated, well past thirty-five, and had seen a lot of life. But not enough. There had never been a slave revolt in St Kitts. However Madeleine must have wept at the news of the murder of her family, it had been no more than news. She had not seen and heard it happen.

Yet her calmness had proved a boon. She had even managed to draw Annette out of the nightmare in which she had lived for so long, had her at least accepting that life must go on. And in her somewhat aloof attitude to the hatred and fear that still, nine months after the revolt, convulsed the white people of Cap François, she had even encouraged Richilde to believe that she might prove a true friend, rather than merely an elder cousin.

Because Kit had failed her. She had suspected that he would, from the beginning, when he had visited her bedroom last November, and said that unfortunately he could not take her with him then, but that he would return for her, before the delivery was expected. It had not made sense, despite his story about a dangerous voyage he had still to undertake. She had wept and she had begged, but he had been adamant. So, he had to be ranked with those who would not and could not understand.

Which included everyone in Cap François, from Etienne and Madame Ramlie, to Monsieur Peynier himself. Coming here had been a terrible mistake. Her heart remained out there in the bush, with Henry Christopher, and through him, with his people. They had murdered, and tortured, and burned, and raped, and they had attempted to flog her. But she now knew, having listened to the unceasing drum roll and the shrill shouts of excited pleasure as each captured

257

Negro, or Negress, was ceremonially executed, that these people, *her* people, were no different. Except that where the Negroes had acted with delirious frenzy, the whites had done so with cold-blooded hatred.

There was not a single redeeming facet to their rule, she now knew. They had seized St Domingue by force, a hundred years before, and they had retained it, by force. They possessed no one with the gentle wisdom of Toussaint, no one with the religious fervour of Boukman, and no one with the heroic stature of Henry Christopher.

She knew she could not stay here. But she knew too that she could never leave St Domingue, and Henry, and Toussaint. And yet the alternative was equally unthinkable. Almost. It was something to be discussed, considered, with a friend. If she could find one. An older, wiser friend, who would understand.

Would Madeleine understand? Richilde had never discussed her true feelings with her cousin. Time enough for that after the baby was born. But Madeleine was divorced from the realities of the situation. Richilde could certainly appreciate why the people of Cap François felt as they did. For nine months now the black armies had held control of the colony, save only for the seaports of Cap François and Port-au-Prince in the south. No help had arrived from France, daily sinking deeper into a revolution of her own, and no one knew for sure what was happening out there in the bush. Certainly the cities were invested, as any reconnoitring parties soon discovered to their cost if they ventured more than a mile from the walls. But the blacks seldom wasted either men or powder any longer in attacking fortified positions. And meanwhile the whole of the richest colony in the entire West Indies was theirs, to plunder to their hearts' content, to turn back into primeval jungle, as it had been when Columbus had first landed here, almost exactly three centuries before.

She wondered what Henry Christopher thought of it all. Or Toussaint. Men who had dreamed, and who knew there was more to life than murder and robbery. But who were dominated by their leaders, like Jean François. How her heart went out to them, and how she wished she could help them. But she could not even help herself, save through the agency of Madeleine. Who was now frowning at her.

'Richilde? Is it time? Your face twisted.'

'I was thinking. I was . . .' but suddenly she *was* aware of cramps in her belly. 'Yes,' she said. 'Oh, my God, yes. Kit.'

'We will take care of you,' Madeleine said. 'Kit will be here for the christening.'

Certainly she was a marvellous midwife – as she should be, Richilde thought, having had five of her own – and with Annette fussing excitedly, and Madame Ramlie returned to help, and an hysterical Louise Ramlie rushing up and down the stairs with water, and Dr Laval coming in to stroke her forehead and approve of what the women were doing . . . the whole event passed off with only a fraction of the pain and discomfort she had anticipated. She was very hot, and Annette bathed her forehead while Madeleine massaged her belly and encouraged her, and suddenly it was over, and a child was wailing its delight at being born.

Richilde closed her eyes, listening only vaguely to the anxious whispers about her. She was exhausted, wanted only to lie there and sleep . . . and then remembered that she dared not sleep. She opened her eyes, stared at Madeleine. 'My child,' she said. 'Let me see my child.'

'My darling Richilde,' Madeleine said, putting both arms round her to kiss her and hug her. '*You* are well. That is all that is important.'

'But my child. I want to hold him.'

'Dear, dear Richilde,' Madeleine said. 'I know you will grieve . . . but God moves in a mysterious way. Your child was born dead.'

Etienne de Mortmain wiped his brow, tugged at his moustache, looked to his sister for support.

'It cannot be considered Etienne's fault,' Madeleine said quietly, staring at Kit. 'No one, no one, Kit, could possibly

259

have supposed Richilde would behave . . . well, she had to have been more demented than we supposed.'

'She had the cunning of a mad woman,' Etienne declared. 'It was uncanny. She did not even weep, when we told her the child had died . . .'

'I do not think she believed me,' Madeleine said. 'I think she had heard it cry, and knew it lived. But Kit . . . I *had* to have it destroyed. You do understand that?'

She spoke, he thought, as if she were talking of a kitten, or a puppy. Not a human being. And yet, it was what he had decreed should happen, by leaving Richilde here in the first place. 'Yes,' he said.

'Then she was even more cunning,' Etienne said. 'She lay there, and said not a word. She lay there, Kit, for three weeks, just waiting, as we now know, for her strength to come back. And then she just got up . . . and left the city.'

'How?' Kit asked. 'That is what I cannot understand.'

'Apparently she let herself out of the house in the middle of the night,' Madeleine said. 'Then she went down to the harbour, took off her clothes, and either waded or swam round to the beach beyond the walls. Then she just walked into the forest.'

'We thought at first she had committed suicide, by drowning,' Etienne said. 'We were beside ourselves with worry, until a patrol found her footprints on the sand where she had come ashore.'

'And then you ceased to worry,' Kit said.

Etienne flushed, and glanced hopefully at his sister.

'You must accept the fact, Kit,' Madeleine said severely, 'that she *is* quite mad. To return to those savages at all . . . but to return to them, naked, just walking through the forest . . . it makes my skin crawl.'

Kit got up, went into the garden. He did not suppose there was any point in being angry. He had failed her, in not taking charge himself. Because he had been afraid of earning her hatred and her loathing. Which was now probably extended to the whole human race. Or at least all of it with white skins.

He could not believe it. And yet, why should he not believe it? He remembered the day of her wedding to Philippe, nine years ago now, when he had suddenly realised that Henry Christopher loved her, as a man should love a woman, and that that was the true reason he would never leave St Domingue. Why, then should he automatically suppose it was impossible for her to love Henry, as a woman should love a man? Because Henry had helped in the destruction of her family? She had never truly considered the Mortmains her family, had always felt an outsider, as had he. Because Henry's skin was black, his standards necessarily so much lower than her own? But whatever crimes he might have committed, could they equal murdering a child merely because its hair had been crinkly? *Destroying* it, as not fit to live.

No, he thought, the real point is that while she might have thought she was returning to Henry Christopher, who was to say she had ever got to him? He was nothing in the Negro army. Just a man. As she was just a woman. A white woman, walking naked through the forest.

'I am sorry, Kit.' Annette stood beside him. 'I am so very sorry. But . . . she seemed to understand them. Even when they were torturing her, she seemed to understand them.'

He frowned at her. Was this some quite unexpected lucidity? Or an utter condemnation?

'If she went back to them,' Annette said. 'If she could do that, of her own free will then there is nothing, nothing at all, that any of us can do about it. At least, not right now.' She sighed, and sat on the garden seat. 'Do you know, I sometimes feel that last August . . . my God, do you realise that it is more than a year ago? . . . the entire world came to an end. That we're just existing, waiting to be sent our allotted ways by God. Do you ever believe that, Kit?'

She was looking up at him. She was twenty-six years of age, and her hair was already streaked with grey. And yet, the touch of false maturity added beauty to the rather pert, youthful features. And she was right, as regards herself. Her world had come to an end. As his was threatening to do.

He acted instinctively, lowered his head, kissed her parted lips. For a moment she hesitated, then her hands closed on his arm, and she drew him down to sit beside her, while she clung to him.

'Kit,' she whispered. 'Oh, Kit. I have been *raped*. By twelve men. Twelve black men.'

'I love you,' he said.

'I have been raped, Kit. And we are first cousins.'

'I love you,' he said again.

'And they call me mad,' she said.

He held her away from him, the better to look at her. 'I love you,' he said a third time. 'We cannot marry, Annette. Not legally. But when I return to Cap François, will you come away with me?'

She frowned at him, through her tears.

'It will mean turning our backs on propriety, even on law,' he said. 'It may mean a quarrel, with Etienne and Madeleine. But it will also mean that we have found something, each other, worthwhile out of all of this hatred and horror. I do not care what has happened to you in the past, Annette. Give me the chance to care for your future.'

'Oh, Kit, my darling Kit. To be yours . . . to forget . . . will you help me to forget, Claudette and Felicité?'

'Yes,' he promised. 'I will help you to forget.'

'And will you help me hang all the black people, when the troops have defeated them?'

Neither her tone nor her expression had changed. Yet that she was deadly serious could not be doubted for a moment. Oh, Christ, he thought, what have you done, Kit Hamilton? But it *had* been done. The invitation had been extended and accepted. So, to set beside a demented sister, he would spend the rest of his life with a demented wife. The alternative would be to watch her sink even deeper into madness.

And promises cost nothing. He had made too many of them before.

'I will stand at your side, always, Annette,' he promised.

'Oh, Kit . . .' she brought him close, and then pushed him

away again. 'When you *return* to Cap François? But . . . where are you going?'

'I must go and find Richilde,' he said. 'When I come back, from there.'

It was dawn when Richilde left the clinging mud of the unharvested canefields behind her, and stepped into the trees. This she had done before. She remembered following the drums, so long ago. And she remembered walking through these trees more recently than that. Yet she could not doubt that this was what she had always been intended to do, by her own will no less than by Fate.

Her feet and ankles were splashed with mud and dust, and insects whirred at her body; she brushed them aside with careless impatience. She did not fear them. She could no longer afford to fear any inhabitant of this forest, not even the human ones. And they were here, all around her. She felt their presence, long before they let her see them.

They were amazed, and uncertain. 'Eh-eh,' someone said. 'But is a white woman.'

'No, man,' said another. 'Is *the* white woman. Is Christophe's woman.'

They gathered around her, staring at her, leaning on their swords and muskets. She was not embarrassed. She remembered none of their faces, but they certainly remembered her. Thus they had seen her before, exactly as she now was. Only now she was not afraid of them, either.

'I seek Christophe,' she said.

'You think she is a spy?' someone asked.

'Maybe we should kill her now,' said another.

'Man, she can't be no spy. Not coming naked so. Maybe she a jumbi.'

'I am neither a ghost nor a spy,' Richilde said. 'I am Christophe's woman. You know this. I have come to be with him. To be with you all. Will you not take me to him?'

They scratched their heads and then began to walk, with her in their midst. She knew where they were going; they had not changed encampments, by all accounts. But it was at

263

least reassuring that they maintained an outpost on the edge of the canefields; if Peynier ever found both the men and the courage to launch a counter assault, he would not take them by surprise. Yet the camp came as a surprise; she had not remembered it being so close to the boundaries of Vergée d'Or. And someone had run ahead, because now she could make out, in the bright and hot morning sunlight, the people gathering to receive her, dominated by the towering figures of Jean François and Henry Christopher; beside them Toussaint seemed a midget.

'She mad,' Jean François declared. 'I said that, this one is mad. I said you were a fool, Henry, to send she off so. And now she has come back. She mad. Well, this time . . .'

'Why you don't be quiet,' Henry said to his commander, and stepped forward. Jean François gave a snort of surprise, but stopped speaking.

'Richilde?' Henry asked. 'Mistress Richilde? What do you want with us?'

Richilde drew a long breath. 'I have come home, Henry.'

'You have come from the white people?' Toussaint asked.

'Yes,' Richilde said.

'Why?'

'They killed my child,' she answered, simply, and looked at Henry Christopher. 'Our child. They killed our child.'

Henry's eyes gloomed at her. 'You have had a child? My child?'

'Yes,' Richilde said. 'But he is dead.'

Henry's hands curled into fists.

'White people,' Jean François growled.

'They are no worse than you,' Richilde told him. 'They merely hate. Do you not hate?'

Jean François did not reply. But Toussaint asked her, 'And do you not hate, us, madame?'

'Yes,' she said. 'But I only hate those who would come between me and my man.'

Jean François would have spoken again, but Toussaint touched his arm, and led him back towards the huts. The other people also melted away, leaving only Richilde, facing

264

Henry.

'You had a child,' he said. 'My child. I did not wish that on you, Mistress Richilde. But I am proud. Even if I wish to avenge his death. Is that what you wish?'

Richilde hesitated, drew a long breath. 'If you mean, did I come here to be avenged, Henry, the answer is no. I came here because I believe that you have a cause, a right to be free, to stand face to face with any white man as an equal. I know *you* are the equal of any white man, Henry. I would have all your people feel the same. But I would also hope to help you.'

'You will tell us how many soldiers Peynier has? What he intends? How many are coming from France?' His voice was eager.

Richilde took his hand. 'I cannot tell you those things, Henry. Because I do not know them. But I do know that they are afraid of you, in Cap François. That you can defeat them, if you are brave, and resourceful, and fight them as your ancestors fought. But I think I can help your people to learn how to use their victory, after they have fought, and won.'

He frowned. 'You mean you would beg for the lives of the white people?'

'Yes,' she said. 'As I am prepared to beg for the lives of the black. But there is more to life than fighting. If you succeed, and I believe you will, you will have to build a nation, here in St Domingue. You and Jean François, and Toussaint. You are the leaders. You must teach your people how to be one, a nation, or they will become nothing more than savages. You must remember Frederick the Great, who built great palaces and cared for his people even while he was fighting nearly all of Europe. You must forge your people into a nation, Henry. For the sake of our dead son, for the sake of all those who have died, all of those who will yet die, that you may be free. You must do this thing.'

He walked beside her, towards the huts. 'Me? Jean François is our general. He tells us what to do. And you know what, Miss Richilde? Toussaint is always saying things

265

like that to Jean François, and it just makes him angry. I think Jean François may kill Toussaint one of these days. Or Toussaint will flee for his life. He and Jean François hate each other. But me . . .'

'You will lead these people, one day, Henry,' Richilde said.

He stopped walking to look at her.

'I know it,' she said. 'I know it in my heart. When Jean François and Toussaint have both been swept away, you will rule St Domingue. Does not the prophecy say this?'

'The prophecy? You believe in that, Mistress Richilde? If you believe in that, then you must believe you are going to stand at my side when the time comes.'

She looked into his eyes. 'Am I not standing here now, Henry?'

Once again the frown of uncertainty.

'I will be standing there, then,' she promised. 'As I am standing here now. But Henry, you must learn to call me Richilde, and not mistress. Because you no longer belong to me; I belong to you.'

She held his hand tightly, as they walked into the village together.

266